BROGNOLA SOUNDED ESPECIALLY WEARY

"On the world stage, meanwhile," he said, "the Man is worried that we can't simply hit Ovan and cut this off at the source, because all of the evidence we have is covert intelligence. We can't afford to point to any more satellite photos of WMD factories that turn out to be anything but…and we can't afford to move against Turkmenistan in an official capacity, not even as a black operation, unless we can turn public opinion against Ovan and show the world he's got his hands in the terror attacks in Iran. If his involvement is exposed, the Iranians will scream bloody murder about the interference, and Magham's fate will be sealed. That's especially true if his own involvement in the plot is outed."

"So what *are* we doing?" Lyons asked.

"A WMD-equipped Ovan would be a nightmare for us all," Brognola said. "His terror network, at this point, quite possibly rivals al Qaeda. But more years of hard-line rule under Magham does no one any favors, either. We need to expose the terror link in Iran and do what we can to ensure an honest victory for Khan while putting a stop to Ovan's terror network and removing him from power."

"Oh, is that all?" McCarter said.

DON PENDLETON'S

STONY

AMERICA'S ULTRA-COVERT INTELLIGENCE AGENCY

MAN®

POWER
GRAB

A GOLD EAGLE BOOK FROM

WORLDWIDE®

TORONTO • NEW YORK • LONDON
AMSTERDAM • PARIS • SYDNEY • HAMBURG
STOCKHOLM • ATHENS • TOKYO • MILAN
MADRID • WARSAW • BUDAPEST • AUCKLAND

Recycling programs
for this product may
not exist in your area.

First edition June 2011

ISBN-13: 978-0-373-61997-9

POWER GRAB

Special thanks and acknowledgment to
Phil Elmore for his contribution to this work

Copyright © 2011 by Worldwide Library

Printed in U.S.A.

POWER
GRAB

PROLOGUE

Rochester, New York

"Quiet!" Nargoly Pyragy ordered. "He is coming!"

The three men watched, crouched behind the concrete-and-faux-marble planter from which projected fake trees covered in plastic leaves. Pyragy, painfully thin, his dark hair thinning, was the oldest and smallest of the trio and was painfully aware of the responsibility he bore. The two others, Kanzi Nihemedow and Gandosi Burdimedezov, were still in their prime and only too eager to strike a blow against the Great Satan. Pyragy would have scoffed had he been alone. He had long since seen the emptiness of such rhetoric. The rest was simply a job, a dangerous job, left to him to conduct.

Nihemedow, who was built like Pyragy but much more handsome, saw himself as the dashing hero of some fantasy. To him the dirty, risky business of such raids was something from a storybook he would read his many children one day. Burdimedezov, the big one, thicker by half through the shoulders than even the second-biggest man Pyragy had ever met, was at least more realistic, though perhaps a bit too willing to rush headlong into danger. That would fade, leaving a skillful operator in its place, for Pyragy knew the large man had in him the ability to go far in intelligence services.

Too many underestimated a fellow Burdimedezov's

size, believing him slow-witted muscle. Gandosi Bur-dimedezov, Pyragy had no doubt, liked it just so. Such a man preferred to be underestimated. Yes, he would go far…and most likely outlive a veteran like Pyragy by decades.

But then, such a thing was never certain in work like this.

Pyragy placed the metal case gently in position. As had been explained to them, the mechanism was per-fectly safe until it was armed. Even then, it should not be fully active, as the technicians explained, until they were well clear. Pyragy wasn't sure how much faith he placed in the pronouncements of men who wouldn't be in the field, next to the bomb, betting their lives on these assurances. He didn't have any choice. At times like these he envied those whose religious faith told them a glorious death in battle against the West would guarantee them a path to Paradise. Pyragy had long ago given up on any such fantasies; he had seen too much, done too much and killed too much to believe in anything but the finality of a bullet or the cold touch of sharpened steel.

He pressed the buttons of the external keypad in sequence. There were five, all blank, lined up for the fingers of a man's hand. He tapped the combination from memory. There was a chirping acknowledgment from inside the box, loud enough for only Pyragy to hear, and he jerked despite himself when he heard it. Glancing left, then right, making sure the two men with him had not seen, he turned his attention back to the case.

The lid opened slowly on small hydraulic pistons, as if the box wished to reveal its contents dramatically. Inside, the flashing lights of the computerized status board blinked slowly as text scrolled across the three backlighted LCD screens in the machine's face.

At the front of the case, dominating the lower half of the hinged mechanism, three stainless-steel orbs were set half flush with the midline of the case. These were the explosives themselves, the warheads. Each was the size of a baseball and each was staggeringly deadly— a shaped plastic explosive core covered in hexagonal shrapnel plates that were in turn layered with solid toxins. On detonation, the shrapnel would excite the toxic resin layer and produce a poison cloud that would linger over the blast radius.

Knowing that there would be no turning back after he pressed the buttons, Pyragy entered the start-up sequence. The machine hummed. Its status readouts responded immediately. Pyragy moved as far from the bomb as he could, which was not very far. Again he hoped that neither of the other two men noticed his actions.

Nihemedow, who was never truly still, began to peer around the side of the planter. Grateful for the chance to focus on more concrete concerns, Pyragy poked him with two fingers and made a sharp gesture of warning. Nihemedow returned the look with one of dire portent but withdrew his head just as the security guard's footsteps grew louder. The man had rounded the corner and would soon pass by their location.

In planning this step of the operation, it was of course Nihemedow who suggested the guard be killed. There was a single night guard known to patrol within the shopping mall at night. There were options for dealing with him. They could wait for him to complete his circuit, plant the device while the man was known to take a scheduled break from eleven o'clock to eleven-thirty and escape before anyone suspected. This option carried with it the risk of discovery during any point. The device would have to be tended while it went through its interminable acclimation program, during which it could not be disturbed. If the guard were to vary his routine, which Pyragy and his team had established during the previous weeks' surveillance, it could ruin everything.

To say he had reluctantly approved the assassination of one fat American would be overstating the case. He didn't care. He wasn't the sort of man to leave any detail to chance or to last-minute decisions, however, so the act had been preplanned right to the man who would do it. Kanzi Nihemedow was eager to blood himself—perhaps too eager—and so he would do the deed. It seemed like such a small detail, in the grand scheme of things, but the death of any single man was no small thing. There was great power in death. This Pyragy understood.

The rasping sound of Nihemedow's knife leaving its sheath set Pyragy's teeth on edge. It was too loud. His thought had been that their silenced pistols would leave behind evidence whereas a knifing could easily be dismissed as a failed mugging or burglary. Looking at it now, in the split second he had to consider the situation, Pyragy decided it would have been better to shoot the guard.

The guard turned his head toward the three men.

Nihemedow, indeed too eager, screamed in bloodlust, his yell almost an ululation. He rushed forward, the knife coming up, the keen blade poised to strike. The guard froze and his eyes went wide. His hands came up as if he would ward off the charging attacker with his fear alone.

The knife flashed downward.

Nihemedow missed.

Had he not been watching, Pyragy would have thought it impossible. The arc of the knife passed down and through the place where the guard should have been. Some analytical part of Pyragy's brain understood what his senses refused to acknowledge. Kanzi had been a half step off in his overeager charge. The two men collided and hit the slick, polished floor in a heap.

"Go, go!" Pyragy ordered Gandosi Burdimedezov. "Stop him!"

Burdimedezov hurried…but it was too late. Nihemedow made a sort of retching, choking noise and fell to his knees, clutching at himself. Burdimedezov threw himself into the fray. There was a moment's scuffling as Nihemedow was knocked flat, then he curled into a ball and screamed in pain and terror. Then it was Burdimedezov yelping, the sound a strange one from so stolid a man. It was a shriek of pain and shock, of surprise. Then Burdimedezov was falling backward, landing painfully in a sitting position, clutching one of his hands. The guard fled beyond him.

Pyragy stood and ripped the Ruger .22 pistol with its attached, handmade silencer from his waistband and began pulling the pistol's trigger as fast as he could. The bullets raised flecks of colored facade from the walls of the corridor leading away from their position as the guard ducked, dodged and scrambled for all he was worth. Pyragy cursed as his pistol ran dry. He threw it to the floor in rage.

"Why!" he demanded, wheeling on Burdimedezov. "Why have you done this?"

"He had a *knife!*" Burdimedezov shrieked. It was then that Pyragy saw the blood streaming from Gandosi's arm and from the hand he clutched tightly in his other palm.

"But," Pyragy argued, "he is a private security guard! They do not carry combat knives. That is absurd!"

"He had a knife, I tell you," Burdimedezov snorted, sounding nothing like himself as he paled from the blood loss. A pool of sticky crimson had begun to widen around him on the floor, and Pyragy realized then how severe the damage must be. "He had a knife clipped to the pocket of his trousers. A folding knife. He flicked it open and cut me."

Pyragy would not have believed it if he had not seen it. Americans were soft. Weak. Everyone knew that. They guarded their airports with soldiers who did not have magazines in their rifles. They apologized to the leaders of nations whose citizens streamed across U.S. borders illegally. They listened to the enemy abroad in their countless wars and "police actions," and prosecuted their own soldiers for killing those enemies too efficiently. How, then, could one fat American fool have been armed and prepared to resist? It boggled the mind.

"See to Kanzi," Pyragy ordered. "He will call for help. We must make sure they do not find the bomb." Heedless of the danger, for in truth there was supposed to be no danger yet, Pyragy used a foot to shove the bomb deep into the planter he and his team had chosen for the purpose. He took a moment to arrange some of the plant fronds to cover it. Glancing at his watch, he cursed. The box was not supposed to be moved for another fifteen minutes. He had been told this over and over again: the bomb required a very specific time for preset acclimation to its environment, to ensure maximum casualties when its sensors and processors were triggered.

Well, there was no help for that now. If he did not hide the bomb, its discovery would render the entire mission a failure. He would not have such a waste on his record. He would not allow himself to fail.

So the bomb would perhaps detonate prematurely. No matter. Even if it killed no one, the explosion would have the desired effect. The Americans would see yet again that the safe little world of illusion in which they lived was not so safe at all. They could be touched. They could be harmed. One of their most precious icons of their sick, capitalist, consumerist world, a shopping mall, a temple to greed, would become a killing ground in their minds, even if there were no victims. Each time one of the lazy Westerners set foot in a shop or in any public place, he or she would be wondering if an explosion was imminent. Wasn't that what a campaign such as this was about?

That was how Pyragy would justify his failure to his superiors, at any rate. With luck, he could convince them that his mission, while not technically successful, was not so horrible a failure as to warrant punishment for him…or for his family.

Burdimedezov dragged Nihemedow up, who still clutched his stomach. "Let me see it," Burdimedezov ordered. "Let me *see* it," he said again, more forcefully. He pushed his partner to a sitting position on a nearby bench.

Pyragy grabbed the heavy duffel bag they had brought with them. His mind began running through what he knew of their situation. They had broken through the glass doors at the rear of the mall, where the periodic parking lot patrols frequently did not come close enough for the drivers to notice such a breach because of the placement of large trash containers and an overgrowth of trees and vines close to the face of the building. The security system's motion sensors, and other electrical components of the obsolete security devices in this structure, were being jammed by the device Pyragy carried on his belt. All of these measures were supposed to have enabled them to break in, place the bomb and get out, disguising their breach as simple vandalism.

Now the guard would be summoning police, and telling those police that armed, dangerous men were in the building. Pyragy pulled back the heavy zipper of the duffel bag and removed a pair of AK-47 rifles with folding metal stocks. He slapped one 30-round magazine home and racked the bolt of the weapon.

"Gandosi," he said. "How badly are you hurt?"

"I will live," Burdimedezov said, his composure returning. Pyragy knew that sensation well. Having temporarily failed, having sustained unanticipated injury, Burdimedezov would be eager to reassert his manhood, to prove that he was no coward and no weakling.

"Your arm looks very bad," Pyragy said, preparing a second AK-47. "You have lost much blood."

"Give me the tape," Burdimedezov said simply. Kanzi Nihemedow sat half crouched on the bench nearby, whimpering.

Pyragy produced a roll of silver duct tape from the bag and threw it to Burdimedezov, who caught it with his uninjured hand. He began using his teeth to break the tape as he wrapped strips of it around his arm and hand. He was still very pale, and his arm and the leg of his pants were stained through with blood, but he showed no signs of slowing down.

"Kanzi?" Pyragy asked.

"He is barely conscious," Burdimedezov said, looking again to his wounded comrade and placing a hand on either side of the man's face to peer directly into his eyes. "He clutches his stomach and refuses to let go. He is bleeding everywhere. I think the American pig gutted him."

Pyragy cursed again. "I do not believe it," he said.

"Kanzi. Kanzi!" Gandosi Burdimedezov shouted. He shook his head. "He does not respond to me at all," he said.

Pyragy, his rifle cradled in one arm, went to stand over them both. He slapped Nihemedow hard across the face.

"Operative Nihemedow!" he bellowed. "Report! You are ordered to report!"

Nihemedow's eyelids fluttered. He finally fixed Pyragy with a sickly gaze, sweat beading on his forehead and cheeks. "Yes...yes, sir," he finally responded.

"Get him a rifle," Pyragy said, not removing his eyes from Nihemedow's.

"But, sir," Burdimedezov said.

"We have moments," Pyragy said. "Unless the guard has decided he fears the legal repercussions of his actions, he will have gone straight for help. We have but one choice, and that is to make the Americans believe we came to attack the mall directly. If we sell our lives dearly, perhaps they will not investigate too thoroughly. They may not find the bomb. It may still do its job."

"Have we no chance to fight clear?"

"There is a chance," Pyragy said. "A slim one. We could, of course, leave now...but the Americans would wonder what we did here. Their authorities would search this place for clues. We must give them an obvious answer, prevent that search from taking place."

"They may still search," Burdimedezov said.

"Perhaps," Pyragy agreed. "But do we dare do less for the cause?"

Burdimedezov thought about that for a moment. "No, sir."

"Then it is agreed," Pyragy said. "Now get Kanzi a rifle."

Burdimedezov brought the third Kalashnikov from the duffel bag, loaded it, racked the bolt, and moved the selector switch to full-auto. He set the rifle aside for a moment and looked up at his leader.

"Help me with him," he said. "I must tape him up."

Understanding, Pyragy managed to lift Nihemedow's arms. The man's resistance, and his strength, were fading fast. Soaked in blood and gore, Burdimedezov managed to wrap layer after layer of duct tape around Nihemedow's stomach.

"Tape his hands to the rifle," Pyragy said.

Burdimedezov looked up at him, then back to his injured colleague, but did as he was instructed. At his leader's direction, he propped Nihemedow up on the bench facing the corridor down which the guard had disappeared.

"They will come from that direction." Pyragy nodded. They could hear the faint wail of sirens in the background now, and knew that the battle was coming. "Take position over there, by that archway. I will conceal myself near the planter once more. Our enemy may be police, and may be their special weapons and tactics personnel. If it is the latter we have much less chance… but if the former, we can shoot our way through them. Be certain to shout slogans. Tell them that God is Great. Tell them you strike a blow with your rifle against the hated West. Anything you think they might overhear."

"If we kill them all, such a tactic does nothing."

"If we kill them all," Pyragy said, "God truly *is* great. Is Kanzi even awake?"

"He may be dead," Burdimedezov said quietly.

"Then he will draw their fire and do his part anyway," Pyragy said grimly. They could hear the sound of glass and metal crashing, echoing down the empty mall hallways. "They have entered the building. Make ready."

When he saw the AR-15-pattern rifles, the helmets and the body armor, Pyragy knew that their chances were not good. He had hoped the first line of response would be city police officers, but this was a tactical response team. They were better armed and better trained, and they far outnumbered Pyragy's team.

Burdimedezov, from his position in the arch, opened fire.

The hollow-metal clatter of the Kalashnikov filled the hallway. The first of the charging law-enforcement officers was stitched across his chest, the rounds knocking him down with a grunt. Burdimedezov began spraying the floor around the man, raising churning debris from the polished floor, trying to finish his enemy. It was possible the 7.62 mm rounds had penetrated the man's vest, but this was not ensured, and thus Burdimedezov hoped to hedge his bets.

The distinctive sound of the lighter 5.56 mm rounds fired from AR-15s filled the corridor, deafening in their overlapping thunder. Pyragy was driven back behind his planter as several rounds found him and chipped away at his dubious cover. He looked around the corner of the planter with one eye, squinting against the dust and grit flying through the air, and saw Burdimedezov leave his place. Fate bless the man, he was screaming about God and capitalists and even the United States President. If they were not all going to die doing this, Pyragy would want to put the man up for a commendation.

Burdimedezov charged the enemy, heedless of the danger. He was shot in the stomach and doubled over, falling to his knees. Struggling to bring up his AK-47, he managed to trigger a final burst from the kneeling position.

Someone shot him in the head.

The big man's forehead opened up and his head snapped back, folding him over awkwardly, still kneeling. He looked, to Pyragy, as if he might be praying.

Kanzi Nihemedow had not moved during all of this. Several bullets had found him. He had jerked in place as his body was hammered this way and that, never once making an attempt to raise the weapon taped into his fists. Pyragy closed his eyes for a moment, crouching behind the planter. There had been in his mind the dim hope that Nihemedow might yet live, at least long enough to die heroically. Instead he had died before the fight had begun…his entrails leaking from him thanks to a single civilian American. It was galling. Pyragy vowed he would never tell Nihemedow's family how this had occurred.

He realized then that there was a chance for him to survive this, perhaps to fight another day. The American justice system was as weak as the Americans themselves. He would be given a lawyer. He would even be read his rights. He could use the many opportunities they would give him, to talk and to talk and to talk, and he could further obfuscate the true reason for the mission as he did so. He would spin the Americans fanciful yarns about his terror cell. Weeks into all of this, the bomb would explode for maximum effect, long forgotten, and only then would the stupid Westerners understand the true reason this attack had taken place.

"I surrender!" he shouted at the top of his lungs in English. "Please, do not shoot! I surrender!" He placed his Kalashnikov on the floor and kicked it away from him, watching it slide some distance before it stopped.

The gunfire continued for a few seconds before shouts of "Cease fire!" and "Hold your fire!" began to echo through the hallway. The men who faced Pyragy kept their distance, maintaining cover, wary of some trick. Pyragy did not kid himself. A sniper would be lining him up for a shot the second he stuck his head out from behind the planter. He would not let them assassinate him. It was said among his people that American police often simply killed their victims this way, after a surrender. Weak as they were, they were also corrupt, and the Americans could not be trusted not to murder unarmed men, women and children if given the opportunity. Some small part of Pyragy's brain wondered if perhaps the bomb he had just planted in this shopping mall would not also kill unarmed men, women and children…but he crushed that thought before it could grow too loud.

"I wish to surrender," Pyragy yelled again. "I am unarmed. I have thrown away my weapon. Do not kill me."

"Come out with your hands on your head," someone shouted back. "Interlace your fingers. Make no sudden moves."

"I want assurances," Pyragy shouted. "I will testify. But I want assurances!"

There was no response to this. Finally the instructions to come out with his hands up were repeated. Pyragy knew that he had only a few moments before they started throwing tear gas or perhaps even stun grenades, if they were equipped with such weapons.

He needed to keep his wits about him. He needed to put on a masterful performance, in fact, if he were to carry out his new plan. Perhaps his people would bargain for his release at some subsequent point…or perhaps, when the attacks began in earnest, his release would be demanded as a condition that the bombings stop. He could not dwell on that now. Now, all that mattered was living through this and making sure his enemies focused on him and his dead teammates. They must not suspect the bomb was here.

He glanced back to where he had concealed the device. He hoped again that moving it prematurely had not ruined things.

"All right," he shouted back. "I am coming out. Please do not shoot."

A high-pitched whine made him turn, again, toward where he had hidden the bomb.

Three metal spheres, propelled by charges of compressed gas, burst upward into the air, one after the other.

"No—" Pyragy had time to say.

And then there was no more time, ever.

CHAPTER ONE

Stony Man Farm, Virginia

Barbara Price, Stony Man Farm's mission controller, seated herself at the large conference table in the War Room, smoothing the slitted thigh-length skirt of the business suit that did nothing to hide her contours. The honey-blonde, model-beautiful Price did not look as if she had been awake since the earliest hours of the morning, but then neither did Aaron "the Bear" Kurtzman. As the Farm's cybernetics expert propelled himself into the room, turning smartly with a practiced motion of his wheelchair, he looked bright-eyed and alert. Clutched in one massive hand was an oversize insulated aluminum travel mug that was, no doubt, freshly filled with his stomach-roiling house blend of overpowering coffee. Kurtzman busied himself with the uplink controls set in the wall next to the giant plasma screen that dominated that end of the briefing room.

The men of Phoenix Force and Able Team filed in moments later, talking quietly among themselves or, in the case of Able Team leader Carl Lyons, sitting stone-faced and watching the room with cold blue eyes while silently sipping coffee from a disposable cup. The big, blond ex-cop, who had more than earned the nickname "Ironman" from his teammates, was flanked by Able

Team members Hermann "Gadgets" Schwarz and Rosario Blancanales.

Schwarz, who pushed his wire-framed glasses up on
his nose while reaching for a coffee cup of his own, was
a computer expert in his own right. He was also a veteran field operative. Many enemies had underestimated
the slim, unassuming Schwarz…and had died because of
it. Blancanales, for his part, looked calm and confident.
He always did. The gray-haired, dark-eyed, soft-spoken
Hispanic, a former Black Beret, was known among the
men as "the Politician" for his ease with blending in
with others, making them believe what he needed them
to believe.

David McCarter, team leader of Phoenix Force, seated
himself next to Blancanales and gave him a neighborly
jab with one elbow, uncharacteristically cheerful by his
usual standards. He emptied the aluminum can of Coca-
Cola from which he was drinking and set it on the table
with a loud, metallic ring. The lean, fox-faced Briton, a
former SAS commando, had changed considerably in
his time as leader of Phoenix, Price thought. While still
something of a hothead, he took his job seriously and
had led his fellow counterterrorist operatives to victory
in mission after dangerous mission.

The other Phoenix Force veterans filled the opposite
side of the conference table. There was Rafael Encizo,
the stocky, well-built Cuban-born guerilla expert. Next
to him hulked Gary Manning, the burly, square-jawed
Canadian who served as Phoenix Force's demolitions
expert. A former antiterrorist operative with the Royal
Canadian Mounted Police, Manning was the sort of
solid, dependable soldier Price was always glad to have
on hand. He was quiet, stable and more than willing to
speak his mind if it was necessary.

To Manning's left sat Calvin James, the lanky knife fighter and former SEAL who would always be the son of Chicago's mean streets. Price mentally chided herself for indulging in such poetic phrasing, even privately. Still, looking at James and watching the muscles play under his dark skin, it was hard not to see him as some kind of predatory animal. Easygoing as he was, he was one of the most dangerous men she had ever met, and that was saying something, considering the company he kept. It occurred to Price that she sat in a room with some of the most experienced warriors on the face of the Earth. There was just one exception, and she would see him soon enough, when he returned from whatever mission had called him away most recently.

Beyond James, just pulling out a chair for himself, was T. J. Hawkins, formerly of the Army Rangers and the youngest member of Phoenix Force. Hawkins's Southern drawl and easy manner belied his abilities as a fighter. He could hold his own with any of the men of Able Team or Phoenix Force, which was why he had been added to the latter's ranks.

Also on hand was Akira Tokaido, the brilliant computer hacker who, with Carmen Delahunt and Huntington Wethers, formed the rest of Kurtzman's cybernetics contingent. Tokaido took the chair next to where Kurtzman was stationed and placed an item on the table in front of them both. The device was about the size of a large universal remote control and bore several LEDs, buttons and knobs, all labeled in neatly printed black permanent marker.

Price unfolded her slim notebook computer, waiting as it connected wirelessly to the secured network that controlled the flat plasma screens on the wall of the briefing room. As she did so, the careworn face of

Hal Brognola suddenly appeared on the screen at the end of the room. Larger than life-size, the face of the director of the Sensitive Operations Group stared out at them with hound-dog sincerity from behind his desk, the scrambled transmission emanating from his office on the Potomac. The big Fed was chewing something, which Price knew was probably an antacid. Dark circles under his eyes betrayed the sleepless night he had no doubt just had.

Not for the first time, Price wondered if Brognola's job was slowly killing him. The man from Justice answered directly to the President, but the covert antiterrorist organization that was Stony Man Farm—from the hidden base in Shenandoah National Park, where they now sat, to the network of resources and assets that included the black-operations soldiers sitting in front of her now—was Brognola's baby before it was anyone's. The troubles of the world rested squarely on Brognola's shoulders before they weighed down anyone else.

"Good morning, Hal," Price said.

Brognola huffed something that might have been a "good morning" of his own. He was looking away from the camera and thus from the microphone when he did it. He found the papers he was looking for and then looked into the lens of his own camera again. "Let's get started," he said.

Price nodded and then looked to Kurtzman, who lowered the lights in the War Room by fifty percent. Price tapped several keys on her notebook computer. The plasma screens on the walls that did not bear Brognola's image came to life with the pictures of three men.

"Now there's a respectable-looking lot," McCarter muttered.

"You're looking at Nargoly Pyragy, Kanzi Nihemedow

and Gandosi Burdimedezov," Brognola said. "Turkmen nationals who, according to our intelligence networks, were part of a terror network run by the recently 'elected' leader of Turkmenistan, officially known as 'President for Life Nikolo Ovan.'"

"'Were'?" Hawkins drawled.

"Were." Brognola nodded. "Because just over eight hours ago, they blew themselves up rather spectacularly in a shopping mall in upstate New York."

Price tapped more buttons and the images shifted to show video footage of a sea of police cars, fire engines, emergency vehicles and SWAT vans parked in front of the blackened entrance to what could have been a shopping center in any part of the United States. A sharp-eyed Calvin James sat forward in his seat.

"Why am I seeing hazmat response teams in that shot, Hal?" he asked.

"Good catch," Brognola said. "This was no ordinary terrorist bombing," he explained. "Aaron?"

Kurtzman nodded and addressed the assembled operatives. "From the point of view of a terrorist," he said, "the hardest part about perpetrating a successful bombing is not finding the materials to make a device. It is not even planting the device, in most cases. It is detonating the device at a time when the explosion will do more than just property damage. In other words, the hard part is figuring out how to kill the most people."

"Timers," Tokaido chimed in as if on cue, "are imprecise. If the bombers are going to be long gone before the bomb explodes, they can't control the conditions at detonation. In Iraq especially, our military have become adept at dealing with one of the ways terrorists circumvent this problem, by using wireless phones to detonate roadside bombs when their spotters see victims in range. Signals of that type can be jammed, and specific locations can be hardened permanently against such technology."

Schwarz nodded knowingly. Price knew that he had been on hand assisting Kurtzman and his team for the past few days, in anticipation of the problem they were now forced to confront directly.

"But what if," Kurtzman said, picking up the narrative again, "terrorists developed a 'smart' bomb, a bomb that can 'learn' over time by sampling its environment and determining the optimum conditions for detonation?"

"You'd have the ultimate terrorist weapon," Schwarz interjected. "A bomb that you can set, leave behind and trust to figure out for itself how to murder the most people."

"Exactly," Brognola said. "And that is just what we're dealing with."

It was Price's turn to address the operatives. She keyed in several more images that were timed to display as she spoke. "Our intelligence and surveillance networks have known for some time that Iran was sponsoring, with just enough plausible deniability to stop world governments from intervening, the production of terrorist bombs and other weapons for use in hot spots like Iraq and Afghanistan. It seems, however, that they're not satisfied with making things worse. A team of Iranian scientists, whose location we have not yet been able to determine, has developed and has been producing, for six months now, these smart terror bombs."

"The bombs are shielded against explosives' detection methods using specially sealed canisters prepared and then cleansed prior to deployment," Tokaido said at Price's nod. Pictures of a briefcase-size weapon containing three inset spheres appeared on the plasma screens. "Central Intelligence Agency operatives have recovered at least two of these devices from potential terror sites abroad, and it was thanks to the CIA that we received the initial hard data that confirmed what our data network sweeps have been turning up as chatter for several months now."

"Each bomb," Kurtzman said, "has electromagnetic, heat, motion and sound detectors, among other sensors, all of it connected to a powerful microcomputer that is devoted solely to figuring out when the most victims will be within range of its payload."

"It's that payload, Calvin," Brognola said, "that is the reason for the hazmat response."

James nodded grimly.

"The bombs," Tokaido said, pointing at schematics that appeared on the screens as Price called them up, "contain three sealed bouncing betty spheres. They're extremely innovative. The plastic explosives are shaped breakaway charges that produce deadly shrapnel, and they're interlaced with a low-level nerve gas, a chemical-warfare agent that ensures the blast radius has an effective kill zone of close to a hundred percent."

"Bloody hell," McCarter said softly.

"And then some," Brognola acknowledged. "The blast radius, fortunately, is only about a hundred yards, but it was enough to demolish a good portion of the shopping mall you see here." The image on the secondary screens returned to the video footage of the upstate mall.

"How many dead in that attack?" Blancanales asked.

"Fortunately, only the terrorists," Brognola said. "There were some wounded among the responding police, but no fatalities. Our assets locally have interviewed law enforcement and the one witness we have, a security guard who seems to be the luckiest bastard in a polyester uniform for miles. In his debriefing, he said that two men who had apparently broken in after hours attacked him and tried to stab him to death. Apparently he used a knife of his own to cut his way out of the situation and flee."

"Three cheers for American ingenuity," McCarter said.

Brognola ignored that. "Something about the attack made our security guard think terrorists instead of burglars, probably because New Yorkers in general are understandably nervous about that kind of thing. He called the cops, the cops sent in SWAT and a gun battle ensued. It was anything but one-sided."

"How so, Hal?" Blancanales asked.

"The terrorists were fielding fully automatic weapons," Brognola said. "The locals say the last of them was trying to surrender when the bomb exploded. The three shooters were the only ones within the blast zone, thankfully, and the locals were smart enough to pull out before they got too much exposure to the toxin. Apparently somebody on hand was worried about conventional chemical weapons or perhaps even a dirty nuke of some kind. Whatever their fears, they got out of the way, and that's what saved them."

"If we're going up against these bombs," James said, "are we looking at dealing with chemical warfare?"

"The toxin used has a very short chemical half-life, to misuse the terminology," Schwarz explained. "Clear the blast zone and wait ten minutes, and there's no danger. That's the only thing working in our favor here."

"What does a new superbomb created in Iran have to do with a Turkmen terror network?" Carl Lyons interjected. "Please tell me the answer isn't what I think it is."

"Sorry." Brognola shook his head. "It is. The bomb used in the attack was, according to our analysis after the fact, the very same bomb the Iranians have developed. Once intelligence services identified the three dead terrorists, the Man gave us the go-ahead to move on this."

"So we're hitting Iran?" McCarter asked.

"Unfortunately," Brognola sighed, "nothing is ever that simple." He waited while Price cued up several more images: pictures of men dressed in formal suits, as well as one man in paramilitary garb.

"This," Brognola said of the latter, "is Nikolo Ovan. He's essentially a warlord. His ultranationalist party has swept to power in the last year and seized control of Turkmenistan, militarizing it and terrorizing the Turkmen people. Ovan fancies himself the next Stalin or something. He's motivated, intelligent, and very, very brutal. His leadership of Turkmenistan threatens the stability of the entire region."

"Recent discoveries of new, more extensive deposits of natural gas," Price said, causing a map of Turkmenistan and its neighbors to display on the screens, "have made Turkmenistan more economically powerful than it has ever been. Our intelligence sources tell us Ovan is negotiating with his neighbors, particularly Iran, to build a pipeline to them and trade in sales of the gas."

"I take it he doesn't want Euros," Hawkins said.

"No," Brognola said. "Ovan wants weapons, specifically weapons of mass destruction. He's been able to purchase enough of them to get them into the hands of the terrorist network he's building. Bad as that is, it could become much, much worse. The CIA tells us that Ovan wants to negotiate a steady supply of these bombs. That, coupled with the buying power a pipeline deal would give him, would make Ovan a real player on the world stage. We can't allow that."

"Ovan hates the West," Price said. "He's a socialist who sees everything about the Western, capitalist world as evil incarnate. His state-controlled television station broadcasts a steady stream of invective and propaganda against the Western world in general and the United States specifically. We know he's been in talks with several dictators of minor countries to see whom he can bring aboard his terror network, too."

"Make no mistake," Brognola said, "Ovan is in this for the long term. He's not just some kill-crazy tin-pot dictator, the type that rises and falls over the course of a summer. He has real plans for something like long-term domination of his region and ultimately the world through terror and violence. If he's allowed to implement them, he'll be that much more difficult to stop."

"So we're hitting Ovan?" Lyons asked impatiently.

"Again, it's not that simple." Brognola shook his head. "The two men you see here with Ovan," he went on, indicating the men in suits, "are candidates for the presidency of Iran."

"This," Price said, causing one of the pictures to glow brighter, "is Khalil Khan. He's the moderate candidate. A series of increasingly turbulent uprisings has prompted calls for yet another election in Iran. The hard-line incumbent, Mohammad-Hossein Magham, is doing everything he can to squelch the press, including attempting to cut off access in Iran to certain social networking sites on the internet, blocking all but Iranian-controlled news media in the country and threatening those news outlets that don't side with him or who dare even to report on the dissidents. Our CIA assets in Iran report that Khalil Khan has a very good chance of winning, if he lives to see election day…and if Ovan doesn't influence the election otherwise."

"It's almost a repeat of the Ahmadinejad-Mousavi election," Brognola said. "Khan's a pro-Western moderate who wants to bring his country into the modern world and improve its human rights record. Magham's a dictator who'd just as soon crush the dissidents and run the country like a prison camp, but he's sensitive to world attention and media coverage. He doesn't just want to run the country—he wants people to acknowledge that he's *right* to run the country."

"Enter Ovan again," Price said. "We have covert intel that says Ovan's terror network is led by two men. These are his sons, half brothers Karbuly and Ebrahim Ghemenizov."

The secondary screens displayed images of a large, bearded man with wild eyes and a thin, balding, sallow man whose eyes shared the other's slightly unstable look. "We have reason to believe Karbuly is heading up the domestic terror network that directed the actions of the three dead terrorists in New York," Price said. "There are unconfirmed reports that Karbuly has been spotted at multiple locations here in the Northeast United States. We think the botched attack, in which the terrorists either set their bomb incorrectly or perhaps used a defective weapon, was the opening salvo in Ovan's long-range plans to hurt the West as he jockeys to better his economic and strategic position worldwide. From the terrorist chatter we've intercepted, we also think he's trying to show the Iranians just what he can bring to the table. They hate us, too, remember, and if he can show the hard-line Iranian government that he's a real force to be reckoned with, they'll be eager to cut a deal with him."

"Ebrahim Ghemenizov is half Iranian by birth," Brognola said, "and the CIA places him in Tehran. Their people believe that Ovan, through Ebrahim, has been behind several terrorist attacks on supporters of Magham."

"But Magham's the hard-liner," James said. "Why would Ovan hurt the candidate who's more likely to sell him the weapons?"

"It's true that Khan would put a stop to the weapons program," Price said, "or at least we hope he would. Magham is behind the program. But he's also working in complicity with Ovan to help stage the attacks on his own supporters. The idea is to create, and spread through the media, the idea that Khan's followers are violent murderers who cannot be trusted. So far the tactic is working. Those few polls we can get that aren't skewed by Magham's government show that, while he's still running behind Khan, the moderates' lead has diminished since the attacks began."

"On the world stage, meanwhile," Brognola said, sounding especially weary, "the Man is worried that we can't simply hit Ovan and cut this off at the source, because all of the evidence we have is covert intelligence. We can't afford to point to any more satellite photos of WMD factories that turn out to be anything but…and we can't afford to move against Turkmenistan in an official capacity, not even as a black operation, unless we can turn public opinion against Ovan and show the world he's got his hands in the terror attacks in Iran. If his involvement is exposed, the Iranians will scream bloody murder about the interference, and Magham's fate will be sealed. That's especially true if his own involvement in the plot is outed."

"So what *are* we doing?" Lyons asked.

"A WMD-equipped Ovan would be a nightmare for us all," Brognola said. "His terror network, at this point, quite possibly rivals al Qaeda. But more years of hard-line rule under Magham does no one any favors, either. We need to expose the terror link in Iran and do what we can to ensure an honest victory for Khan, while putting a stop to Ovan's terror network and removing him from power."

"Oh, is that all?" McCarter snorted, half grinning. Brognola rolled his eyes fractionally but ignored the comment.

"Gadgets, working with Aaron, Akira and our friends at the CIA who provided the sample bombs," Brognola said, "have performed extensive analysis on the bombs, and there's a vulnerability we can exploit. The devices have a unique electromagnetic signature that changes as they go active and increases as they reach their full sensor capabilities."

"The signature is difficult to pin down among the background noise of the electromagnetic spectrum," Schwarz said, "but it *can* be detected."

"The Pentagon has, overnight, retasked its War-lock network of surveillance satellites," Brognola said. "They're going to provide us with the detection we need to home in on each terrorist attack site. Able Team, using this intelligence, will intercept the cells before they can carry out the series of attacks we believe to be imminent."

"That's where this come in," Tokaido said, holding up the handmade device.

"Gadgets and Akira have built this scanner-jamming

unit," Price said. "It reads the bombs' signals at close range and retards the function of the processors in the bombs. It can be used, at extreme close range, to deactivate it, provided you can hold it on target long enough."

"The problem is," Schwarz explained, "you've got to get close enough and point the unit directly at the bomb as you approach to prevent it from going off. Then you've got to touch it to the casing and hold it there until it gives you the all-clear that the bomb has been neutralized. The rest happens within the bomb's processor as it interacts with the wireless signal from our unit."

"Are you saying," Lyons asked him, "that the bombs could go off because they sense us coming?"

"That's exactly what I'm saying," Schwarz confirmed. "Also this device is one of a kind. There isn't time to build more, nor to test this one. So nobody drop it." He looked at Blancanales and then back to Lyons.

"Wonderful," Lyons said.

"Phoenix," Price said, "will deploy to Iran. The CIA has operatives placed within Iranian security who will conduct you from there. You'll enter the country as Canadian journalists and then fall off the radar to conduct your operation covertly with the CIA's assistance. Able Team will use the Warlock surveillance feed to perform terrorist interdiction here."

"The goal," Brognola said, "is to stop the terrorist attacks centered in Tehran and, if possible, uncover Ovan's network there. We also want to prevent an outright assassination of Khan if we can. If you can expose the terror connection there, we'll redeploy you to deal with Ovan directly. If you can't get anything on him, however, there's little we can do except find and destroy the source of the Iranian bombs so that Ovan cannot continue to make use of them. Able, meanwhile, will deal with the threat at home using the more direct approach."

"At least there's that," Lyons said.

"Jack Grimaldi is standing by," Price said, referring to Stony Man's senior pilot, "and he'll hop you from target to target. The Warlock network has produced a priority list, and the signals we receive will help redirect you once you get closer to each potential strike point."

"All right, then," McCarter said. He stood. "What are we wasting time here for?"

"Good luck," Brognola said. "And good hunting."

Price lingered as the rest of the teams filed out, their conversations growing louder and more businesslike as they began to discuss the missions ahead of them. Kurtzman shot a salute to Brognola as he wheeled in front of the screen, and Brognola nodded in acknowledgment.

"You okay, Hal?" Price asked, stopping Brognola as he reached for the disconnect button.

"I'm always okay, Barb," Brognola said. "You know how it is. This job is never easy."

"I do," Price said. "Just...take care of yourself, Hal. We all count on you."

"And the country," Brognola said, "counts on *them*." He pointed at his camera, and Price knew he meant the soldiers who had just left. Brognola's extended finger came down on his unit's disconnect button. His screen went blank.

"Another day," Price said to the empty room, "another mission to save the world."

She shook her head. Enough introspection. There was a lot of work to do.

CHAPTER TWO

Ithaca, New York

The twin rotors of the massive Boeing MH-47G Chinook helicopter flattened the grass of the field in which ace pilot Jack Grimaldi brought the big bird down. With a top speed of close to 200 miles per hour, the heavy chopper was overkill for ferrying Able Team around—the helicopter could lift and transport a bulldozer or an M-198 howitzer—but it had been readily available while time was of the essence. The chopper had a 450-mile range, and with the Warlock network and U.S. intelligence projecting their targets to be clustered in the New England area, this Special Operations Aviation version of the Chinook would serve well to hop them from site to site. The chopper boasted an advanced avionics system, a fast-rope rappelling system and was no slouch as an assault chopper. A single Chinook so equipped could, Grimaldi had told Able Team enthusiastically, replace multiple UH-60 Black Hawk helicopters.

Carl Lyons just wished the damned thing was a little smaller.

It was no small feat to land a chopper somewhere other than an airstrip or helipad, that much he knew. The wires and telephone poles, not to mention the trees, that dotted their landing zone made Lyons decidedly nervous as Grimaldi deftly fitted the machine into the space available.

The members of Able Team filed out of the chopper, weapons at the ready. There was no attempt at subtlety here, and there would be no hiding in plain sight in civilian clothes, trying to keep those around them from seeing what they were doing. No, there was no time for niceties of that kind. The Warlock network indicated that one of the Iranian bombs was online in the area, and Carl Lyons could see why terrorists might have selected this location.

Men and women dressed for spring gasped and backed up as Lyons, Schwarz and Blancanales approached. All were dressed in combat boots and black BDUs, although Lyons had foregone the BDU blouse for a brown leather bomber jacket over a black T-shirt. Each man carried web gear or, in Lyons's case, a canvas shoulder bag bearing extra magazines and other weaponry. Lyons's bag was stuffed with 20-round polymer drum magazines for the Daewoo USAS-12 select-fire 12-gauge assault weapon he favored. In a leather shoulder holster under his left arm, he carried his .357 Magnum Colt Python. Schwarz and Blancanales both carried M-16 rifles, although Schwarz also had his Beretta 93-R machine pistol in shoulder leather, and Blancanales had a Beretta M-9 in a dropped thigh rig.

Each member of Able Team wore a microtransceiver earbud in his ear. The processors in the little devices cut the sound of gunfire but transmitted even a whisper from the owner, amplifying such sounds so that each member of the audio network could hear them. The effective range of the little earbuds wasn't very great, but it was more than enough for the typical combat ranges in which the team typically fought.

Schwarz moved out in front as Blancanales and Lyons flanked him, weapons at the ready. Somebody in the crowd screamed. The three men of Able Team found themselves among the hedgerow parking lot of the Ithaca Farmer's Market, which would have been a peaceful scene if not for the roar of the Chinook's rotors, the artificial windstorm caused by its presence and the rushing crowds hurrying to avoid the armed men now approaching them.

Lyons wasn't happy about terrifying civilians in this way, and he was keenly aware of the danger presented by a spooked crowd. As the three advanced, each one of them shouted, "Government agents. Remain calm. We are authorized Justice Department agents. Do not panic."

He wondered if an armed man shouting "Do not panic" was likely to produce the desired effect. He doubted it.

Still, there was nothing they could do about it. There was a job to do, and Schwarz, in front with his whiz-bang techno-remote, was following some sort of sine-wave graphic on its tiny LCD screen. Carl Lyons didn't care how it worked; the device was the domain of Gadgets Schwarz. As long as the device kept them from exploding when they got near the bomb, he was satisfied.

Someone shouted to call the police, and Lyons shot the woman a baleful glare. "We *are* the police," he said.

She just stared at him, then repeated her appeal to call the police.

Well, that figured, and some part of him was proud of her for not simply bowing to asserted authority. Too many people could be fooled into doing what they were told by people who meant them harm, simply because the predators of the world counted on bullying their victims into submission.

The farmer's market was an open-air covered pavilion that stretched in two different directions, forming an L-shape. It was quite large, and secondary sections containing booths and display tables jutted out at different points along the building. There was food for sale, some of it obviously still cooking as those preparing it fled their posts. There was also a ton of flea-market-style junk. Everything from garage-sale electronics to new, Chinese-made tourist-trap merchandise was arrayed for sale on line after line of folding tables.

"Have you got it?" Lyons asked.

"Tracking a firm trace signal," Schwarz reported.

Blancanales shooed an attractive young woman in a halter top out of his way, somehow managing to be charming while doing it, and Lyons shook his head. Blancanales could get lucky in the strangest places.

They searched up and down each aisle. All the crap on the tables was starting to look the same, as far as Carl Lyons was concerned. Then, suddenly, the device in Schwarz's hands seemed to light up like a Christmas tree. He stopped, examining a table covered in old, obsolete video game consoles that looked like they had been rolled down a hill and then run through a rock tumbler.

"Here!" Schwarz said. "It's right here!"

Lyons realized then that he was pointing with the scanner at a gunmetal-gray box on the table that he had first thought to be one of the console games. It was, on closer inspection, one of the Iranian smart bombs.

Blancanales and Lyons took up stations on either side of Schwarz, covering a flank. The three men had worked and fought together for so long that very few words needed to pass between them; they knew their jobs, and they knew how to protect their own.

"Leave the area immediately," Lyons ordered the few brave souls who still stood and watched, milling around nearby. "You won't be in any danger if you leave immediately, but this device could produce noxious fumes. You don't want to inhale them."

The crowd moved off. Schwarz shot Lyons a look. "'Noxious fumes'? Underselling the whole nerve-gas thing, aren't you?"

"Shut up, Gadgets," Lyons said. He smiled, though. This was an old game they played. Both men knew they didn't want to create a panic—or any more of a panic than they had already caused with their arrival. Already he could hear police sirens in the distance. If Price was doing her job, and she of course would be, the Farm would even now be relaying orders to the local authorities, instructing them to maintain a cordon around the target site but not to interfere with the government agents operating within it.

The locals always hated that, and Lyons didn't blame them. He'd worn the badge and been part of the thin blue line himself. Nobody liked the jurisdictional crap from the Feds. There was simply no other way, and this was going to play out again and again as Jack Grimaldi ferried them into and out of one municipality and then the next. They were going to stomp a lot of feet before this was over. The alternative was wading through the usual bureaucratic red tape, and he was not going to allow that. People would die before the folks keeping chairs warm with their asses figured out what had to be done to keep the populace safe from Ovan's terror network. He supposed he couldn't blame the local law enforcement for not understanding the threat of a net-work they didn't know about; Ovan and his terrorists were classified government information, their existence a closely guarded U.S. intelligence secret at this point.

By the time Able and Phoenix were done with Ovan, it was Lyons's hope that no American civilian would ever *need* to hear of Ovan's network. The men in it, and perhaps Ovan himself, would be extinct.

Schwarz, careful to keep the scanner device trained on the box as he approached it, was already holding down a switch, and Lyons thought he could hear a high-pitched whine coming from the scanner. Schwarz then placed the unit in contact with the smart bomb and pressed several more buttons. Lights began to cycle in a definite pattern.

"This bomb," Schwarz said, "is fully active. According to the scanner it hasn't completed its acclimation algorithm."

"It's what now?" Lyons asked absently. He was watching for threats over the barrel of his Daewoo.

"The bomb has to do a bunch of computer sampling," Schwarz said, still holding the scanner in contact with the device. "The CIA first told us about it, and Akira and I verified in testing with devices not carrying explosive charges. When it's placed, it has to go through an orientation phase, if you want to call it that, so its computer brain can get its bearings. It can't be moved during the orientation or the calibration is all screwy and it just goes off at a random interval."

"That what happened to the three puddles they pulled out of that shopping mall?"

"No way to tell," Schwarz said, "but it's the most likely explanation. Of course, we don't know for certain that trying to deactivate the bomb like this won't set it off."

"We don't?" Lyons asked. He caught the wink that Schwarz shot Blancanales, though.

"How long does it take?" Blancanales asked. He waved off a pair of women in shorts and tank tops who were starting to edge closer from the hedgerow parking lot. "Please, ladies," he ordered. "Move along."

"Still pulling the chicks, eh?" Schwarz said without looking up from his work.

"You know it," Blancanales said smoothly.

The status LEDs on Schwarz's scanner suddenly turned green. There was a metal clicking noise from inside the bomb casing. Schwarz looked at Lyons, then to Blancanales, and placed the scanner back in a padded pouch on his web gear.

"What are you—?" Lyons started to say.

Schwarz reached out and pressed the buttons on either side of the case. He opened the bomb like a suitcase and let the top rest against the table, revealing the inset spheres of the explosives.

Blancanales whistled.

Schwarz reached inside and, as Lyons winced, pressed a catch that released each of the spheres. Then he removed them. A contact wire trailed from each sphere. Schwarz produced a multitool from his web gear and used the wire cutters to snip the wires just aft of the connection to each sphere. Then he placed the spheres gently back in their receptacles.

The Able Team electronics genius pointed to the bomb case.

"The bouncing betty balls here," he said, "have simple contact switches connecting their fuses to the computer's brain. When they're expelled from the bomb through breakaway hatches in the outer casing, they pull free from the fuses, and that's what causes them to go off. They're harmless now."

"Really?" Lyons asked.

"Well, as harmless as a sphere of plastic explosive laced with solidified nerve toxin ever gets. I'm not saying I'd leave them out for the neighborhood kids to play with."

"Good call," Lyons said. "Let's collect those and get the hell out of here." He was grateful for the chopper still beating the air in the field nearby, its rotor thrum a heartbeat to the action here in the market. Getting on that chopper and flying away meant they wouldn't have to deal with any awkward questions from the local law enforcement.

"Wait!" Schwarz said. He pulled the scanner from his web gear; it was beeping. "I'm getting…yes, I'm getting another localized signal. It's not a full trace, just back-scatter, but it's strong. The profile fits that of a device that's online but not activated."

"Another device…here?" Lyons asked.

"Yes, somewhere close." Schwarz nodded.

"Go," Lyons ordered. "Find it."

Schwarz was off again, the scanner in his hands pointed in front of him. His M-16 was still slung and he used his free hand to pull the Beretta 93-R to allow him to track and shoot at the same time.

"This way," Schwarz directed.

They followed the electronics expert as he made his way into the hedgerow parking lot. Here, winding rows of man-tall shrubbery separated each curving dirt path. Cars were parked on either side of the paths, and to exit the market, drivers would have to take a circuitous route through the twisting rows and back around the rear of the market to reach the nearest paved road.

Schwarz began moving back and forth among the rows of parked cars, spooking even more civilians. Lyons and Blancanales urged them to get back beyond the police cordon, the flashing lights of which he could see beyond the hedgerows.

"Get out of here!" Lyons snarled at one group of teenagers.

Schwarz moved like a dog following a scent, this way and that, watching the telltales of the scanner unit rise and fall. At the end of the furthest hedgerow, Lyons put a hand on Schwarz's shoulder and told him to stop.

"What?" Schwarz asked.

"There," Lyons said. He pointed.

Sitting at the end of the parking lane was a battered black cargo van. The windows were tinted, darker than was probably legal, and a cardboard sun screen bearing the cartoon image of a giant pair of sunglasses obscured the front windshield.

The van rocked slightly to the left, then the right.

"Signal's coming from there," Schwarz confirmed. "And obviously there's someone in there."

"Or a lot of someones," Lyons said. He nodded to Blancanales, who nodded back and broke away, moving around to cover the rear right quarter of the vehicle. "Now for the part I hate."

"What part is that?" Schwarz asked from his position at the front of the van.

"The part where they start shooting after I demand they come out," Lyons said. "You in the van!" he roared at full volume.

Lyons was hitting the dirt even before the shots came, but they came. The hollow metallic clatter of a

Kalashnikov beat the interior of the van like a drum. Bullets sprayed from the rear windows and even blindly through the body of the vehicle. The engine started.

"Go for the tires," Lyons ordered.

Blancanales and Schwarz immediately fired into the front and rear tires of the vehicle, which was already moving. The dirt and gravel beneath the shredded wheels flew up in great plumes as the vehicle's powerful engine urged it forward. Lyons pushed himself to his feet and jogged ahead; the van might be moving, but it wasn't doing so very quickly. Lining up his shot carefully to prevent catching his partners' positions, he lowered the barrel of the USAS-12, flicked the weapon's selector switch to full-auto and held back the trigger.

Heavy 12-gauge slugs poured from the barrel of the weapon. Lyons rode out the tremendous muzzle-rise of the weapon, firing from the hip, watching the heavy slugs tear apart the grille of the van. The hood was blown up on its hinges as the engine screamed in torment. The van shuddered to a halt.

The sliding door was shoved aside, as the rear doors were thrown open.

"Here they come," Lyons said, his words carried to Able Team by his transceiver.

"Got it," Blancanales said.

"Let 'er rip," Schwarz said.

The terrorists spilled out, almost falling over each other. There were three of them. The one who scrambled out the side door was easy pickings; he tried to level his Kalashnikov at Lyons. The big cop let his USAS-12 fall to the end of its single-point sling and withdrew his Colt Python with deadly speed, pulling through double-action to send a Magnum round punching through the man's face.

Schwarz and Blancanales fired short, measured bursts of their own, dropping their adversaries. Lyons holstered his Python and reloaded a new drum magazine in his shotgun. He advanced on the van.

"Check them!" Lyons said. "If anybody's still alive we need medical attention rolling." A live prisoner might mean valuable intelligence about the terrorist network Ovan was fielding. Lyons didn't like the idea that technology was their only lead in this mission. The cop in him told him they needed something else, some human element, some information that would give them an edge over their enemies. With only an electronic leash to lead them around, they were vulnerable. If they lost the initiative he wasn't sure they'd be able to get it back, and that worried him. Too many lives were riding on this… and the terrorist attack on the mall was already all over the news, cycling through the twenty-four-hour cable networks. More attacks would raise public response to the level of panic. Nobody wanted that…and Able Team, thanks to their one-of-a-kind gizmo and the Warlock network, were the three men standing between Ovan's terrorists and complete chaos in the United States.

No, he didn't like the idea at all. But he would do his job, and so would Blancanales and Schwarz. They always did.

"Nothing here," Schwarz said.

"Mine's dead," Blancanales reported.

Lyons didn't bother to look at his man; there was no surviving the head shot that gunner had suffered.

Inside the van, he found another one.

The gunman was slumped in a corner of the cargo area, a Makarov pistol on the floor beside him. There was a bullet hole in his temple and a spray of blood on the interior of the van above and behind him.

In his free hand was a cell phone. A voice on the other end was still speaking.

Lyons picked it up and listened. He handed it to Schwarz, who listened. The connection was terminated from the other end.

"Probably Turkmen," Schwarz guessed. "Not in my repertoire."

Lyons pocketed the phone. "Jack," he said. "Are you reading us?"

"Loud and clear," Grimaldi answered from the chopper.

"Have a courier detailed to meet us, soonest," he said. "Coordinate with your flight plan, however we can work it out. I've got a cell phone here that I want analyzed."

"Will do."

Lyons glanced into the back of the van. Two of the suitcase-size bombs were inside. "They're not active?" he asked.

"Not according to this," Schwarz said, pointing the scanner at the bombs.

"Then let's pack them up and get back on the chopper," Lyons said, looking around. "We're only just getting started."

CHAPTER THREE

Tehran, Iran

The Volkswagen diesel microbus pulled up to the curb as the men of Phoenix Force, completely unarmed and traveling under the false papers of Canadian reporters from a fictional news outlet, left Imam Khomeini International Airport. Named for the leader of the 1979 Iranian revolution, the airport had been closed and reopened several times in the scuffle over whether or not the facility was run by foreign contractors. David McCarter remembered reading some years back that the airport's runway had supposedly been built over ancient subterranean waterways and was therefore somehow unstable. Nothing had given way when their Kish Air flight from Dubai had landed, however. McCarter was grateful for that, and grateful that they were done bouncing around all over the globe to complete their successful transit into hostile territory. He grew tired of the secret-agent games and sometimes wondered if they ever truly fooled anyone for long.

Unarmed as he was, McCarter knew a moment's concern when he sat in the passenger seat of the van. If the man meeting them wasn't who he was supposed to be, there would be little they could do about it.

"Hello," the man behind the wheel said as he guided the van away from the loading and unloading area. "My name is Ghaem Ahmadi. I am officially a well-placed operative within the Iranian Internal Security force."

"Officially?" McCarter asked.

"Unofficially, Uncle Sam asks me to extend his greetings on behalf of the Central Intelligence Agency." Ahmadi smiled. He had a gap-toothed grin set wide in a smooth, olive-skinned face. His dark eyes and round face gave him an almost somber look, as if he was in mourning, and the smile that creased his features seemed incongruous. He wore nondescript civilian clothing and a light windbreaker, much as the members of Phoenix Force did.

"Pleased to meet you," McCarter said. "A little birdie tells me the weather here's doing okay lately."

"It is hotter than Texas but drier than Arizona," Ahmadi said, and grimaced at the awkward code phrases. "You are satisfied?"

"I am," McCarter said. "I imagine you'd be hauling us to a dungeon somewhere if you weren't."

"I imagine as much, as well," Ahmadi said.

They traveled in silence for a time. It was a relatively clear day in a city known for its cloying smog. McCarter could see Milad Tower in the distance, and beyond that, the Alborz mountains were visible. As they moved through the city he was struck by how modern and cosmopolitan it looked and felt. It wasn't at all the type of backward, repressive society he knew it to be, not from the outside. Of course, you didn't have to look far to see the fear in people's eyes whenever one of the uniformed paramilitary Iranian Internal Security goons neared. The IIS had been one of the innovations Magham's government had brought to an already oppressed people. The paramilitary IIS squads strutted through the streets of the city as if they owned it—which, for all intents and purposes, they did.

The city was home to some eight million people, thirteen million if you included the surrounding metro area. It was also the governmental capital and economic hub of Iran, although McCarter thought he remembered reading that the government was still mulling over moving the seat of government to another location. He didn't suppose that would make too much difference in terms of the mission ahead of them. He was, however, only too aware that he and his men were deep in a country that was no friend to the United States, with very little recourse should things go awry. They were heavily dependent on the extensive network the CIA had developed covertly in Iran.

"You are fidgeting in your seat," Ahmadi said. "I believe I know why." His round face again crinkled into something like a smile as he gestured to the men in the rear bench seats. His accent was pronounced, but he was clearly fluent in English.

"Let's just say I am very attuned to our situation," McCarter said.

Ahmadi laughed. "I like how this is put. Yes. I like it." He gestured again. "Very discreetly, look under your seats. I received a special request for you, Mister…?"

"David," McCarter said. The team would use their first names only in a covert situation like this.

"Mr. David." Ahmadi smiled again. "I received a special request for the leader of my guests, and I did what I could to provide for the others."

McCarter reached under his seat and felt a familiar shape: the grip of a Browning Hi-Power, as it turned out. He checked the weapon as best he could, keeping it low near the floor to prevent it from being seen by pedestrians and other drivers. There was a clip-on holster that he affixed inside his waistband, under his windbreaker, and a small mountain of extra magazines that he placed in his pockets.

He glanced back to see that his teammates had been provided with similar setups and Glock pistols, the compact Model 19. He nodded his approval to Ahmadi.

"The Glock 19 is the pistol of the IIS," he explained. "Relatively easy for me to get. Untraceable except back to the armory of the IIS. The Browning was more difficult, but all things are possible with motivation."

"Much appreciated." McCarter nodded. "Were you able to get us anything heavier?"

"There is a bag containing two folding-stock AKS-74U rifles in the back," Ahmadi said. "Loaded magazines for both, as well. It was the most I could get and, realistically, the most you can expect to carry without raising suspicions."

McCarter was inclined to agree. The 5.45x39 millimeter Krinkov rifles had short barrels and were designed to be compact; they would fit into a small bag easily enough. That would be more or less the limit of what they could display openly. If the Phoenix Force veterans were trooping all over Iran's largest city carrying bags large enough to house assault rifles for all of them, it would look out of place. One man with a duffel bag was a man with a duffel bag. Five were suspicious.

"So where do we begin, Ghaem?"

"First, I have one last item for you all," the Iranian said. He reached into the pocket behind his seat and pulled out a small cloth bag. He handed it to McCarter, who looked inside and discovered five personal radios. The radios had wireless headsets. They weren't as small as the self-contained transceivers Phoenix Force often used, but there had been no way to smuggle those into Iran without risking giving themselves away. The team did have their secure satellite phones, which provided them with a very important data link to Stony Man. The encrypted units could pass for ordinary Iridium satellite phones, and only the access codes known to Phoenix Force would enable an operator to use the phones at all.

"What's the range of these?" McCarter asked.

"A few city blocks," Ahmadi said. "No more. These are scrambled. They are reasonably secure unless someone with similar hardware chooses to make it his business to listen."

"Someone…like whom?" McCarter asked.

"One of my good friends from the CIA, for example." Ahmadi waved one hand. "It is unlikely to be a problem. I do not foresee anyone going out of the way to help us."

"So, mate," McCarter asked again, "you're our guide. To where can you guide us?"

"There is a safehouse," Ahmadi said. "We have traced its rental to a holding company that we believe is ultimately owned by agents of Ovan's government. Now is a very good time to strike that safehouse."

"Why is that?"

"There are three rallies scheduled for supporters of Magham today. The safehouse, which is being used by Ovan's terror network, is the logical place for them to prepare for their attacks. We can intercept them and perhaps deal a very telling blow to the entire network in a single day. Without your operatives such a move would not have been possible before. There was thought in Washington that the situation here in Iran was best dealt with…quietly. I imagine there are those within the agency who think your intervention is akin to using a hammer to kill ants. You may get some of the ants, they will say, but you will miss many more, and you will anger the colony."

"Do you feel the same way?"

"I do not," Ahmadi said. "I have fought long and hard to help bring about, in whatever small way I can, a free and democratic Iran. I was a young man when I became a traitor to my country and allowed myself to be recruited by the CIA. But the slow approach is… slow. We have seen so little real change, and every time my people shout for democracy, for freedom, they are crushed under boot heels with greater force. The beginning of the IIS was the beginning of the worst wave of terror and oppression we have seen. It is time for more direct methods. I welcome them."

"Fair enough," McCarter said.

"Do your men require rest before we can go?" Ahmadi asked. "We could spare perhaps an hour or two and still have enough time before the first of the rallies."

McCarter glanced back at his teammates, who shook their heads or otherwise silently indicated no. He did the same. "We're ready," he said.

"Then so am I."

Ahmadi drove them through ever-narrowing streets, and McCarter was struck by the age of Tehran, by its mixture of architectures, by the weight of its past pressing in from all sides. He laughed at himself, wondering why he was doing so much bloody woolgathering, and reminded himself to focus on the task at hand.

"Comm check," McCarter whispered. He listened as each of his men responded in kind, their whispers amplified in the wireless earpiece he wore. "All right," he said as Ahmadi continued to delve deeper into the city, squeezing down alleyways that McCarter thought for certain would rip the side mirrors from the microbus. He finally stopped in a dimly lighted corridor between two recently built concrete buildings. He pointed through the front windshield.

"There," he said. "The safehouse is there, accessible only through the front door, on the street opposite, and by this metal door at the rear."

"How secure is that door?" McCarter asked.

"Not at all," Ahmadi said. "The lock is…damaged. It will give with enough pressure."

"Damaged, eh?" McCarter asked. "I wonder who might have damaged it for us?"

"I would not know." Ahmadi looked up and in any direction but at McCarter. "Perhaps a man with a small, quiet cordless drill could damage the lock in the night. Who is to say? The ways of vandals are mysterious."

"Indeed they are," McCarter said.

"It's a bottleneck," Rafael Encizo said.

"Unfortunately," Ahmadi agreed. "But works against us also works for us."

"Works for *us*," McCarter agreed. "You stay here, Ghaem. We need you at the wheel for a fast getaway, mate."

"This I understand," Ahmadi said, although he looked somewhat disappointed. "I shall keep the engine running."

McCarter nodded. "Let's go, then, lads."

The only concealment for the operation was provided by the alley itself. Under other circumstances McCarter would have detailed at least two men to take the front while the remaining three breached the rear. As it was, he had to hope they could overcome the enemy within using only surprise and ruthlessness.

"Rafe, T.J., take the rifles," McCarter directed. "You're the exterminators, lads. Go in first, spray the bugs out. We'll follow and mop up."

The men of Phoenix Force hit the pavement and arrayed themselves on either side of the door.

"Gary." McCarter pointed. The big Canadian's tree-trunk legs were just what the situation called for. Manning moved into position and, with his Glock drawn, planted one foot solidly against the door.

The metal door sprang inward as something gave. Encizo and Hawkins were immediately through the opening, their Krinkov assault rifles chattering.

McCarter came through the doorway with his Hi-Power ready. There were several tables, each really a tall counter, and on these tables were arrayed a variety of weapons. Most were AKs, some of them stripped. There were a few pistols, some of them exotic or obscure enough that even McCarter would have had to pause to identify them. There were boxes of ammunition, maps, and on the wall, he caught a glimpse of a map of Tehran with certain targets marked in red felt pen.

A burst of gunfire nearly took his head off.

He ducked behind the cover of one of the tall counters. These were solid, not standing on individual legs, but they couldn't be more than studs and drywall, because bullets were passing right through them. At the opposite end of the room, several gunmen were blazing away, and midway between McCarter's position and theirs, Encizo and Hawkins were holding their own.

McCarter bided his time. He waited, sensing the rhythm of the gunfight. A burst from the enemy…an answering burst from his men…a few shots from the

Glocks held by James and Manning. They were firing from the rearmost position, from outside the doorway, covering the exit. From where he crouched McCarter could see the front door, and he could see that their opposition was pinned down. Going for the front door would expose the enemy and allow Phoenix Force to take them down.

Stalemate.

Not on my watch, McCarter thought. He stood and braved the gunfire as he half crouched and ran from table to table, zigzagging this way and that. The maneuver did what he had hoped it would: it drew the attention and the fire of the enemy at the opposite end of the room. That was the break that Encizo and Hawkins needed. They worked their way forward with their Krinkovs and began firing anew, advancing as they covered each other.

One man went down in a hail of bullets. Another fell over him as he, too, was tagged. McCarter threw himself behind the dubious safety of the closest counter and was covered in drywall dust as bullets from the remaining shooters punched through it.

The gunfire stopped.

"Clear!" Encizo shouted.

"Clear!" Hawkins repeated.

He heard Manning and James sound off, as well. Standing cautiously, McCarter didn't bother to brush himself off. He kept the Hi-Power at the ready while he made sure there were no lurking targets behind him or on his flanks. The other men of Phoenix Force had presumably done the same before sounding the all-clear.

"Everyone intact?" McCarter asked.

Again the team members sounded off; no one was injured badly. James had taken a scratch across the forearm that was not truly a graze. It was bleeding but not badly. He was careful to use a handkerchief from his pocket to make sure he didn't leave a telltale puddle of blood behind, though. It was unlikely any of the Iranian authorities would conduct DNA analysis, but it paid to be meticulous. The men of Phoenix Force took their jobs seriously and were well experienced in them.

Ahmadi entered the back, careful to announce himself. "We do not have much time," he said. "We must move quickly. The gunfire will have attracted attention, and even here, where IIS raids are common, someone will have called the authorities. They will come to investigate."

"Then let's get what there is and get gone, lads," McCarter said. "Rafael, watch the front. T.J., you monitor the rear. The rest of you, let's sweep this room. Turn up anything you can. Turn it inside out if you must, but let's do it with haste."

McCarter, James and Manning began working their way from one end of the room to the other, like searchers beating a field for a missing person. They tossed the gear on the tables and checked every piece of furniture in the Spartan room, looking for anything that might be squirreled away.

"Nothing," James finally said. Ahmadi had produced a first-aid kit and was wrapping the tall black man's arm tightly in gauze. James tucked the bloody handkerchief in a pocket; he would dispose of it later.

"Something about this is not right," the Iranian agent said.

"Do I hear sirens?" Encizo asked from the door.

They heard it, then, the foghorn cadence of the peculiar sirens the Iranians used.

"That is IIS, without doubt," Ahmadi said.

"Then let's go right now." McCarter pointed to the door.

They filed out. As they were climbing into the microbus, Ahmadi had a thought and actually slapped his forehead.

"What?" McCarter said.

"The lights," he said. "I did not check the lights."

McCarter didn't bother to ask what that meant. He simply gestured for Ahmadi to move. The Iranian operative leaped from the vehicle and went back through the rear door, while McCarter seated himself behind the wheel.

"David." Manning pointed from his seat. At the end of the alleyway, they could see the flashing lights of what had to be security vehicles.

Ahmadi came running from the building. "Go!" he shouted. "Go!"

McCarter stepped on it. The little microbus was surprisingly responsive. He put the vehicle into Reverse and accelerated, putting distance between them and the alleyway. At the first junction, he took a hard reverse left, scraping the side of the van against a concrete building as he did so.

"Switch with me!" McCarter told Ahmadi. "I have no bloody idea where I'm going!"

Ahmadi managed to move himself into position and take the wheel as McCarter slid out of the seat, then planted himself behind the controls. The van careened from one side of the alley to the other, and this time one of the mirrors did get ripped off. Ahmadi muttered something that was definitely a curse, though it was apparently in Persian.

"What was it you went looking for?" McCarter asked as Ahmadi brought the little microbus back under control at last. The Iranian did not answer until he took several more turns, then looked back to make sure they were not being pursued.

"That," he said at last, "was much closer than I might have liked."

"Well?" McCarter asked again.

"My apologies," Ahmadi said. He reached into his jacket and removed a device. It was a pair of wires connected to a small metal box. He handed it to McCarter, and the Briton put the box against the metal of the door frame on his side, watching it stick there.

"Magnetized."

"It is a bug," Ahmadi said. "We have had good success with that particular model. It is preferred to fit it somewhere there is electrical wiring, such as in light fixtures."

"A bug?" McCarter asked.

"Yes," Ahmadi confirmed. "There were far too few men at the safehouse. And we found weapons, but not nearly enough. Ovan's terrorist network is much more advanced, much better equipped than this."

"Offhand," James said, "I think I'm glad there weren't more of them in that particular room."

"This I understand," Ahmadi said. "But I do not think you realize what this means."

"The room was bugged," McCarter said. "Understood. But there's nothing they can use against us. How does this line up with there being too few men present?"

"No." Ahmadi shook his head, spinning the wheel as he took one hard turn, then another. "Iranian Internal Security, even Ovan's terrorist network, they do not use this equipment. This is *my* equipment."

"The bug is—" McCarter began.

"That is standard-issue CIA surveillance equipment," Ahmadi said. "I have used its like many times. I have never seen this particular unit, nor am I aware of any success in attempting to bug this structure. It has always been too well-guarded for us to risk it. At least, that was my understanding."

"So you didn't put this here and you don't know of anyone else who did," McCarter said.

"Correct." Ahmadi nodded.

"And you think our boys were tipped off to expect trouble and effected at least a partial evacuation of the premises?"

"Unless they have moved up their timetable, it is the only explanation. They may be deployed at the rallies, which means we will meet greater difficulty in attempting to safeguard Magham's people and supporters from the terrorists. Or it may be another problem entirely. There may be a mole within the CIA."

"Bloody hell," McCarter said.

CHAPTER FOUR

Syracuse, New York

The local minor-league baseball team was featuring a promotional night when door prizes were offered to fans. Carl Lyons couldn't tell what the door prize was as they neared, but he didn't suppose that it mattered.

Grimaldi and the Chinook waited in the middle of a vacant parking lot for a nearby weekend market. Fortunately they had not yet drawn a crowd, but that was inevitable. Mindful of the huge crowd inside the stadium, however, the men of Able Team had opted to leave their long-arms in the chopper. Lyons was already going through shotgun withdrawal as they took the steps leading to the stadium two at a time. Schwarz was trying to be discreet with his scanner, but Lyons couldn't see any point in trying to hide too much. There was no way they could pass off as normal what was essentially a raid on a civilian location.

"Lead on," Lyons urged as Schwarz once more took the lead.

Lyons felt exposed and worried that Schwarz was especially vulnerable. He liked that phone in the hands of the dead terrorist even less. The Warlock network had indicated that signals were coming from this location, and Able Team had opted to investigate the stadium first because it offered huge target potential. If the terrorists had come and gone, leaving their bombs behind, it was just possible that the smart bombs hadn't yet detonated and could be neutralized without a gun battle. Much as he hated the thought of the terrorists planting their bombs and escaping undetected, Lyons had to admit that it would be preferable not to start spraying bullets in the company of…how many people? The stadium looked like it easily held a few thousand as he ran his eyes over the vacant and occupied seats.

They'd flashed their Justice Department ID coming through the gates, and now security personnel in black polo shirts were wandering around nearby, obviously wondering what was going on. Lyons figured his team could afford to ignore them for now. As long as they didn't get in the way and as long as nothing went boom, it hardly mattered if a few of the locals gave Able Team the stink eye as they passed.

As they moved from the upper decks to the lower, and then to some access areas that were on the basement level of the stadium, Lyons fought an uneasy feeling of being watched. He hoped it was just his imagination. But if he was that dying terrorist and he'd had a chance to make one last phone call before he died, wouldn't he have tried to warn the others in his network? It only made sense. And if they had been warned, and they were on-site, there was no telling what they might have planned.

Screw it. Lyons was disgusted with himself even for spending so much time dwelling on it. No matter how dangerous the job, of course, he and Blancanales and Schwarz would do it. The idea of worrying about their own hides when American lives were at stake never even entered into the equation. It was just that he, as team leader, had to worry from time to time. He had to worry about what would happen if they failed in their mission. That was the one thing Stony Man Farm could never do: fail. They had lost battles before and the ugly reality was that they would lose them again. But they could not afford to lose the war. The war was why Lyons had given up any hope of a normal life to dedicate himself to Able Team and to the Farm. He knew his teammates shared his drive and had made the same sacrifices.

They had lost many good men and women getting to this point. And it was all worth it. They fought because they had to. They fought because their country needed them. They fought because predators, monsters, killers like Ovan's terrorists, sought to murder innocent men, women and children, and there had to be warriors like the men and women of Stony Man Farm to stand between those killers and the rest of the world.

"This door is locked," Schwarz said. He was facing a fire door. The corridor of the access level was getting smaller. Lyons couldn't tell where it went, but it was probably used for maintenance purposes. "This padlock looks brand-new." The chain on the doors was indeed bright and polished, while the rest of the metal on that level looked scuffed and slightly rusted.

"I have a key," Lyons said. He planted his combat-booted foot against the door, hard. Then he kicked it again. Then he did it again.

"You're not going to break the padlock like that, Carl," Schwarz said dryly.

"Don't care about the padlock," Lyons grunted. He heard the shriek of metal on metal as something started go give. "Care about the hinges."

The hinges gave. The door, which had never been designed to sustain such an onslaught, fell aside at an angle, hanging on twisted flanges. Lyons shoved it aside and then waved down the corridor.

"Why, thank you, sir," Schwarz said with an exaggerated flourish.

"Shut up and find me a bomb," Lyons growled.

At the end of the corridor, they found a cluster of machinery whose purpose Lyons couldn't guess.

"Sprinkler system," Schwarz said.

"Thought they used AstroTurf in all these stadiums," Lyons argued.

"Don't you ever use the web browser on your phone?" Schwarz teased, referring to the secure satellite phones they all carried. "Read up on your local history, Carl. This stadium has had real turf for a few years now."

"And I'm very happy for them." Lyons's growl turned deeper. "Find me a frigging bomb."

The bomb casings looked like the ones they had found in Ithaca, New York, and they were chained together through the suitcaselike handles in a cluster at the rear of the machinery.

"Pol, the door," Lyons directed. "Cover our backs. I'll keep an eye on Gadgets."

"And I get bomb duty," Schwarz said. He pressed the scanner he had used to track the bombs to each of the devices, running the scanner across each bomb in a constantly moving pattern.

"Can't you do one after the other?" Lyons asked.

"I'd rather get them all moving toward neutralization at once," Schwarz said. "It helps disrupt the processors so that if the bombs are, well, thinking of going off, they won't."

"Great," Lyons said.

"These are fully activated," Schwarz explained, "and they've almost completed their calibration cycles. We were lucky. These could have gone off down here and spread a toxic cloud through most of the stadium." Not far above them, they could hear the roar of the crowd as the home team did something worth cheering. The music playing over the PA reverberated through the ceiling. Lyons could feel it in his chest.

"We've got company!" Blancanales shouted from the doorway.

"What?" Lyons asked.

"Hostiles!" Blancanales yelled. "Coming down the corridor!"

Lyons cursed under his breath. Well, there was one way to handle it.

"Come on!" he shouted to Blancanales. "Gadgets! Watch your ass!"

"Thanks for thinking of me!" Schwarz called after them.

Lyons pulled his Colt Python from its shoulder holster. Blancanales, understanding the bold play the Able Team leader was running, raised his own weapon. Lyons just needed to verify that they weren't staring down some errant security guards or even local police called to see what the hell was going on.

A pistol fired in their direction. Lyons could feel the bullet pass his face.

There was a knot of men moving down the corridor, all of them armed with handguns. Lyons could see one particularly large man behind the others. They were shouting to each other in something that almost sounded like Russian to Lyons's ears; it was like the voice he had heard on the phone. It was probably Turkmen, and that meant that these men were Ovan's operatives. It also meant they'd been lying in wait for Able Team, and that was very, very bad.

Forward, toward the danger. That was the only way.

Lyons roared, flattened himself against the wall of the corridor and started shooting.

The boom of the .357 Magnum rounds was deafening in the corridor. His first shots took out one, then another terrorist, and his crazed charge broke the enemy's forward momentum. They had thought they were cornering their quarry. They had thought that, while the men they had waited to kill or capture weren't helpless, they were at least at a disadvantage.

Lyons made his own advantages.

Screaming like madmen, the two Able Team soldiers continued to press their charge. Each time Lyons reloaded his Colt Python, Blancanales picked up the slack with his Beretta, filling the corridor with 9 mm destruction.

The tide turned. The men coming down the corridor began to back up, then broke, then fled. Lyons and Blancanales pursued. Foremost in Lyons's mind was the fact that Schwarz was back there by himself, trying to defuse bombs that could kill thousands of people if he didn't succeed. They had to make sure nothing interfered with that. They would have to shield Schwarz with their own bodies, if necessary.

Another man fell to a bullet. There were several ricochets around them, and Lyons ducked, taking a round in the arm that had expended most of its energy bouncing from the corridor wall. He gritted his teeth against the pain. There was some blood, but it didn't feel as if the slug had penetrated very far.

Then all of the shooters were down, except one. He turned as if to run, and Blancanales tackled him.

Or he tried.

As he hit the big man's legs, Blancanales realized

that their opponent was almost a giant. He had to crouch to avoid scraping his head on the top of the corridor, and he seemed almost as broad through the shoulders as Blancanales was tall. The giant grunted as Blancanales hit his legs…and then he straightened, reaching around with one grizzly-bear-size palm to grab the back of Blancanales's head. He threw Blancanales into the corridor then, and the Able Team warrior went slack, knocked out cold.

The gun that came up in the giant's fist looked like a toy. There was an audible click as the hammer of the 1911-pattern .45 automatic failed to fire. It wasn't locked back, but Lyons wasn't going to wonder what gods of fate had prompted this misfire. He pulled the trigger of his Colt Python.

It clicked. He was empty.

The giant roared in laughter then, his whole body shaking. He had a lion's mane of naturally curly black hair framing a face that could have been chipped from granite. Strangely piercing blue eyes stared out from his craggy face, and Lyons recognized that look. This was one of the two brothers mentioned at the briefing. This was Karbuly Ghemenizov, son of Nikolo Ovan and leader of Ovan's terror network here in the United States.

Ghemenizov wasted no words. He threw himself at Lyons, the sheer weight of the man knocking the former L.A. cop onto his back. The Python skittered across the floor. The second he hit the corridor, Lyons understood the lethal danger. Going to the ground with a larger opponent like this was a sure way to get killed. If Ghemenizov mounted him and started to pound him with those ham-size fists, he would never get up again.

Lyons brought his feet up, scooting to one side, keeping his feet between Ghemenizov and himself. He fired several vicious kicks from that position, several times catching Ghemenizov painfully in the shins. The giant roared, then simply waded through the defense of Lyons's legs. Lyons's had just enough time to roll to the side to avoid being pinned when Ghemenizov landed on the floor of the corridor.

He was not fast enough to escape. The big terrorist grabbed him and hooked an arm around his neck. Lyons ducked through that, going for the crook of the elbow, escaping before the giant could apply pressure. That was the only thing that saved his life.

He wriggled free and managed to get to his feet as the giant also rose, still on top of him. Then a fist the size of a small moon was rocketing toward him. He tried to bring up his arm to block and felt the fist smash right past his guard and into his face. The blow bounced him off the wall of the narrow access corridor. Stars exploded in his vision and bright spots swam in front of his eyes.

One of his martial-arts instructors had once counseled him, "Never celebrate the hit." It was the sensei's way of telling him not to waste time reacting to a blow, no matter how painful. The appropriate response to being hit was to hit back harder.

Lyons fired a punch with everything he had. He felt as if he'd struck a brick wall, but he put all his power behind it anyway, following through with every fiber of his being. Ghemenizov howled and actually rocked back slightly.

Lyons didn't know how much damage he was doing and didn't care. Half blind, he began punching and kicking, throwing knees and round kicks and elbow strikes, anything and everything he could summon. He mixed in ax-hand strikes and hammer fists, too, fighting for his life, driving back the monster who towered over him.

He felt something give in the big man's torso, possibly a rib.

With a bellow of inhuman fury, Ghemenizov started to drive Lyons back. He fought with little technique, using his natural strength and ferocity, but this he had in abundance. Lyons felt the shock wave of every blow as the giant hammered away at him. Then, as he reeled under the onslaught, he heard the giant speak.

"You wonder, don't you," Ghemenizov whispered, his accent sounding like nothing so much as thickly Russian. "You wonder why I waited. Why I watched you tamper with my little bombs. I know you stopped the bombs in the little market. We were warned. I wanted to see. I like to see my foes, see who dares to challenge me, before I crush them."

Then he was done talking, apparently. Ghemenizov grabbed Lyons, now dazed, by the throat with one hand, wrapping his fingers in the leather of Lyons's bomber jacket with the other. He started squeezing, and Lyons could only hammer away ineffectually at the big man's arms. He tried to reach for the tactical folding knife he kept clipped to his pants' pocket, but he could not find it; it had apparently been dislodged during the struggle.

"You are very strong," the giant said in his ear, still squeezing.

Lyons could feel his vision start to go gray around the edges. Black spots replaced the bright blobs he had seen before.

"I like a good fight. You have given me one. But you, like everyone who faces me, have lost. I enjoy making people lose. I enjoy hurting them. I have enjoyed hurting *you*."

He threw Lyons to the floor, and the big cop felt the floor strike his face with unyielding finality. Some part of his mind could picture Ghemenizov raising a large foot to stomp him. A man like this would relish stomping on a fallen enemy.

Schwarz would have been able to deactivate the bombs by now. He and Blancanales would be able to continue the fight. He, Carl Lyons, would not be the first Stony Man warrior to fall in the line of duty, at the hands of a brutal foe.

He only regretted that he would not be able to complete the mission and destroy Ovan's network—

The shots, when they came, sounded strangely distant. Lyons realized then that he was hearing the triple bursts of Schwarz's Beretta 93-R. He faded for a moment, then came back, then faded again. Finally he opened his eyes and looked up at the face of Hermann Schwarz.

"Oh, thank God," Schwarz said. "I thought I was going to have to give you mouth to mouth."

Blancanales's face came into view. He looked sheepish. "Come on, Ironman. We've got to keep moving."

"Did you get him?"

"No," Schwarz said. "He got away. With you and Pol both down I didn't dare go after him and leave you and the bombs unattended."

"It was…Karbuly Ghemenizov. Head of their terror network here. Should have…gone after him."

"And let your brains leak out all over this floor?" Schwarz said with a half grin. "Not likely, Carl. Come on. We've got to get the deactivated bombs back to the chopper."

"Police?"

"Not coming unless somebody thought we should have paid at the gate," Schwarz said. "The noise down here was probably nothing like gunfire to the folks upstairs." They could still hear the music and cheering of the game above.

"You saved my life," Lyons said.

"Pol's, too," Schwarz said. "I keep reminding him."

"Help me up," Lyons said.

His teammates helped the big blond cop get to his feet.

"How do you feel?" Schwarz asked.

"I just got the shit beaten out of me by a giant Cossack," Lyons said. "How do you think I feel?"

"Well, you're alive enough to be grumpy," Schwarz said, helping him down the corridor as Blancanales covered them both. "I imagine you'll live."

"Shut up, Gadgets."

"It looks like he mostly pounded on your skull," Schwarz went on. "That should mean you'll be fine in just a little while."

"Shut *up,* Gadgets."

They continued bickering as they made their way back to the Chinook. Grimaldi wasted no time asking questions. He simply put the heavy helicopter back into the air. "We've got our next target," he reported. "The Farm says Warlock has pinpointed another set of signals in Albany, New York. That's where we're headed."

"All right." Lyons nodded wearily.

Blancanales retrieved the chopper's well-equipped first-aid kit and went to work. He started probing at Lyons's chest. The big cop breathed in heavily but refused to give in to the pain any more than that.

"I don't think your ribs are broken," Blancanales said finally. "Although I couldn't say why not, from what

Gadgets says happened. All I remember is a sensation of flying, and then the wall and I got to know each other."

"He wasn't the most fun person you'll ever meet," Lyons said.

The chopper was headed east. Lyons could tell from the position of the sun. They spoke over the noise of the chopper as Grimaldi flew them. Lyons hoped there would be enough time. Whoever was in position in Albany, Karbuly Ghemenizov wouldn't be there…but there was no point in searching the city of Syracuse for him. He wouldn't be staying there, unless it was to plant more bombs, and if he did so, the Warlock network would find him.

Lyons hoped so.

"You're looking pretty grim, Carl," Schwarz said, less teasing now. "You all right?"

"I don't like getting my ass kicked."

"Did you see that guy?" Schwarz asked. "He could beat up a marching band and have energy left over for the color guard."

"That has to be the strangest comparison I've ever heard."

"Quiet," Schwarz said. "Your brain is scrambled and you're not in my right mind."

"Gadgets?"

"Yes, Carl?"

"Shut up."

CHAPTER FIVE

Tehran, Iran

The irony that they were fighting to protect supporters and party officials belonging to the hard-line tyrant now holding Iran's presidency was not lost on David McCarter. The strange complication of the surveillance equipment, unaccounted for, worried him a great deal, but there was nothing to be done about that now. They would have to play out the hand they had been dealt. It would do no good to concern themselves with factors whose import was not discernible yet.

The small cafeteria hall that was the site of the first rally boasted a crowd of a few hundred people. Phoenix Force, at Ahmadi's urging, insinuated themselves into the crowd toward the back. There were a few token security personnel here and there, from what they could tell. These men wore no uniforms and, while they carried wireless radios, did not appear to be armed.

The front of the cafeteria hall had been decorated with banners bearing Magham's photograph and some sort of slogan. None of McCarter's team would have been able to understand it even if they could read the writing, but of course that was irrelevant. A podium had been erected, and one of several speakers who Ahmadi had said was a minor party functionary was now going on in Persian. He sounded boring even in an incomprehensible language, McCarter thought, and it didn't surprise him that politics was dull no matter what the cultural environment.

The plan, inasmuch as they were able to create one, was simply to stay among the crowd unless and until a terrorist hit was enacted. It was a stopgap measure; McCarter would much have preferred to go directly to the heart of the matter but, as Brognola had said, there were certain political concerns. The big Fed would not come right out and say it in so many words in the briefing, but they all understood that there were certain political exigencies at stake. It wasn't enough to destroy Ovan or to smash Magham. The men involved had to be exposed so that the world would know why such men had been destroyed and smashed. Thus the weight of public opinion would not be thrown too hard against those few industrialized nations still willing to combat terror in the world.

The real difficulty here would be in pulling off armed resistance to the attack without ending up in the hands of the Iranian authorities. At the thought, McCarter realized it was odd that this rally, supporting as it did the current government's regime, boasted no Iranian Internal Security agents. He edged closer to Ahmadi, who now wore a radio just as did Phoenix Force's members. Their conversation would be inaudible to anyone not wearing such an earpiece.

"Ghaem, lad," McCarter said softly. "Where is the IIS in all this?"

"It is indeed curious," Ahmadi said. "Usually, Magham's operatives travel with them in plentiful number."

"Not that I'm complaining, mate," McCarter said,

"but just how do you suppose we would pull this off if the place were crawling with IIS men?"

"I assumed you would think of something." Ahmadi managed to sound sheepish, even whispering. "You came highly recommended."

"Can't argue that," McCarter said with a mental shrug.

The audience began to close in around the podium as the speaker made as if to wrap up his comments. Apparently he was some sort of preliminary figure, for the crowd perked up considerably when the next man strode to the podium. He began without apparent preamble, making sweeping gestures with his arms, doing his best to animate the crowd. For the most part, they responded, and the men of Phoenix Force played along, shouting when the crowd shouted, waving when the crowd waved.

McCarter was starting to feel silly when he saw the first of the killers.

He would not have been able to explain, if asked, what first drew his attention to the man. It was something in his body language, a quality visible to a soldier with years of battlefield experience. The man who stood in the midst of the crowd, playing along as McCarter was doing, was focused entirely too much on everyone but the speaker at the podium. He kept brushing his hand across his shirt just above his waistline, too, a dead giveaway. It was a tell that he was carrying a firearm or some other weapon there.

"David," Enciso said in his ear. "I have a possible shooter."

"Describe him," McCarter said. He listened. It was clear that Enciso was describing an entirely different person.

"I've got another," James said. "He's just to my left, in a black shirt and tan pants."

"Me, too," Manning said. "In fact, I see two, close to the podium on the far right."

"I've got one, as well," Hawkins drawled.

McCarter worked his way farther to the rear of the hall. He looked out over the assembled group and, with the positions of his team still fixed in his mind, ran down the approximate positions of the potential shooters. "Calvin," he said, "I need you to take the two closest to you. That's yours and the one Rafe spotted." He ran down assignments for Manning and Hawkins, too. "That leaves one for me. Get ready."

Ahmadi had assumed McCarter and his men would think of something.

McCarter reached the rear of the cafeteria and pulled the fire alarm.

The response was immediate. Most of the crowd began filing out of the room, conditioned as were most people to respond to a fire alarm. But in that moment when most people stop and look up in reaction to such an alarm, the possible shooters had looked, not to the alarm, but to their target at the podium. McCarter knew what they were thinking; it was what he would be thinking in their place. They were wondering how to complete their mission.

Well, they wouldn't be. He and Phoenix Force would make certain of that.

"Now!" McCarter ordered.

The Phoenix Force commandos drew their weapons and leveled them at the would-be gunmen. The shooters went for their own weapons, but they weren't fast enough. The pops of pistols were almost anticlimactic in the seconds that followed. Phoenix Force moved in

on their targets, crouching low, moving smoothly, confident in their ability to engage enemies in close-quarters
handgun exchanges and come out the winner.

As soon as the battle had begun, it was over, and the
members of Phoenix Force stood over a dozen dead
bodies.

Someone screamed.

The few people who had not responded to the fire
alarm began to flee from the cafeteria. The speaker
at the podium and the political operatives with him
looked around in dismay. Some of them fled and some
of them didn't; the ones who remained looked confused
or frozen.

It was time to go, before they met more resistance.

"Go, go, go, go," McCarter urged. The team backed
away, leaving the stunned speaker still at his podium.
"Do we have anyone else?"

"No one that I can see," Encizo reported. There were
calls of assent from the other team members.

"Let's fade, lads," McCarter said. "Ghaem?"

"Meet me at the rear entrance, please," Ahmadi reported. "I have secured alternate transportation." The
foghorn sirens of Iranian Internal Security were closing
in. Ahmadi could hear them better than he could, Mc-
Carter was certain.

He stepped over one of the corpses—and it grabbed
him. The terrorist was not yet dead, and he was determined to take someone with him. McCarter went down
and suddenly found himself wrestling for possession of
his Browning with a man possessed. The strength of
adrenaline, fear and imminent death made the man's
hands iron as he clawed at the Briton.

"Keep going!" McCarter yelled. He slammed a palm

heel up under his adversary's chin. "Don't wait for me! Go!"

The sirens were more insistent now; they sounded as if they were immediately outside. This was what McCarter had feared: doing their jobs only to end up handing themselves to the Iranian security forces. To be prisoners under those circumstances would be a fate worse than death. The Farm would have to disavow knowledge of them, and the Iranians, realizing they had high-value military personnel from the United States, would never let them go. They would probably use their captives for whatever propaganda value they could get, first torturing each member of Phoenix Force to break them.

Everyone could be broken. Many times McCarter and the men of Phoenix had found themselves in the clutches of determined enemies, and at times those experiences had been decidedly unpleasant. They had remained strong through them, but he had no illusions. The members of Phoenix Force were human, not supermen, and they could be broken by persistent torture as could virtually anyone else. It could take years of privation and steady mistreatment…or it could take hours of brutal, maiming torture, depending on the methods used.

He did not intend to end that way, nor would he allow his team to be captured and so abused.

A driving horizontal elbow to his wounded enemy's jaw hammered him back down to the floor. McCarter snatched up his Hi-Power and put an insurance round through his enemy's head. Then he hurried off, leaving behind only dead men and a very confused political operative standing openmouthed at the podium. On im-

pulse, McCarter turned in the doorway at the last second
and threw a jaunty half salute to the stunned man.

He was glad the other team members hadn't seen that.
He wouldn't want them to think he hadn't completely left
his younger days behind, with the mantle of leadership
on him now.

Bloody stodgy, he'd become.

Almost laughing to himself, he found Ahmadi waiting in the alley behind the cafeteria in what appeared
to be a brand-new black Range Rover. He piled in.

"What's this?" he asked as Ahmadi pulled away. The
sirens of the IIS were practically on top of them. "And
I thought I told you all to leave."

"T.J. fell," James said, deadpan. "We had to stop and,
you know, help him up."

"Bloody hell," McCarter muttered. He looked to
Ahmadi. "I approve of the new wheels, lad."

"An IIS patrol one block over found the Volkswagen
where I left it," he said apologetically. "I am not sure
what roused their interest, but I thought it best to find
us another vehicle. If I were to show myself and claim
it, they would want to know what I am doing here, and
that would have been difficult to explain. More questions, more potential for discovery. As you know, I hold
a position within the IIS. It was from its ranks that I was
recruited. I dare not do anything to bring suspicion on
me, for once such scrutiny is leveled, it is very difficult
to crawl out from under."

"So you boosted this?" James said from the seat
behind the driver. "Nice, man."

"Well, I do have standards," Ahmadi said. His
strangely incongruous grin split his features again. He
was enjoying himself, and McCarter thought he knew
why. He finally felt like he was part of the war, finally

felt like he was striking a real blow against the forces of totalitarian oppression that had held his country for so long. A few moments on the periphery of battle were worth years of working covertly for the CIA as a deep-cover operative.

Ahmadi rounded a corner and suddenly slammed on the brakes. McCarter followed his urgent gaze and saw the roadblock: there were several white-painted IIS trucks and uniformed personnel parked on either side of the narrow street, with a portable barrier erected across the roadway.

"They've seen us," James said from behind Ahmadi.

Indeed they had. The security personnel began pointing and shouting. Then their Kalashnikovs came off their shoulders.

Ahmadi slammed the gearshift into Reverse and stomped the Range Rover's accelerator. With surprising skill he whipped the vehicle around and shifted again, propelling them back the way they had come. Gunfire rang out as the IIS gunners began chasing them down the street, firing as they went. In the mirror on his side, McCarter could see the IIS patrol cars pulling into position to pursue.

"Can you lose them?" he asked.

"Yes." Ahmadi nodded. "This I can do."

"Lads, let's get some rifle fire out those rear windows," McCarter said as bullets spanged and whined off the body of the Range Rover.

Manning, who was seated in the rearmost section of the vehicle, accepted a Krinkov from Encizo, who was not in a good position to fire it. Hawkins joined him. Bullets had already starred the rear windshield as the IIS vehicles closed in, so the two Stony Man fighters simply let their rounds go through what was left of the pane.

"We are rapidly burning a trail straight to us," James said.

"I know." McCarter nodded. "There's nothing to be done about it, mate. Just remember what will happen if they catch us...and make sure they don't."

James exchanged glances with Encizo. "Understood, David," Encizo said solemnly.

"Chin up, there," McCarter said, exaggerating his own accent. "It's not come to that yet. Still some life in us yet."

A bullet passed through what was left of the rear windshield and blew the rearview mirror to plastic shrapnel. Ahmadi cursed in Persian but kept going.

"Stop tempting Saint Murphy, man," James grumbled.

"We are almost there," Ahmadi said.

"Almost where?"

"Here," Ahmadi said, and whipped the wheel hard to the left. The Range Rover almost went up on two wheels as the Iranian operative pushed it through the corner. McCarter looked back and could see skid marks on only one side; they *had* left the ground on the other side, if only by inches.

"Bloody hell," he murmured.

Slamming the accelerator to the floor, Ahmadi took two more hard turns, a right and then a left, and guided the now bullet-pocked Range Rover into a parking garage that had no attendant. He raced up the ramp to the next level, then the next. Then he threw the machine into Reverse, backed all the way to one end of the parking garage and stopped.

"Out," he said. "Hurry. I will join you in a moment.

Take the ramp down two levels, to one above the street. Find a vehicle there that is suitable."

"And do what?" Hawkins asked.

"Steal it, of course." Ahmadi grinned that strange grin of his.

As Phoenix Force jumped out of the Range Rover, Ahmadi tromped the accelerator again. McCarter watched as, at the last possible moment, the Iranian dumped from the vehicle, hitting the pavement hard and even rolling for a half turn. The Range Rover hit the guardrail at the opposite end of the parking garage and careened over the side, making an ear-splitting crash at street level when it hit.

McCarter whistled. "Just park that anywhere, mate," he whispered. Then he was moving again, following his teammates to the level Ahmadi had suggested.

Calvin James had selected what appeared to be a late-model Peugot, until McCarter got close enough to see that it was a Semand Soren, an Iranian-made car built on the Peugot platform. It was a fairly large vehicle, big enough to accommodate them all, though it would be a tight fit for anyone squeezed between Manning and, say, Encizo. James was under the dashboard on the driver's side, hot-wiring it. That was a skill he possessed from long experience, growing up on Chicago's South Side.

McCarter got in. Ahmadi was not far behind. He took the wheel from James once the car was started, glanced down at the ignition wires neatly twisted together and nodded his approval.

"I could not have done better myself," he said.

"You're an interesting dude, Ghaem," James said.

They pulled away, and this time Ahmadi was careful to drive placidly, attracting no attention to them. Several times speeding IIS vehicles passed them with their yellow lights shining and their siren-horns bellowing, but they paid Phoenix Force's new vehicle no mind.

"I will take us to the second of the three rallies," Ahmadi said. "This one is…problematic. Unless you wish to rest first?"

"No," McCarter said. "We're game, mate. No point slowing down until the job is done."

The Iranian brightened visibly. "I am glad," he said. "We travel now to one of the lesser offices of Magham's People's Party. It has gotten a reputation of late for protests."

"Protests?" James asked.

"Student protests," Ahmadi said. "The young. They are the most brave of my people, because perhaps they are too young to know just how bad it can and has been. They have openly defied Magham's laws and edicts concerning displays of dissent. Magham's people have labeled them seditious, said their speaking out is harmful to our theocratic republic. I fear that eventually, when he believes he has more support behind him, he will crack down and crush them under his boot heels. But for now he allows them to protest in vain. It is only a matter of time before their defiance is rewarded with death."

"We'll need to be careful to safeguard them as we go in," McCarter said. "Ovan's operatives, not to mention the IIS, could well take armed intervention as an excuse to start whacking protestors, believing they can blame it on someone else. Misfortunes of war and all that."

"Yes," Ahmadi agreed. "It is very possible."

They parked the car in yet another alleyway, this one accessible to the party headquarters storefront a few blocks away. Ahmadi immediately disappeared again, telling them he was going to find yet another vehicle, which he would park some distance away in the other direction.

"Man, I hope that dude is really on our side," James said as Phoenix Force assembled at the rear entrance of this new target. "I'd hate to think he's running us around from place to place just to turn us over." From around the corner of the small building, through an accessway between towering buildings, they could hear the protesters at the front of the storefront. Chanting protesters were another group that sounded the same in any language, McCarter decided.

"According to the briefing files we received from the Farm," McCarter said quietly, "he's a trusted operative. Has been for some years now."

"I know," James said. "I'm just sayin'. What's the plan, David?"

"The IIS is already riled up," McCarter said, "and we're not likely to have much time to play around waiting. If we go in hot, it will prompt Ovan's operatives to show themselves if they're present. If not, it will get everybody out of here and disrupt the rally, but either way, the threat will be over for the time being. We'll have a brief window to hightail it out of here to stay one step ahead of Internal Security, too."

"I'm starting to feel like a smash-and-grab man," Hawkins said quietly, a grin on his face.

"We're counterguerrillas," James stressed. "Or maybe counter-counterrevolutionaries. Something like that, man. You got to get into the gun-and-go mind-set."

While he couldn't disagree, McCarter still felt as if they were missing something…as if they would never truly get ahead of the operation playing reactive games like this one. "Everyone ready?" he asked.

The team members voiced their assent.

"Go!" McCarter ordered.

Manning kicked the door, although it was not locked. Whether that was another of Ahmadi's late-night preparations or just luck, McCarter couldn't say. Clearly the CIA operative had been preparing for their arrival and anticipating what he would be taking them to do as their local contact.

Manning and Encizo went in low, while McCarter, James and Hawkins went in high. Their weapons were at the ready.

They burst into the headquarters building ready to fire.

And they stopped short.

The room was completely empty. There were desks, and chairs, and the protesters beyond the storefront, visible through tinted glass. There were more posters for Magham.

There was absolutely nobody living in the place.

"This is seriously uncool," James said.

"Out the back, lads," McCarter directed. "Back the way we've come. Quickly now!"

Ahmadi was waiting with an imported Mercedes SUV of some kind. He'd broken out one of the rear windows to gain access to it, a detail McCarter filed away for possible future reference. Phoenix Force again piled into the vehicle and once more pulled away as Ahmadi drove them to relative, if dubious, safety.

"What is wrong?" Ahmadi asked, seeing the looks on their faces.

"It was a bust, mate," McCarter said. "Nobody home."

"That is…unusual," the Iranian said.

"You know anything about that?" James asked.

"I do not." Ahmadi shook his head.

If he was not sincere, McCarter concluded, he was the

best actor the Briton had ever encountered. He looked completely crestfallen, as if he'd applied for membership to an exclusive club only to be turned down. That stood to reason. If Ahmadi was on the level, and McCarter's instincts told him the Iranian was just what he claimed to be, then of course he would feel he'd let his visiting commando friends down.

"I am unsure what to do," Ahmadi said. "There is the third rally. We may yet find more of Ovan's operatives. I am at a loss to explain why the rally here did not take place as scheduled. I have no other opportunities for you. It was certain we would have our hands full with these attacks."

"Then we keep the appointment," McCarter said. "Until something new shakes loose, it's all we've got."

Ahmadi nodded, frowning. McCarter knew how he felt. The game they were playing was a dangerous one, and the stakes had just been raised.

CHAPTER SIX

Albany, New York

The New York State Museum in Albany, New York, was located not far from the city's famous Egg, a sculpture-like performance center designed in the late 1960s. As the capital of New York, Albany wasn't much to look at, Lyons decided, but he liked the Egg and he almost wished he could spend some time looking through the exhibitions in the New York State Museum, among the oldest and largest in the nation. He would of course never admit this urge to his teammates. Blancanales wouldn't comment, but Schwarz would give him no end of teasing, probably accusing him of having some inner pencil-neck nerd and then suggesting they take a day trip together. He had endured Schwarz's banter for so long that he could hear it in his sleep.

As soon as Able Team neared the museum, it was obvious that something was wrong.

Albany Police Department vehicles surrounded the building, and the police had fashioned temporary barriers and caution tape to erect a cordon. There were spectators crowding around, but not too many, and the local police were discouraging those who got close from getting any nearer.

"Looks like we're late to the party," Lyons said.

"You sure you're okay, Carl?" Schwarz asked.

"Dammit, Gadgets, stop fussing over me," Lyons growled. "It's not my first rodeo. I've lost fights before."

Schwarz traded looks with Blancanales.

"Now," Lyons said, "let's get control of this situation. You're getting clear readings from the museum?"

"Unfortunately, yes," Schwarz said. "There are definitely smart bombs inside. The readings indicate they're reaching the climax of their calibration cycles, too. We don't have a lot of time."

"Pol, get on your satellite phone and call the Farm. Have Barb get through to the locals and throw every government credential you can at them. We need to get in there and we need to make sure nobody interferes with us."

The Chinook circled, attracting a lot of attention from the ground, as Blancanales made arrangements through Barbara Price. It didn't take long for the team to secure clearance to land nearby with assurances that the local cops wouldn't attempt to stop them. Lyons unlimbered his USAS-12 and loaded a fresh drum magazine.

"Let's go," he said. "Take her down, Jack."

"Roger," Grimaldi answered.

"Barb confirms that terrorists have seized the museum," Blancanales reported. "They've made a lot of conflicting demands that don't make a lot of sense, she says. Sounds like they're just buying time with the locals in order to get the bombs placed."

"True to form, from what we know so far." Schwarz nodded.

"Then, let's get in there," Lyons said.

The Chinook made a dramatic entrance, but the authorities had been given a little time to get used to the idea. Lyons knew that Brognola himself had spent plenty of hours on the phone smoothing the way with countless arms of government and law enforcement, although in a situation like this, Price would have handled most of the negotiations. Brognola was usually called out when feathers were ruffled and international incidents had occurred. It was no wonder the man looked as if he had a permanent ulcer.

In transit, they had considered fast-roping into position once they arrived, but in practice, it was easier simply to land the chopper neatly in an intersection near the police cordon, where civilian traffic was being rerouted. As they moved into position, they consulted their secure satellite phones, for floor plans of the museum the Farm had transmitted.

The police passed them through the cordon. If the jurisdictional breach meant anything to them, the grim looks on Able Team's faces and the weapons they carried kept the grumbling to a minimum. Once past the cordon, Lyons directed Schwarz and Blancanales to take secondary entrances at the side and rear of the museum while he went straight for the front doors.

The standard procedures in play here assumed the terrorists wanted something and would preserve their leverage—the hostages—until they got it. Able Team and the Farm, however, knew that taking hostages was simply a means to an end. Ovan's terrorists didn't care about any demands they may have issued, and they would just as soon kill the hostages, but they needed to shield their activities and prevent law-enforcement intervention until the bombs had finished their calibrations.

What that meant was that there was no reason Able Team could not mount a full-on assault. The breach of the facility would not prompt the terrorists to murder their hostages, for they would perform those killings in their own time anyway. The best chance those innocent men and women had, therefore, was for Able Team to kill the men holding them, and to kill them quickly.

If the terrorists didn't murder them, the smart bombs would, for the clock was ticking down and there was very little time left. Schwarz confirmed that as he looked over his handheld scanner while the teammates mounted their assault.

"From this angle," Schwarz reported over his earbud transceiver, "it looks like the bombs are on the second floor somewhere."

"Start working your way up there," Lyons said. He pushed past the glass doors of the entrance, walking as if he didn't have a care in the world. In reality, he was grim and determined, full of righteous anger and the desire for justice. The damage Ovan's terrorists had done turned his stomach, as did the continued threat Ovan's men and their weapons of mass destruction posed to the innocent populace of the United States.

There were guards on the ground floor, wearing ski masks and carrying AK-47s. Lyons brought the USAS-12 up and stroked the trigger on semiautomatic, unleashing 12-gauge slugs that punched each man in the chest and put him down forever.

The noise brought more gunmen. They were no longer human beings to Lyons—not because he dehumanized his enemies, but because enemies with guns bent on killing him were no longer feeling, breathing people so much as they were a math problem, a physics equation. Each man carried so much ammunition that could be delivered in so many ways, and each of these was a target vector that Lyons would need to avoid to stay alive. He, in turn, had so many ways to deliver his own payload of offensive weaponry to the enemy, and each time he did so, the odds against him decreased.

It was time for some exponential improvement in the odds.

Lyons burst into the nearest exhibit hall, following his nose, trusting that Schwarz would be working his way toward the bombs and would report as soon as he had something to relate. Blancanales was similarly quiet, no doubt eliminating enemies of his own. The three men of Able Team would work their way from three directions leading always to higher floors, clearing the building as they went, carving a path through Ovan's terrorists and liberating any hostages they found.

It was as direct a plan as any, and it was serviceable. It needn't be complicated, especially with the motivated veteran soldiers of Able to drive it.

The hall in which Lyons found himself boasted elaborate displays of early humans and woolly mammoths, exactly the sort of stereotypical thing he expected to find in such a place. He saw movement in his peripheral vision and knew the enemy was trying to be clever.

They came at him from the displays, hiding among the life-size mannequins. One man wielded an entrenching tool as if it were an ax. Lyons used the Daewoo to sidestep the attack, slamming the butt of the USAS-12 heavily against the side of the man's skull. There was a sickening crack as the man folded, his eyes rolling up into his head.

Whipping the big weapon around, Lyons fired once, then again, then again. He winced as one of his slugs blew the head off a mannequin dressed in animal furs and carrying a bow...until the man behind the mannequin, a crater in his face, completed his fall from behind the dummy, slumping to the floor like a sack of wet flour.

Lyons hit the fire doors at the end of the exhibit hall and found himself in an access corridor. Vending machines hummed on either side of him. He stopped. He could hear breathing.

Was it a hostage? It was possible some of the men, women and children trapped in the museum might be hiding from the armed killers who had taken control of the building. He was about to call out when he heard the distinctive metallic clack of a Kalashnikov's heavy bolt being pulled back.

So. That was how it was. Ovan's people were all lying in wait, and there was only one explanation for that. They would be confident that the threat of killing the hostages would keep ordinary law enforcement at bay. Lyons would feel that way were he in their position. This meant that Karbuly Ghemenizov or one of his people had warned his killers that an opposition team had been fielded. Obviously, while placing their bombs for eventual destruction of the museum and its patrons, they had hoped also to put an end to the interference Able Team had proved to Ghemenizov it was capable of offering.

Well. Lyons would teach these clever murderers that they weren't nearly as smart as they thought. Lining up the shot, he aimed at the center of the bottled-water machine sitting diagonally from him. He pulled the trigger on full-auto.

The vending machine exploded, spraying water and partially shredded plastic bottles. The terrorist behind it stumbled out, his chest a bloody ruin, and collapsed on the floor. Lyons took a step forward—

He thought he heard Schwarz say something quietly,

but before he could ask the man to repeat his transmission, a second terrorist charged him. A knife was clenched in the man's fist. Lyons brought the USAS-12 up to shield his face and the man grabbed the rifle, wrenching it this way and that. The blade of his knife inched closer to Lyons's hand, and the big cop was forced to let that end of the weapon go to prevent having his fingers sliced off.

He directed a brutal front kick into the man's midsection, knocking him to the polished floor. The knife wielder still clutched his weapon and made as if to gather himself for another lunge. Lyons had had enough of him. He roared.

He reached out and, with one arm, tipped over the soda machine above the man.

The heavy vending machine crashed down, crushing the terrorist underneath.

One of the man's feet started jerking spastically. His head had been crushed by a corner of the vending machine.

Lyons stepped over the twitching corpse and cautiously strode through the doors.

HERMANN "GADGETS" SCHWARZ followed the scanner he and Akira Tokaido had designed and built, moving up the stairwell that would take him to the second floor. He had affixed the custom suppressor, built by the Farm's armorer, John "Cowboy" Kissinger, to the threaded muzzle of his 93-R machine pistol. With the weapon in one hand, his M-16 slung across his back and the scanner in his off hand, he carefully crept up the stairs.

The mission, like so many Able Team had undertaken, was fraught with challenge and risk. That was nothing new and Schwarz had no issue with any of it.

He was, however, deeply concerned about the threat the Iranian smart weapons represented. As familiar as he was with the technology, it now seemed very simple to him, and he was tormented by images of similar weapons being created in other rogue states. If they didn't succeed in intercepting the terrorist attacks in the United States, and if Phoenix Force could not disrupt the pipeline poised to carry those weapons out of Iran and into the global terror landscape, a new age of destruction could shift the balance of global power for the foreseeable future if not forever.

It was heady stuff.

Schwarz knew he spent a lot of time in his own head, so to speak, and sometimes he envied the single-minded determination of Lyons or the calm, detached, always-cool way Blancanales accepted every challenge with equanimity and resolve. But he had always managed to get things done in his own way, and his career with Stony Man Farm had been a long one.

With luck, it would have the chance to get even longer.

At the top of the stairwell, he paused just outside the door. It was a heavy metal affair with a standard push bar. He started to move forward to push the bar…and noticed the gap.

The door was wedged open slightly. A screwdriver poked through the bottom of the opening on one side. He waited and, watching the shadows beneath the bottom of the door, was rewarded with movement.

There was someone on the other side. He very quietly placed the sensor in its padded pouch and took a two-handed grip on his weapon.

Schwarz stood back and lashed out with a kick. While he would never be able to put the force into a door kick that Lyons could, he wasn't such a slouch himself and he knew how to generate power with his body. The door whipped open, slamming into whoever waited, and Schwarz burst through with his pistol ready.

It wasn't one man; it was three, and all of them carried a Kalashnikov. Schwarz put a 3-round burst into one of them, hitting him in the chest, and then stitched the second through the neck and face. The third tried to bring his weapon up in the close confines of the hallway in which they stood and only managed to jab Schwarz with the barrel. The electronics expert shoved the barrel aside just as it went off. He felt the barrel grow warm as the full-auto burst hammered his eardrums and blew a gaping hole in the drywall beyond him.

The terrorist let his AK drop to the floor. He and Schwarz were suddenly grappling for the 93-R. Schwarz dropped his center of gravity, trying to get more leverage, and as he extended one hand, his fingers found the screwdriver propping open the door.

The tool came up and around. Schwarz buried it in the killer's neck. He fell to the floor, gurgling and spraying crimson across the polished faux-marble.

Schwarz looked left, then right. Looking down at his dead foe, he covered his transceiver with one hand and said, in his best impersonation of a famous action movie star, "Screw you, buddy."

Then, glad nobody had seen that, he removed the sensor from its pouch and continued on.

Rosario "Politician" Blancanales put his finger to his earbud, shook his head and continued across the floor of the automotive history exhibit. He passed an old, beautifully restored Model T Ford, his M-16 set to 3-round burst and ready in front of him.

The hall he faced was quite large, and as he crouched to survey what lay ahead of him, he realized the entire affair was a setup. The terrorists were waiting. He saw them crouched behind various show cars and mock-ups at the far end of the hall. They were simply waiting for him to come within range, waiting for a clear shot at him.

He needed to clear the hall and keep going. So far he hadn't seen any hostages, but they were probably with the bombs. He had no sooner thought that than his earbud buzzed to life.

"Carl, Pol, this is Gadgets," he said. "I've got the bombs and I'm moving in. There are half a dozen tangos here, and at least that many hostages. They're moving around a display of the solar system. There's an alcove and the hostages are corralled there."

Blancanales consulted his satellite phone's records of the floorplan. He was not far from a stairwell that would take him to Schwarz's position, if he could just cross this hall.

"I'm on my way," Lyons said. "Will be to you in moments. You focus on the bombs, I'll take the tangos. Pol, status?"

"Give me a second and I'll be right behind you," he promised. Glancing to his right, he saw a mannequin on a rolling dolly underneath a mockup of a DeLorean, which was not quite life-size. "Okay, found what I need."

He pulled the dolly out as quietly as he could and kicked the mannequin from it. Then, with his M-16 in front of his body and lying on his belly, he pushed the dolly back so he could coil his legs against the bumper of the Model T.

Okay, he thought. Here goes nothing.

He gave the hardest shove he could, and suddenly he was being propelled quickly across the polished floor of the hall on the dolly. He fired bursts from his M-16 as he went, picking off shooter after shooter, moving faster than they could track him and faster than they thought to lead him. When he hit the far wall and spilled over the side of the dolly with an earsplitting crash, he had taken out all of his foes.

He wondered if he should give in to his action-movie impulse and say something sarcastic or witty. No, he decided. He doubted even Schwarz would indulge in such a thing, and certainly Carl Lyons would not even think it.

He hit the stairwell at a run. It was reckless. As he reached the second-floor fire door he pushed it open and almost tripped over a gunman. Clubbing the man down with the stock of his M-16, he reversed the weapon and fired point-blank into the man's head to keep him there. Then he took cover behind a half-wall divider and started shooting, pinning down terrorists that Carl Lyons was simultaneously mowing down with his automatic shotgun.

Schwarz was crouched over a cluster of smart bombs, pointing his magic technological wand at the devices. With Lyons keeping the terrorists fully occupied now, Blancanales made his way to the alcove. As he ran past the solar system exhibit, errant fire put bullet holes in the surface of the Earth and blew Venus clear out of the system.

He shielded the hostages with his body, covering them with his weapon. A last terrorist broke free from the knot of armed killers Lyons was neutralizing and Blancanales tagged him, walking a 3-round burst up his torso. As he fell backward, his Kalashnikov disgorged a burst that did even more damage to the model of the solar system at the side of the alcove.

"The bombs are disarmed," Schwarz announced. "They were very nearly ready to detonate, too."

"Did you say bombs?" one of the hostages, a slight, balding man, asked.

"No, sir," Blancanales said smoothly. He moved between Schwarz and the man. "That's a SWAT term, sir. It's kind of an inside joke. Now, if you'll just accompany me to the nearest exits, we'll get you back to your families. Anybody hurt? No? Excellent. Follow me, folks…"

CARL LYONS STOOD outside the museum surrounded by curious police officers who were apparently too intimidated or impressed to bother him. He made a quiet assessment of his aches and pains. Either he was older than he thought he was, or the day had been rougher than even he was willing to admit.

He hurt. He hurt bad, and the mission was only just getting started. The Warlock network was computing their next target and Grimaldi would be on hand with the chopper as soon as he knew where to ferry them. For the briefest of moments, however, Lyons was content just to stand there and ache.

He watched Blancanales plying his trade in dealing with people, making sure things were smoothed over with the locals. He watched Schwarz carry the bomb casings back to the chopper. Most satisfyingly, he watched as the hostages were reunited with their family members—those who had family waiting for them beyond the police cordon.

For the moment, that was enough for him.

Lyons shouldered his USAS-12 and marched on.

CHAPTER SEVEN

Tehran, Iran

Ghaem Ahmadi had told the Phoenix Force team members that the building they were now entering was a social center. T. J. Hawkins didn't like it. Nothing about Tehran seemed particularly social to him, although he had to admit that the city was a lot more modern in appearance and in pace than most people would imagine when thinking of the Iranian metropolis. Maybe it was because he'd seen too much of this kind of life. Tehran was far richer than the filthy hopelessness that was Somalia, but he saw, in the eyes of so many of the citizens here, the same deadened spirits, the same resignation, that had characterized so many of the Somalis. In his glimpses of the IIS and the supporters of the oppressive regime, he could also see the same fanatical devotion, the same implacable, devoted madness, that had characterized the Somali fighters he and the Rangers had been pitted against.

The whole thing made him uneasy and set every one of his combat instincts ablaze. The Glock 19 was a reassuring weight in his waistband under his jacket, but as the members of Phoenix Force moved casually through the rear entrance of the social center, trying to look as if they belonged, the background noise of the crowd gathered inside reminded him too much of a preriot crowd of desperate Somalis. Someone with less training would probably find himself reaching for an M-16 that was not there; the fact that Hawkins recognized the urge buried deep in the back of his mind was enough to make him wish for the Krinkovs, which were with Ahmadi in the Mercedes SUV. The Iranian had said large bags would be checked for explosives, which meant the weapons would have to stay in their vehicle.

The security setup didn't make any sense to Hawkins. There were no metal detectors and no armed guards that he could see, although to assume they weren't there simply because they weren't visible would be an amateur's mistake. Not that he was complaining—metal detectors would make the operation to interdict Ovan's terrorist operatives almost impossible. But Ovan's people had been hitting hard-line rallies for a while now. According to the briefing files he and all the team members had been given, they had left a series of anonymous calls to Iranian media claiming credit for the attacks in the name of supporters of Khan. If Magham's people knew they were the targets of such attacks, why weren't they imposing stricter security? Could they be gambling with the lives of their supporters because they knew the attacks were making Khan look bad?

The social center was a two-tiered open hall with half-stairways leading to the upper deck, an elevated stage of sorts. More Magham banners and some large posters of the man had been arrayed at the lip of the stage. Hawkins paid particular attention to the upper deck, which ran from the rear of the room around the perimeter of the hall about a third of the way deep. Something about that stage was bothering him. He wasn't sure why.

He glanced behind him to see Manning and followed

the big Canadian's gaze back to the stage. The two of them exchanged the briefest of nods. James and Encizo met Hawkins's eyes, too. McCarter was ahead of him, but the team leader's body language told Hawkins that McCarter, like the rest of the team, was on edge. There was something about this scenario that wasn't adding up.

Hawkins stepped past a grizzled, hard-looking man with a gaunt, deeply lined face, who gave him a blank look as Hawkins left him behind. As he looked around, he realized what was wrong.

The crowd was all wrong. It was sparse for the size of the venue, and the men ranged from their twenties to middle age. There were no senior citizens and no young people.

"David," Hawkins started to whisper.

"I see, lad," McCarter breathed back.

"We're burned," James said.

"Gary," McCarter said quietly, "work your way to the back. Get back to the Mercedes if you can."

"David—" Manning started.

"You know what to do," McCarter said. "Go now, mate."

"Affirmative," Manning said.

"He's not going to make it," James said quietly.

"No," McCarter said. "He's not. But he may get close enough. Work to the perimeter, lads."

Hawkins immediately understood. One man could conceivably back out of the trap, but two or more would alert the enemy that their prey was onto the setup. It might already be too late.

Hawkins started moving through the crowd slowly, doing his best to look as if he was simply milling around. There were no speakers assembled at the front of the hall, and if this was indeed a trap, there probably would not be. Hawkins nonetheless did his best to look as if he was watching the front eagerly for the first appearance of someone there.

He backed into someone and remembered not to excuse himself reflexively in English. He started to turn, to move around the man in his way, and felt a viselike grip on his arm.

The shout in his ear was clear enough in intent if not in its words. As he felt his left arm being grabbed, he yanked it free, driving a vertical elbow up into the face of the man trying to stop him. As his opponent closed in and tried to grapple with him, he kept his elbow up between them. The Glock came out of its holster as if by reflex, and at close quarters, Hawkins fired from retention. With the Glock pressed at an angle against his body, he pulled the trigger again and again, blasting the opponent off of him as the 9 mm rounds entered at an angle centered on the enemy's pelvis.

Battle erupted all around him.

Wooden platforms covering hatches in the stage opened up at intervals across its length and along the sides. The men lifting them from within wore the uniforms of the Iranian Internal Security forces. In their hands they held Kalashnikov rifles.

The room exploded in the fiery white blooms of muzzle-flashes from every direction. Either the IIS forces lacked discipline, or the men who had been planted in the hall as audience members were expendable, for several of them were taken down with the first volley.

The men of Phoenix Force, with little to use for cover, substituted mobility, weaving in and around the enemies around them as they scattered for the outside walls of the hall. To reach the shooters and gain the higher ground was the goal; it was the only tactical choice. They did not need to communicate to do it, either, for every man of Phoenix Force was an experienced combat soldier who understood the principles of fighting against the odds.

Hawkins ran and fired, acquiring targets on the move, emptying his Glock's 15-round magazine. With a practiced movement he retracted his arm until the elbow rested against his body, ripped the lightweight plastic magazine free and brought his off hand up with the fresh one to slam it home. The force of his movement caused the Glock's slide, which was locked open, to slam forward, but by long habit he was already racking the slide as if trying to rip it from the gun. He scarcely noticed the live round that he jacked over his shoulder as he pushed the Glock out again to full extension. In combat, practiced movement was the key; the moment he might have taken to process the slide moving forward on its own was a moment he did not dare waste. He had many more magazines. He had only one life.

The Glock fired, fired again and fired three more times as Hawkins moved slowly with heel-to-toe steps, gliding this way and that, making himself a difficult target as he half crouched. The gliding gait kept his upper body stable so he could fire accurately. Aimed fire won battles; the men of Phoenix Force did not spray and pray.

He vaulted the steps leading up to the upper platform and mounted it high on the right side, shooting down an IIS gunner and knocking the man back into his wood-framed hiding hole. Hawkins dived in after the man, landing hard on the concrete floor underneath the stage. The dead man stared up at the trapdoor as if his last thoughts had been of escape. Hawkins quickly relieved him of his Kalashnikov and spare magazines, shouldering the bandolier as he pushed himself back up through the hatchway.

He fired out the rifle and swapped magazines before doing so again. The center of the room was a sea of bodies now as men fell and stayed where they hit the floor. Hawkins quickly judged the positions of his teammates, noting that Manning was not among them.

"Withdraw!" McCarter ordered, and Hawkins heard the command over his earpiece despite the ringing in his hearing caused by the storm of indoor gunfire.

The men of Phoenix Force converged on each other, covering one another as they moved to the rear. The resistance from within was withering. They hit the doorway, filing through, covering each other in pairs.

The vehicle was gone.

Ahmadi and their transportation were nowhere in sight. Several white-painted IIS vehicles, their sirens blaring, were closing on their position.

"Go for broke, lads!" McCarter shouted.

They laid down as much fire as they could. Crouching in twos by the doorway, the man behind standing taller than the man in front of him, they emptied their weapons into the Iranian enforcement troops. James, like Hawkins, had secured a Kalashnikov while inside, but the others had only the pistols Ahmadi had provided.

Hawkins could see where this was going. The IIS were forming a cordon around them, and once it was complete, they would simply move in, walking their fire straight into the killing bowl that trapped the men of Phoenix Force. They couldn't go back into the social center, either. Bullets were already hitting the closed door from behind. Only the threat of being caught in their own cross fire prompted the IIS operatives within from bursting through that door, Hawkins suspected.

As his Kalashnikov ran dry and he loaded the last of his field-acquired magazines for it, Hawkins wondered if pinned down on an Iranian street was going to be how he, and the rest of the team, finally went out. There wasn't a mission that each man didn't consider the possibility, of course, but they always won. No man could buck the odds forever; no man was immortal. It wasn't so far-fetched to think they would die in combat. Given the horrors that awaited them at the hands of Iranian Internal Security, death here and now would be preferable.

But he was not about to give up. That wasn't the Phoenix Force way. That wasn't how the men and women of Stony Man Farm operated.

Hawkins braced himself. Over the chatter of the gunfire there was very little chance McCarter could hear him, but he shouted anyway.

"David!" he yelled. "I'm going to break left and draw fire. That should give you a chance to punch through!"

McCarter looked over at Hawkins just as the slide of his Hi-Power locked back. He started to shake his head, and then grim realization flashed across his features. They were out of options. Somebody would have to do it, and Hawkins had just volunteered.

McCarter, loading a spare magazine into his pistol, nodded.

Hawkins could feel his feet coiled beneath him as he prepared to spring. In his mind, he visualized the path he would take, weaving this way and that, firing out his last magazine on full-auto. He picked the closest IIS vehicle, its flank parked facing them. He would run to that. He visualized reaching the vehicle, vaulting over its hood and smashing aside any resistance with the butt of the Kalashnikov, which would be empty by the time he reached it.

Yeah. That was how it would go. And if he was cut down by a hail of bullets before he reached it, well, those were the breaks, and Phoenix Force would still get its chance—

The Mercedes SUV, its engine howling with the abuse it was taking, suddenly reappeared, smashing between the rear of one IIS vehicle and the nose of another, tearing off most of its own front grille and ripping off the security vehicle's front bumper. Hawkins, as he threw himself to the pavement, had the fleeting impression of Ghaem Ahmadi behind the wheel, crouched beneath bullet holes that were appearing in the windshield as if by magic.

Gary Manning was leaning out of the rear windshield. With his legs braced on the rear seat and his upper body projecting through the rear windshield opening, he had a Krinkov in each hand. Using the roof of the vehicle to support the two weapons, he was laying down a hellfire burst of high-velocity cartridges.

"Bloody hell!" Hawkins heard McCarter exclaim.

The bullet-riddled SUV whipped to a halt in a wide arc of burning rubber and screeching brakes as Ahmadi leaned hard on the wheel. Using the SUV itself as cover while Manning put down withering cover fire, the other Phoenix Force men ran for the car. Brass rang off the dented metal of the SUV's roof. Manning, cool as ever, his expression one of focused intent, walked his twin Krinkovs from left to right and back again.

Rare as it was for a car to explode from gunfire, something volatile in the rear of one of the IIS vehicles caught and burst. Flames leaped up, scattering the security operatives gathered behind that vehicle. Ahmadi used the distraction to tromp the accelerator to the floor. The battered SUV burned rubber as it gained momentum, smashing aside an IIS man with a pistol. He hit the pavement with a sickening cracking noise.

The streets of Tehran blurred as Ahmadi pushed the Mercedes to its top speed, barely missing pedestrians and small obstacles that Hawkins assumed were post boxes. McCarter, in the front seat squeezed between Ahmadi and Hawkins, began yelling something that Hawkins couldn't hear. He realized his ears were ringing badly.

Manning slid down into the backseat, both Krinkovs empty. Encizo and James, on either side of him, helped pull him back in. The SUV jostled them from side to side as Ahmadi began making hard turns, left, then right, then left again, wheeling this way and that with crazed abandon.

"Slow the bloody car down before you kill us all!" McCarter was yelling. Hawkins put a useless thumb up to his ear, willing his hearing to return.

"We must reach the garage," the Iranian said. "Or it is a slow death for us all!"

Hawkins didn't know what "the garage" was, but assumed it would allow Ahmadi to park the vehicle out of sight and hide all of them from pursuit. The carnage they had left behind, coupled with Manning's and Ahmadi's grandstand play, seemed to have forestalled pursuit, but he could hear the braying of security vehicle sirens in the distance. The Iranians were stirred up like hornets. The job had gone bad. It was inevitable that open military operations, even small-scale covert ones that were Phoenix Force's specialty, would draw heat from the powers in Tehran, but their entire mission to expose Ovan's terrorist network here in Iran was based on the element of surprise. Something had caused them to lose that element of surprise too quickly, and Hawkins immediately thought of the surveillance gear they had found—not to mention the strangely abandoned rally.

If he was thinking it, McCarter would be thinking it. He set his Kalashnikov with its single magazine on the floor between his legs, barrel down, and checked his Glock. He offered one of his spare magazines to McCarter, who thumbed the cartridges out and into an empty magazine for his Hi-Power, nodding his thanks.

They may not be surrounded by hostiles at this moment, but they were far from clear. They were also deep within the territory of a hostile, arguably rogue nation whose security personnel would consider their intrusion an act of war. If they were caught, finding a way to kill themselves would be critical, for under torture they would all eventually break. That was just a fact of life, even if it took years to do it.

The garage was in a curiously mixed commercial and residential neighborhood whose architecture was a confusion of ancient and modern elements. Ahmadi pulled the Mercedes from the tiny street into the garage with only inches to spare on either side of his mirrors. What they would have done had another car been going the other way, Hawkins couldn't guess.

From the street it was obvious the garage was the lower floor of a two-story building, the top floor a residence or shop. Ahmadi hurried from the SUV and pulled the windowless, wooden-slat garage door into place, throwing a bolt from inside to secure it. He turned with a sigh of relief.

"We will be safe—" he started.

McCarter was waiting for him as he turned around. Ahmadi stopped short with the barrel of McCarter's Browning Hi-Power pressed against his forehead.

"You walked us into a trap, friend," McCarter said.

There was no melodramatic thumbing back of the trigger. Ahmadi, for his part, did not immediately launch into an indignant you-can't-do-this routine, which Hawkins and the other Phoenix men had seen plenty of times. He simply became very, very still.

"I understand your concern," Ahmadi said simply.

"Do you, now?" McCarter demanded. The fox-faced Briton was wound up; Hawkins could see that much. Most trained men would not press a gun to an enemy's body at contact distance like that, for there were several desperate plays that someone in Ahmadi's position might try from that range. McCarter was certainly aware of what those might be, however, and at the first indication of even the most barely perceptible movement on the Iranian agent's part, he would doubtless pull the trigger.

At least, that's how it looked to Hawkins. That was how it was supposed to look. McCarter wanted Ahmadi to know that the operative's life depended on telling the truth.

"Where are we right now?" McCarter demanded.

"It is one of my safehouses. A CIA facility," Ahmadi said.

"Who knows we're here?"

"No one," Ahmadi said. "I did not report my use of this place."

"What do you mean, mate, 'report'?" McCarter asked.

"Per standard procedure," Ahmadi said, "I have

reported our progress to the CIA network here in Tehran. This is essential, I am led to understand, to making sure CIA assets do not interfere with our activities in the city, and so they can mount whatever obfuscating campaigns available to protect your identities. Disinformation released through official and unofficial sources regarding your descriptions, for example. Anonymous tips that lead nowhere. To distract the Iranians from the operation they must know where we are and what we are doing, so they can lead the Iranian authorities away from us. Is this not logical?"

McCarter didn't comment on that. He looked at his Phoenix Force teammates and then back at Ahmadi. The pistol didn't waver. "I don't like that you magically found surveillance equipment just before things started going to hell, mate," he said.

"Would I have shown it to you?" Ahmadi said. "That would make no sense."

"I'll grant you that," McCarter said. "So explain to me where you disappeared to."

"I saw the IIS closing in and removed the vehicle before they took notice of me," Ahmadi said. "Your man," Ahmadi said, indicated Manning, "exited the vehicle just as violence erupted, and I intercepted him as he took to a side street in search of me. We quickly decided to use the fortunes of the moment to our advantage and mounted the...er, the rear attack that rescued you."

"So now what?" James put in.

"The only possible explanation," Ahmadi said, "is that there is a leak in the CIA. This is the only thing that can explain how our operation was discovered so quickly. For the IIS to mount a counter-operation intended to corner and capture you means that someone must have informed them of what was going on."

"You said," Encizo offered, "that the surveillance device you found is standard CIA manufacture, but you weren't aware of it."

"Yes." The Iranian agent nodded. "Which means someone within the CIA is mounting an operation of his own, one that is not knowledge to the rest of the Tehran network. It is likely that whoever did that is also the leak. At least, that is the simplest explanation."

"The simplest explanation," McCarter said, "is that you're the leak, Ghaem, and that you betrayed us."

"If that were true, I would not have rescued you," Ahmadi replied.

"Gary?" McCarter asked.

"It's true," Manning said. "I wouldn't have found him if he hadn't rolled up on me."

McCarter thought for a moment, then raised the pistol, engaging the safety before putting the cocked-and-locked weapon back in his waistband in its clip-on holster. "All right," he said. "But operating on the assumption that you're clean, Ghaem, and that someone else among your intelligence boys is gunning for us, we have a very serious problem. We will have failed to complete our mission under these circumstances if we don't think of something, and fast. And just because you haven't checked in, don't think your boys won't know this is a likely spot for us to be."

"The thought has occurred to me," Ahmadi said. "I will procure another vehicle so we can make haste to leave."

"Gary," McCarter said, "go with him."

Ahmadi looked at McCarter, then Manning, then back. "Of course. You do not trust me."

"It's nothing personal, mate," McCarter said. "Now, what can you give us for our next move?"

"There is only one that I can think of," Ahmadi said. "Magham's most trusted officials, his upper echelon, are holding a conference tomorrow morning. They would be a tempting target for Ovan's operatives, and while the blow would not be a crippling one, it would look very bad for Khan's campaign to be linked to such an attack. Many of these men of Magham's are very old, some almost legendary in Iranian political circles. It would be seen as an attack on the virtually helpless."

"Hard-line dictators," Encizo said. "The world is a cruel place for them and their followers."

"Right." McCarter nodded. "We'll need more ammunition."

"I have it here," Ahmadi said, pointing to the residence above.

"Then let's get cracking, lads," McCarter concluded.

CHAPTER EIGHT

The American-Canadian border

Hermann Schwarz watched the streets slide by on the American side of Niagara Falls, a bit surprised at just how run-down the area looked. Why one of the biggest tourist attractions in this part of the country should translate to such a practically bombed-out, burned-out neighborhood he couldn't guess. The few people he did see on the streets looked like anything but tourists. While it was true that the Canadian side of the falls offered a more spectacular view, there was no reason this side of the border should be in such disrepair. At least, that much seemed obvious to Schwarz.

The signals provided by the Warlock network were strangely scattered when Stony Man had relayed the target data to Able Team. They had arranged for a courier to have a rented Chevy Suburban waiting for them just outside of town. There Grimaldi had landed the Chinook with a minimum of fuss and alarm. With Lyons behind the wheel, driving like a man possessed, Schwarz hung on to the ceiling strap on his side for dear life as the Able Team leader hunched over the wheel and pushed the vehicle for all it was worth. The courier had left a dash light, which was even now strobing red through the front windshield, but how much difference that was making, Schwarz couldn't tell. He imagined that if he was one of the drivers unfortunate enough to share the roads with Carl Lyons that day, he'd get out of the way for his own safety.

"Carl," Schwarz asked, "perhaps this would be a good time to remind you of the benefits of decaffeinated coffee…."

"Shove it, Gadgets," Lyons snarled. His tone was so severe that Schwarz stopped talking out of surprise. Lyons had a temper, but normally he didn't take things quite so personally.

Lyons cut off an ancient Volkswagen microbus with a giant peace symbol emblazoned on its spare tire cover.

"Okay," Schwarz said despite himself, "you did that one on purpose. Admit that much."

"Do you really need to ask?" Blancanales offered. Lyons didn't comment.

Schwarz shrugged. He held the sensor in his hands. It was providing sporadic readings that were leading them closer and closer to the border. The signature profile looked different than any he had yet encountered, however.

Then he realized. Just as he did so, he heard the rumble. A vibration passed through the car, perceptible even as they moved.

"Hey," Blancanales said. "Did you guys just hear—?"

"Oh, no," Schwarz said.

"Oh, *shit*," Lyons said at the same time.

The big blond ex-cop slammed a heavy foot down on the brake pedal. Car horns behind them blared their drivers' outrage. The Suburban squealed to a stop just as a uniformed officer staggered toward them waving his arms. As Able Team watched, he collapsed, his hands at his throat.

"Nerve agent!" Blancanales snarled.

Lyons threw the gearshift into Reverse and burned rubber backward. The Suburban's powerful engine roared in response. They hit the car immediately behind them, shoving it backward, and that car hit yet another. Schwarz realized that Lyons was doing this intentionally, one arm wrapped around the back of Schwarz's seat as Lyons craned his neck to look out the rear window. With a deft pull of the steering wheel he managed to push the Suburban and the cars it was shoving into a makeshift roadblock.

"Everybody out!" Lyons ordered, grabbing his shotgun. Blancanales took his M-16 and Schwarz, his 93-R in one hand and the sensor unit in the other, piled out behind the two of them.

There were screams and murmurs of alarm as the armed men began moving down the street, back the way they had come. Lyons and Blancanales began shouting to the crowd that the trio were federal officers, and that for their own safety, anyone on the street should move in an orderly fashion away from the mess ahead.

The next few minutes were a blur to Schwarz as they did their best to keep the crowd clear of the blast zone. He consulted his secure satellite phone, which contained briefing notes and maps of the area. Up ahead was the entrance to an observation platform on the American side of the falls. What he had feared was obviously what had come to pass: the strange, unfamiliar readings Warlock and then his handheld sensor had detected corresponded to the signature of a bomb during the final detonation sequence.

They were too late.

In the distance, where they dared not go lest the nerve toxin still be viable, they could see bodies. Smoke was rising from the entrance to the plaza at the end of the street. As some of this receded in the wind—the fact that they now stood upwind from the destruction was probably why they were not dead, Schwarz reflected— they could see the wreckage of civilian vehicles that had been thrown this way and that in the explosion.

Schwarz glanced down at the sensor. What he saw hit him like a slap in the face.

"Carl," he said, "I'm seeing back scatter here."

"What?" Lyons asked.

"Trace signals," Schwarz explained. "More bombs!"

Blancanales used his own phone to contact the Farm, but Price and her team were already on it, and Blancanales relayed to Lyons and Schwarz that a hazmat team was already on scene. Only minutes after he said it, the first of the brightly marked vans, accompanied by a National Guard escort, started to arrive. One of the National Guard Hummers pushed a couple of the civilian vehicles out of the way.

"Gadgets," Lyons said. "We need someone to coordinate with hazmat on scene, and you've got more up here—" he tapped the side of his head "—than Pol or I do."

This was no time for flippant comebacks. Schwarz only nodded. "I'll cover it, Carl."

"Give me the thing," Lyons said.

Schwarz handed him the sensor. He had reviewed its operation with both Lyons and Blancanales on the Chinook in-flight, just in case he was injured.

"Be careful, Carl," Schwarz said.

"No," Lyons said ominously. "I don't imagine I will be. Pol, get the truck out of their way." He pointed to where the National Guard were still clearing the makeshift roadblock, replacing it with armed Hummers. Men from the hazmat team, looking like astronauts in their protective gear, were starting to file out of the nearest of the vans.

Blancanales ran for the truck, conferred with one of the guardsmen and then drove the vehicle free. Lyons swung himself up and into the passenger seat even as the Suburban started to pull away.

Schwarz watched them go. He turned back to the hazmat teams, rehearsing his "I'm a federal agent and I'm here to help" routine in his mind as he strode toward the vans.

He wasn't looking forward to what he was about to see.

This was going to be ugly.

CARL LYONS FELT his left fist clench around the stock of the Daewoo automatic shotgun.

Those bastards. Those filthy bastards. He was going to make them pay for what they'd done.

Watching the handheld scanner, doing his best to make sense of the data it displayed, he pointed silently, first left, then right, then straight ahead, trying to follow the signals. Blancanales piloted the Suburban through the traffic. Lyons and Blancanales realized, at the same time, where the trail was leading.

"Carl, we're going to get caught in traffic here." Blancanales pointed. They were on the ramp to the bridge leading across the border.

Lyons put his finger to his earbud transceiver, an unnecessary gesture. "Gadgets," he said, "can you still read me?" The transceivers had limited range.

"Barely," Schwarz said.

"Sitrep?"

"It's bad, Carl," Schwarz said. "No casualty figures

yet, but the place…it's a mess. The guard is on its way to secure the bridges."

That made sense; a major terrorist attack had just occurred on U.S. soil, and one of the first responses would be to stop the flow of traffic across the border on which the target zone sat.

Lyons looked left, then right. Blancanales was right. They were snarled in traffic and becoming increasingly boxed in. It was possible that the Canadians had shut down or at least temporarily suspended crossings into their country, which would explain why the lines of travelers were no longer moving from the American side.

Blancanales nosed up a little farther, bringing them even with a white cargo van in the lane to their left. Suddenly the scanner in Lyons's hand lit up like a Christmas tree. Right hand squeezing the scanner with a viselike grip, he pointed it across Blancanales's line of sight and at the van.

The readings spiked again.

The dark-skinned man in the passenger seat looked over. His eyes grew wide as he realized that Lyons and Blancanales were looking at him.

Blancanales reached down and slammed his seat's backrest lever. As he fell backward, almost lying prone, Lyons brought the barrel of the automatic shotgun up and aimed through Blancanales's window.

Lyons was forced to duck as automatic gunfire punched holes in the window. He shoved the muzzle of the Daewoo forward and pulled the trigger back. The blast of full-auto shotgun shells was deafening inside the Suburban, but it had the desired effect. The gunman, who held an old Skorpion machine pistol, was driven down, the frame of the open window sprayed with blood.

Blancanales hit his door handle and rolled out, staying low. Lyons shoved his own door open and dragged himself and the shotgun to the pavement. People were yelling and pointing, some getting out of their cars and fleeing, moving either back toward the United States proper or forward along the bridge to Canada. Lyons was only too aware of how many innocents were in the potential cross fire. They had to get these shooters off the bridge.

Blancanales and Lyons met as both men circled to the rear of the Suburban. Lyons held the scanner out to Blancanales. "Take this," he said. "Get inside that van. Defuse anything you find."

"Where are you going?" Blancanales asked.

"After them." Lyons jerked a thumb toward the bridge. "Go!"

Blancanales nodded. Lyons took off, the shotgun heavy in his hands, weaving in and out of the idling cars essentially parked on the bridge.

"Back in your car!" he shouted as he passed by. "You, down! Federal officer! Back in your car!"

There were four hardmen, all carrying Kalashnikovs. Some part of Lyons wondered if those rugged but sloppy assault rifles were just on a permanent fire sale in some corner of the Third World, but he dismissed the thought. The customs booths were coming up fast, and uniformed agents were waving wildly and trying to flag him down.

Gunfire ripped back his way and tore up the asphalt, flattening the tire of a passenger car and stitching another car across the hood. That was no good, no good at all. Lyons had no choice.

He changed the angle of his pursuit so that he was standing between the enemy and the closest targets, shielding the civilians with his body. Swapping magazines in the Daewoo and being very careful of his aim, he triggered single shots in the form of 12-gauge slugs, taking the rear man in the throat and the head, blowing the skull apart. The body hit the pavement like a sack of sodden grain.

That left three.

The men ran for the customs booths and then through them. The border guards there wisely chose not to intervene.

Lyons shouted "Federal agent!" as he ran through, the shotgun held in front of him barring further discussion on the matter.

No one chose to interfere with him. Hal Brognola was going to have a coronary over this, Lyons decided. There was no way this wasn't an international incident in the making.

He didn't care.

The three shooters crossed the bridge and hit the duty-free area in what was nominally a kinder, gentler no-man's-land between the two nations. An imaginary line crossed between the two countries here, and sitting on the width of that line was a shop that sold tax-free goods. The gunmen ran into the parking lot and, using the cover the vehicles parked there, started firing back.

Lyons would not be deterred. He zigzagged, narrowly avoiding gouts of automatic fire, and returned fire with aimed shots of his own. The automatic shotgun thundered. A pair of tourists ran for the safety of the duty-free shop, and gunfire followed them. They only just missed it.

That made an already angry Carl Lyons that much more furious. Target innocent civilians on purpose, would they? He'd show them. He'd show them hard.

He dived for the cover of a nearby minivan, which the shooters immediately started filling with holes. A few bullets found the gas tank and started spreading gasoline across the pavement.

Wonderful, he thought.

It was only a matter of time before they started shooting under the bodies of the cars, if he stayed where he was. The biggest mistake a man could make in combat was to fail to stay mobile. Gliding in a half crouch to make his upper body a stable shooting platform, he moved from car to car, flinching away as broken glass peppered his face and the sparks from bullet ricochets filled his vision. If civilians in the area were reacting to the violence, he couldn't hear them over the gunfire. But he moved so that the gunfire aimed toward him would be away from the duty-free shop, where he was certain there would be multiple innocents.

He could hear sirens in the background. That would be the local Canadian police, probably, as chances were the Americans had their hands full on the other side of the border. At the thought, another spasm of anger seized his features and made his lip curl. All those people, innocent Americans, cut down by scum...

He channeled the anger, turning it into a cold, pitiless rage that fueled his steps as he pushed out from behind a vehicle and unloaded a stream of slugs from the 20-round drum magazine in his shotgun. The weapon clicked empty, leaving the SUV behind which two of the shooters were hiding a smoking ruin. One of the men staggered out from behind the truck with a bloody, gaping wound in his chest. He collapsed, his Kalashnikov clattering to the ground.

Two down, two left, Lyons ticked off in his mind.

He moved again, placing his back to the flank of a full-size van bearing an advertisement for locksmithing services. His hearing, battered by gunfire, was acute enough that he could hear the steps approaching. Whoever was walking in on him was breathing heavily, and he had heard that sound before: it was the ragged edge of terror, as experienced by a man who was fighting for his life against an enemy who was entirely capable of fighting back. So many of the terrorist bastards Stony Man went up against were used to shooting only unarmed men, women and children. Faced with an opponent who could shoot back, they turned into mewling children.

Just before they turned into dead men.

Lyons pushed himself up and, as the man dashed around the side of the van, the big ex-cop threw up one muscled arm, slamming it onto the man's neck. The clothesline stopped him cold and he slapped the pavement wetly, his head actually bouncing off the asphalt. Lyons paused to drive the butt of the USAS-12 into the man's face. He was rewarded with a sickening cracking noise. The body underneath him went deathly limp, still clutching an AK-47 in its nerveless fingers.

One.

He heard the car door open then, and willed whoever was exiting the vehicle to think better of it. It didn't work. His faith in psychic powers would be forever shaken if not for the fact that he didn't believe in any of that crap. He moved across the parking lot to the shelter of an old Cadillac, a vehicle from the 1970s roughly the size of an ocean liner. The terrorist, predictably, called to him.

"You!" he said. "American?"

"American," Lyons yelled back. He risked a glance over the hood of the car. His last shooter had an elderly man in a headlock, with a Makarov pistol shoved into the man's temple.

"Back off, American!" the man shouted.

His English was heavily accented. He sounded Russian, but not quite. Something was off. It was a Turkic accent, which meant these were definitely Ovan's men. Lyons didn't believe in coincidence any more than he believed in psychics.

"Let the old man go," Lyons yelled back. He placed his shotgun on the deck, drew his Colt Python and checked the loads. Then he cocked the hammer back. Precision work was called for here. The sirens that had been in the distance were now much closer, and he thought he could see flashing lights from around the corner of the duty-free building. The Canadian police were here.

"You don't have a lot of time," Lyons warned.

"This man does not have a lot of time!" the terrorist shouted. "You will let me go or I will kill him!"

"I want to look you in the eye," Lyons said. "I want your word, man-to-man, that you'll agree to let him go."

"Very well, American," the terrorist shouted.

Lyons stood. He held the Python in his fist, low against his body. He started walking toward the terrorist.

"That is close enough!" the shooter cried. "You stay back, or I kill him!"

"I told you," Lyons said. "I want to look you in the eye. Only then will I take your word that you'll set him free if I let you go."

The gunman stood, nervous, practically shaking as the big ex-cop approached. Lyons's stride never wavered.

"Ironman." Blancanales's voice was strong in his earbud transceiver. The distance across the bridge was not that great.

"Go," Lyons said, almost subvocalizing.

"Found two more bombs in the van," Blancanales reported. "I would need Gadgets to confirm, but I think the bombs had started to activate themselves. I don't think these guys realize what they're playing with. These smart bombs aren't so smart."

"Stop where you are!" the terrorist demanded.

Lyons was still walking. The distance was very close now. "Give me your word," he said. "I want your solemn promise."

"Very well, I promise—"

Lyons, still walking, whipped his right hand up and triggered a single shot. The .357 Magnum round punched a bloody hole through the shooter's right eye and dropped him to the ground. The old man, still standing there, shook on his feet, looked down and ran for it.

Spry old fellow, Lyons thought. He nudged the dead gunman with his boot as he swiveled his head in all directions, checking for further threats. Finding none, he spared the dead and now one-eyed man a final glance. If you were going to shoot them cold, you were going to look at them, and if you couldn't, you didn't have the nerve for Stony Man.

Psychics, coincidence and promises from terrorists. Those were three things he didn't believe in.

The Canadian police converged on him then, their squad cars squealing as they pulled to a halt surrounding the duty-free. Lyons placed his Python very gently on the asphalt so as not to scratch its finish and stepped away from it, standing perfectly still with his hands clasped behind his neck. He had been through this drill before.

"Lay down your weapons!" someone called over a bullhorn. "Put your hands up!"

With a sigh, Carl Lyons waited for more redundant instructions. The locals were fit to be tied; that was certain. One other thing was certain.

Brognola was going to kill him.

CHAPTER NINE

Tehran, Iran

Garret Aimler leaned back in his ripped leather office chair, closing his eyes as the chair squeaked loudly. From the upper right desk drawer of his dented, fifty-year-old metal desk, he removed a pack of cherry Blackstone cigars. The little filtered cigars were hard to get here in Tehran, but then almost everything was hard to get in Tehran.

The office, buried in a congested commercial district of Tehran, was part of the ultrasecret covert CIA network in the city. Most Americans would be surprised to learn that the Central Intelligence Agency maintained such an elaborate setup here in one of the most infamous rogue nations in the world, but most Americans would be shocked and horrified at a great many things their government did. Garret Aimler knew that only too well. He'd been party to more horrors than he would ever be able to forget.

An intricate system of bribes and payoffs, threats and bargains, favors and debts allowed the CIA to continue to operate within the city. On some level, Aimler suspected that the Iranians knew the CIA were in their midst. It would explain a lot of their behavior, really. The brinkmanship politics played by the Iranian regime and the Americans was so pitifully pointless at times that it seemed only too possible the Iranians knew that the Americans were there and the Americans knew that the Iranians knew. Aimler had pestered his superiors through channels as often as his infrequent communications with them would allow, but of course they would never admit it.

It would bother him that any number of Iranians, supposedly turned to the American cause, could betray the network here in Tehran and bring the full force and weight of the Iranian government down on his head— if he didn't believe firmly that they already knew. It made sense. The Iranians constantly pushed things with the world body and with the United States, skirting the boundaries of provoking yet another undeclared war. They would push until the United States blinked…or didn't, and then they would back off, confident that they had gotten what they wanted: loosening of sanctions, more "attention" on the world stage, whatever a tight-ass like Magham thought he was gaining with the interminable political games that he played. He was an amateur compared to the puppet masters in the United States, of course. Everybody was.

Aimler had been playing the intelligence game for almost twenty years now. He was a seasoned professional, and in those two decades, he had learned only too much about what his government was doing. Oh, most of what he had learned was still being disclaimed or otherwise dismissed as a collection of conspiracy theories. But Garret Aimler knew better.

For years he had worked his way up in the Tehran network, a CIA operations group put in place since shortly after the American hostages were returned in what was the biggest photo opportunity ever orchestrated by the world's power-broker puppeteers. Aimler knew only too well. He didn't have proof, but he didn't need proof. He understood how these things worked. One administration had cut a deal with the Iranians to prolong the crisis just long enough for a subsequent administration to claim credit, giving the American people a delightful narrative to follow that was all so much smoke and mirrors. The Iranians, meanwhile, secretly continued to receive arms shipments from the United States, even during the tense months and years that followed the supposed hostage drama. Aimler had his doubts about the hostages themselves, too. He suspected most of them were plants, paid to cool their heels on Iranian soil until it was profitable and beneficial for them to come home again.

The thought reminded him of a passage he had intended to include in his book. Firing up his computer, which was networked to the few other computers in the building under heavy password encryption, he accessed his own secret files. Aimler was in charge of operations here in Tehran, so there was nobody to question his maintenance of personal files on the network and nobody to question his loyalty. Not that Garret Aimler was disloyal. He loved the United States. He just hated and feared what it had become after years of puppet government by those in power.

He called up his manuscript and paged through its contents, reviewing what he had written already and considering the notes he had left in chapters that he had yet to fill in. Twenty years in the CIA, coupled with Aimler's own research into his country's wrongdoing, was a long time to accumulate secrets. When he finally left Tehran and published his book, he was going to be a millionaire many times over. But more importantly, the truth would finally be exposed.

That was what drove Garret Aimler. He believed in the truth before he believed in anything else.

Typing out the paragraphs before he forgot them, Aimler saved his manuscript and filed it away. He stood, carrying his pack of Blackstone cigars, and went to the filthy window. A shaft of sickly yellow light streamed in through it despite the grime on its face. He considered the street outside. The other window offered a view of only the alley behind his office, where he always kept a vehicle fueled and waiting, and the satellite antenna taped to its surface.

The car was an imported French sedan with a powerful engine. He had made other arrangements related to the vehicle, as there was always the chance he would need to cover his escape, but he doubted very much that these backup options would ever need to be activated. He, Garret Aimler, was truly master of this domain, a spider at the center of a web that touched every part of the city.

The thought made him angry. He had spent years developing the Tehran network, nudging first one politician here, then another leading figure there. Iranian politics, corrupted with religious fanaticism and dictatorial totalitarianism, could only be moved gently, steered almost invisibly, over the long term. You did not move a heavy shelf laden with fine china all at once, or you would cause the china to fall and break. You did not dictate to the Iranians their election policy overnight, or you would cause more harm than good. Frankly, Iran was a nation that needed a strong leader like Magham. Were that idiot moderate Khan to take office, the power vacuum created would lead to chaos. The smaller dogs would start to nip at his heels, domestic terror would run rampant and the nation would devolve into the type of quagmire that Iraq had become in the wake of Hussein's defeat.

Why his CIA superiors could not see it never ceased to frustrate Aimler. They had the evidence of an entire country in ruin in front of them; why could they not see that inserting a weakling into power would have the opposite effect? Aimler firmly believed that peace in the Middle East was possible. And if his job was to secure peace to secure the welfare of American citizens, despite what those citizens and their government might want, well, he would just go ahead and make sure he secured that peace. A strong Iran was to be the lynchpin of his new Middle Eastern order.

He had outlined all of this in his manuscript, and once he had the chance to implement it, he could surface and take credit. The government would try to assassinate him, as it assassinated secretly anyone who bucked the system. President Kennedy had been killed in just such a conspiracy, Aimler was certain, and any number of military and political failures had been laid at his doorstep to discredit him before the Agency had decided to eliminate him. Again Aimler had no proof of this, but he had spent enough time reading about assassination conspiracies to know truth when he heard it. He had analyzed this and countless other "world falsehoods," as he called them, and devoted several chapters to them.

He took the Zippo lighter from his pocket. It had the CIA emblem on it, faded now. The lighter was a foolishly reckless affectation, of course. It tied him to the very agency that was not supposed to be here in Tehran, and if any of his superiors knew he was walking around with it, they would reprimand him. Imagine, over something stupid like that! As if the Iranians were too stupid to know a very extensive intelligence network was set

up in their midst. Aimler theorized in his book that the
highest levels of the Iranian government had given their
consent for the network's establishment. It helped them
to better organize and coordinate the puppet show for
the television cameras, as Iran rattled its saber and the
United States danced to the tune Iran played…all while
distracting the American public from their real problems
at home and abroad.

But his real message was that America was built on
torture.

The freest nation on Earth was in actuality a gulag.
Aimler was firmly convinced that the United States
maintained secret black-ops prisons throughout the
world, into which were placed political dissidents who
threatened to reveal how the game was played. Illegal
wars were just the start. Anyone who stood in the way
of the New World Order was systematically tortured or
simply murdered and disappeared. So many famous pol-
iticians who had died of "accidents" were in fact suicides
or murders, all of it covered up by the illuminati.

They went by many names and they operated under
many organizations, all of which Aimler had described,
or would describe, in his book. The Council on Foreign
Relations, the Trilateral Commission, the heirs to the
Rockefellers. Secret societies such as those to which
the last twenty presidents had all belonged. Secret deals
cut behind the scenes among nations that were supposed to be enemies but which were, in fact, working
to keep their populations docile and distracted so that
the men and women in power could continue to enrich
themselves.

The torture aspect bothered Aimler the most, and
he intended to hit that angle hardest when he promoted
the book. Perhaps he would open one of those micro-

blogging accounts so that he could post daily about the torture that the United States condoned. Oh, yes, Garret Aimler would expose them all. He would tell the world. It was unfortunate that he had to expose so much that was wrong with the United States in the process, but that was too bad. He loved his country too much not to hate it.

Many times he had asked himself if what he was doing was treason in the traditional sense. He was, after all, circumventing CIA policy to impose his own will and his own intentions. But with those in power beholden to hidden masters and anyone who spoke out tortured and imprisoned, Garret Aimler's only hope to survive and avoid one of those black-ops prisons was to expose the whole charade. Once he had named names, once he had become famous, he would be untouchable. They would not be able to kill him for fear of validating everything he had tried to tell the people.

What the government and the hidden masters of the world *would* do, however, was paint him as a crank. He would dismissed and grouped alongside those people who believed reptilian space aliens lived at the center of the Earth and orchestrated world affairs through a series of sympathizers and disguised aliens living and working among the human population. Aimler had given serious thought to that theory, of course, as anyone interested in truth should do, but ultimately he had discarded it as too complicated. Occam's razor, after all. The traditional conspiracy theories were the ones most likely to be true.

Aimler considered his reflection in the grimy mirror. He was pushing his late forties but still looked good, with a traditionally handsome face, broad features and a naturally curly lion's mane of hair that was still all his own. He touched it up with dye, but he imagined once he hit the published-author's circuit, he would allow some salt-and-pepper to creep in for that distinguished, scholarly look. It would drive the women wild. Did famously published authors get groupies? He liked to think they did. He may be forty, but he kept himself in good shape, despite the boredom and the long hours of piloting a desk that his job demanded.

Flicking the Zippo lighter to life, Aimler lit the end of his filtered cigar and took in a lungful of the cherry-flavored smoke. As he stood there, considering Tehran, it dawned on him how arrogant his superiors were. They actually thought they knew better than him, the man who had lived and breathed Iranian power politics for twenty years, what should be done.

They had brought those…those mercenaries into the country. Aimler was supposed to just let them walk in here and run roughshod over everything he'd built? And what did his bosses back in the States think would happen when a heavily armed team of commandos, from some branch of the government so secret that Aimler still could not verify who had fielded them, started running amok in Iran? While it was possible they would succeed in their goal of ensuring Khan's win for the presidency, it was much more likely they would just louse everything up. Magham would go on the defensive rather than believing his power base was secure. The clampdowns he would order would make it that much more difficult for Aimler to do his work behind the scenes. Were he deposed, the country would descend into chaos…but even if he managed to pull out a presidential victory, the attacks would make him feel very insecure. Magham, feeling insecure, would take steps to shore up his power, and the IIS would become even more problematic than they were now.

Aimler was proud of the work he had done to infiltrate the IIS. Recruiting Ghaem Ahmadi and turning his loyalty to the United States had been a very real coup for him, and the intelligence that Ahmadi produced while working within Iranian Internal Security was very valuable. It was therefore a source of great regret to Aimler that he had been forced to assign Ahmadi to the commandos. The orders had come down from Langley: he was to assign his senior operative, the man with the best leads in Iranian intelligence circles, to facilitate the work of a special forces operator unit. He was to render all possible assistance to them.

Aimler did not know how much the commandos, or the agency running them, knew about the Iranian situation. It was likely they suspected, or even knew for certain, that Ovan was behind the terror attacks, and that Turkmenistan was trying to leverage the election to broker a deal for Iranian smart weapons. The Iranians never did tire of building bombs that would take the lives of Westerners. Garret Aimler knew exactly where the laboratory was that produced the weapons Ovan so coveted. He had recordings of the initial negotiations through which Magham had sold his first batch of smart bombs to Ovan's regime.

Such information was so powerful that he had no choice but to conceal it from his handlers in the United States. They would probably have ordered an air strike, which was just the sort of ham-fisted, shortsighted option the current administration seemed to favor.

Something else that Ahmadi's commandos probably did not know was just how complicit Magham was in Ovan's operations. Aimler had surveillance positioned in venues so highly placed that he had tapped Magham's personal communications. He had extensive audio and even video damning Magham for sacrificing his own people to influence public opinion and defeat Khan. If the files tucked away and protected in Aimler's computer were ever to come to light, they would be the kiss of death for Magham's administration…and they would as good as gift wrap whatever military operation the Western world chose to mount against Iran and Turkmenistan.

Aimler had no intention of letting that information come to light. He had deliberately soft-pedaled his own intelligence reports coming from Tehran, manipulating the data to make him look good but to avoid revealing the true extent of what he knew. The files he had on Magham were his leverage. He would use them, eventually, to secure Magham's cooperation as a strong Iran moved forward into the brave new world he would help create with his exposé on America's treachery. He would, in effect, facilitate a new peace in the Middle East.

He bet *that* was good for some groupies.

But first he had to eliminate these meddling mercenaries before they did serious damage to Magham's operation, and so far that had proved frustratingly difficult. He had many of the relevant facilities bugged, most of these off the books, so he was not worried that Ahmadi would realize what was happening until it was too late. Ahmadi's own status reports, filed by encrypted text message directly to the CIA network here in Tehran, had been invaluable in tracking the commandos' movements and intercepting them.

It should have been simple. He had tipped off Ovan's men and the Iranian Internal Security service in discreet, scrambled, anonymous phone calls. The tips to the IIS alone should have resulted in the deaths of all concerned. He had followed the security forces' preparations with interest in laying their trap at one of the rallies to which Ahmadi had led the mercenaries. How they had managed to fight their way clear, he wasn't sure. His off-record sources within Iranian Internal Security told him that heads were going to roll, quite literally, over the failure to capture armed foreigners operating on Iranian soil.

He wondered briefly if Ahmadi's assistance might have made the difference, but Ahmadi, while a capable field man, was not a special forces soldier. It was doubtful he would do more than get killed alongside the interlopers he was helping.

Aimler did regret that. Ghaem Ahmadi was a good man, if far too trusting of the United States government. The company he kept was going to get him killed, but so be it. It was necessary for the long game, and Aimler was no stranger to making sacrifices. Perhaps the Iranians, believing Ahmadi had died a loyal IIS officer, would give him a state funeral for getting shot in the line of duty. It was possible, depending on the circumstances.

Aimler crushed his little cigar out on the windowsill, where it joined other crumpled filters and a collage of burn marks in the plaster. He went to his computer and checked for Ahmadi's latest status report. There was nothing, and there should have been an update.

Well. That didn't take as long as he thought it might. Ahmadi had realized something was up and had gone dark. Well. He would just have to up his game. From the drawer of his desk he retrieved an Iridium satellite phone, which he connected to the antenna mounted on the rear window.

There was only one possible move Ahmadi could make, given the information Aimler had gleaned from the man's earlier reports. In Ahmadi's shoes, Aimler would direct his mercenary charges to the only target left, which was also the most tempting: the upcoming conference of Magham's senior staff.

Magham may be complicit in the deaths of his supporters, but he would never sacrifice his top personnel for the sake of gaining votes. The conference would be safe, by previous arrangement. Aimler had intercepted wireless phone calls between Ovan's terrorists and Magham's people establishing that very fact. The recordings were more fuel for the fire on which he would threaten to burn Magham's empire if the man did not cooperate with him in establishing Middle Eastern peace… but of course that was later.

Using the satellite phone, Aimler dialed a number from memory. He could picture the gaunt, sunken face of Ebrahim Ghemenizov as he did so. Ghemenizov was coordinator of Ovan's network in Iran and operated with the protection of IIS personnel for the duration of his time in the country. Most of the security operatives had no idea who the man was; they simply followed orders and didn't ask too many questions when terrorist attacks took the lives of low-level Magham supporters while boosting Magham in the polls. The Iranian political atmosphere did not exactly encourage inquisitiveness among its enforcers.

"Yes?" Ghemenizov answered.

"It's your friend again," Aimler said.

"My friend?" Ghemenizov spit. "I lost good men to the attack on our safehouse!"

"I warned you about that," Aimler said, "and I know you evacuated some of them. You can hardly blame me for not taking me seriously enough to remove them all."

"How does one trust an anonymous voice on the telephone?" Ghemenizov asked. "An anonymous *American* voice?"

"You can trust results," Aimler said. "If you want to take revenge on the American mercenaries who attacked and killed your people, I can tell you precisely where to find them, and when."

"I am listening."

Aimler explained about the conference and identified the location and time of the meeting.

"This is known to us," Ghemenizov scoffed. "You will have to do better than that, Anonymous Voice."

"You've been told you're not to harm the men attending the meeting," Aimler said, imagining he could see the surprise on Ghemenizov's face in being told his own instructions. "But the men who attacked you do not know this. They will be waiting for you to appear at the conference. They will be eager to stop the violence they think you will do there. You can use this knowledge to intercept them and kill them."

"Where will they be? I want details."

"I don't have them," Aimler said. "But you're quite the capable...warrior." Aimler almost tripped over the word. He was not fond of the concept and considered most soldiers to be hired thugs. Ebrahim Ghemenizov was a sociopath with a gun, not a freedom fighter or any sort of warrior. Still, it never hurt to flatter the help.

"You expect me to trust you still?"

"My information has been accurate," Aimler said, "and I'm willing to bet you want to make the American mercenaries pay. They'll be waiting for you at the conference. You won't want to pass up this opportunity."

"I do not—"

Aimler hung up.

Whatever it was that Ghemenizov "did not," Aimler didn't care. In these relationships, one had to assert power. Authority was taken, not granted. He had no doubt that despite his misgivings, the Turkmen terrorist would act on the information. He would be too eager for blood to turn it down. Men of Ebrahim Ghemenizov's particular mental bent were not known for their restraint.

Aimler whistled quietly to himself. He perhaps had some more time to work on his manuscript. After all, he had assured that his problems locally were about to be solved, and permanently.

It was difficult to be a patriot...but not so difficult as some might have one believe.

CHAPTER TEN

The New York–Pennsylvania border

The travel plaza just over the New York/Pennsylvania border would be coming up in just a few minutes, Grimaldi reported. The men of Able Team, strapped into their seats in the Chinook, communicated with earbud transceivers, which canceled the noise of the big chopper's twin rotors.

Carl Lyons took a moment to examine the satellite surveillance footage that had been transmitted to Able Team's phones as soon as Warlock had identified the travel plaza as a likely target. There was some construction present, and a large fuel tank of some kind had been placed near pits dug by the truck stop area of the parking lot. Old tanks were being excavated. Lyons made mental notes of the areas that would provide cover outside the structure. He also checked the schematics of the travel plaza itself. There were no obvious points in the plans that looked ideal for planting the Iranian smart bombs but Able Team would deal with that once they got on-site.

Lyons thought back to his recent contact with Stony Man Farm.

"Yes," Price had said through the secure connection, "Hal's been on the phone with the Canadian authorities. They're not too happy, but when he explained the circumstances to them, they relented."

By the time the Canadian police had released Lyons, grudgingly returning his weapons, the news was also out that six Americans had been killed in the attack on the observation platform near Niagara Falls. The Canadians knew better than to poke their southern neighbor with a stick when it was wounded.

The death toll could have been a lot worse, but Lyons was furious. They had known all along that the reactionary game they were playing, even with the advanced warning of the Warlock network, afforded them no margin for error and no guarantees. They had stopped attacks that would have been far worse, but Lyons— still aching from his firsthand encounter with Karbuly Ghemenizov—considered no losses acceptable. Until they rooted out and stopped Ovan's network completely, he would not be satisfied.

The Canadian cop who had returned Lyons's shotgun and pistol looked as if he was holding two live rattlesnakes. Lyons would never understand that attitude about the tools of the trade, but there it was. Not everyone was as committed to results as were the counterterrorist operatives of the Farm. Hell, not everyone was as committed to results as the average American beat cop, of whom Lyons had known plenty, to say nothing of the soldiers and special forces operators he and Able Team had worked with over the years.

Lyons simply sat and cursed. He cursed anyone and everyone who was part of the problem. Able Team, Stony Man, Phoenix Force…these were components of the solution. The problem was global terror and the network of societal predators across the globe that facilitated it.

"Gentlemen, we are over the target area," Grimaldi reported.

"Uh-oh." Blancanales, from his position near the chopper's open doorway, held up a hand. "I have smoke. Repeat, I have smoke."

"Jack," Lyons ordered. "Down! Down now!"

Some of the vehicles in the lot were on fire. A cordon of police vehicles, spaced far from the travel plaza itself, had cut off the plaza from the highway. Law-enforcement officers milled around those vehicles but were making no attempt to enter.

"What's holding them up?" Lyons asked. "Did the Farm transmit orders through channels?"

"Nobody said anything," Grimaldi reported from the cockpit.

"I don't like it." Lyons shook his head.

The big chopper swooped down and into the trucker's parking lot, where the largest space was available. Able Team jumped clear with their weapons hot, ready to engage the enemy. Lyons took the lead. He watched the cops in the distance, watching him and Able. They made no move to assist. He was going to get to the bottom of this.

They encountered a man holding a bloody handkerchief to his forehead, staggering out of the building. "Are you, like, SWAT?"

"Sir," Blancanales said, "what happened here?"

"Buncha guys came in, shot up the joint," he said. "Terrorists, like. They left already. I think I'm the last one. Nobody left but me. Cops all pulled out. Don't know why."

"Left already? Did you see where they were going?"

"Got in a truck and went north on I-81," the man said.

"Have you been shot, sir?" Schwarz asked.

"No." The man shook his head. "Broken glass."

"Anyone else injured?"

"No, sir, Officer," the man reported. "I don't think so."

Lyons contained the sigh of relief he felt. "All right," he said. "See those police vehicles, sir? I want you to go to them with your hands out and visible. Someone there will see to it you get medical attention."

"Thank you, Officer," the man said. He sounded dazed. He was probably in shock.

Lyons watched him go.

"Pol, take the left. Gadgets, the right. I'll sweep down the center. We need to make sure the site is secured and defuse any bombs we find. Keep sharp. Something's wrong."

"I'm getting a scattered signal," Schwarz said. He looked around at all the construction through which they were passing on foot; the parking lot was torn apart. A maze of orange cones and safety barriers described a twisted path through all of the wreckage.

"Let's follow it down, then," Lyons said. He looked around suspiciously, hand on his weapon. Something sure didn't feel right.

"Pol," Lyons said. "Contact the Farm. Find out what's going on with the local first responders. There should be fire and medical on-site. One of the left hands hasn't told one of the right hands what it's doing."

"On it." Blancanales nodded, removing his satellite phone.

The trio split up per Lyons's directions. He took the front entrance of the travel plaza. The shattered glass doors, really just metal frames now, slid aside automatically to let him pass. He stopped to survey the damage, the USAS-12 in his fists. Bullet holes pocked the lounge area and dotted the walls. Plaster dust, glass pebbles, brass casings and shattered tiles crunched under his combat boots. There was an information desk at the far end of the room, and he went to this. Something didn't feel right, and now something didn't *smell* right.

He peered over the edge of the desk. The coppery smell in the air was blood, just as he'd feared. Two employees wearing the polyester blazers of state employees had been shot down where they sat, from the look of things. The civilian Able Team had encountered was wrong; there were casualties.

The terrorists had come and gone. That meant that they'd had time to plant their bombs, and the window for defusing those bombs was small. Then again, if the devices malfunctioned, as the ones in the van near the falls had seemed likely to, they could all go up at any minute.

"Terrific," Lyons whispered to himself.

He decided to check all the obvious hiding places here in the main building. He swept the ladies' room first, then the men's room. There was nothing in any of the stalls. There was some sort of central planter, a big, square, tiled eyesore with soil and green plants blossoming from it, out in the lounge area. He checked this over and poked through the plants with the barrel of the Daewoo. Nothing.

A vending machine area led from the main lounge, and across from that was a tourist counter with several shelves full of travel brochures. Lyons checked the counter first, and then moved into the vending area. There was a soda machine, a machine that dispensed hot foods like pizza and a coffee machine whose coffee probably tasted like plastic. Most vending machine coffee did. Lyons wondered if—

Something clicked.

Lyons froze. The audible click had been accompanied by pressure against his shin, a pressure so slight as to be almost unnoticeable. He looked down.

His leg was pressing against a trip wire.

Somebody had booby-trapped the vending area. He stopped then and pictured Ovan's men. They hit the travel plaza. They shot up the place, greased the employees to give them space to work, scattering the civilians here and there, creating confusion and panic. It was purposeful; this was not terror for terror's sake, as in each case the goal had been to plant a bomb that would do much more damage *later,* after the danger of the attack was seemingly past. That was the information contained in Able Team's briefing from the Farm.

He put himself in the terrorists' position. The biggest obstacle to their plan would be having their bombs discovered early. They would need to prevent an extensive search. They would have come in, fired their shots, taken provisional control of the site…and then, on the way out, they would have planted booby traps to cover their tracks and slow any response.

"Carl," Blancanales said, "I just got confirmation from Barb. The cops pulled back to await federal response. That's us. One of them apparently stepped on what they called a mine, after the terrorists cleared out and the first squad cars hit the scene."

"Yeah," Lyons said. "About that."

"Carl?"

"I've got a problem."

Lyons looked down and assessed the situation. The

trip wire was taut against his shin, leading back to a metal housing that had been nailed to the wall. There were cracks in the plaster around the nails, as if the world's strongest man had hammered them in. They'd probably used a nail gun; it was a quick and efficient way to mount a device like this across a narrow pathway. The device itself Lyons couldn't see very well from where he stood, but the sound he'd heard could only be a mechanical detonator. The first click, the line going taut against the mechanism, would be followed by an explosion when pressure was released. It was not unlike stepping on a land mine, arming it and then raising your foot only to have it blown off.

"Gadgets," Lyons said, "have you found the bombs?"

"Negative, Carl," Schwarz reported. "The signal is all over the place. I think all the construction is bouncing the readings around. There's a lot of metal out here—the fuel tanks, conduit, rebar. That may be the issue. I'm not sure."

"You and Pol freeze. Right now."

"Carl?" Blancanales asked. "What is it?"

"This place is rigged. I want you both to be extremely careful where you step."

"Affirmative," Blancanales answered.

"Got it," Schwarz reported.

"Okay," Lyons went on. "Gadgets, I want you to give the scanner to Pol and have him continue looking. I'm in the main building in a little hallway where there are some vending machines. I have just armed an explosive trip wire."

There was a pause. Then Schwarz said, "On my way."

"Watch your ass," Lyons said calmly. "We don't know how many of these little surprises are waiting."

Lyons felt sweat trickling down his forehead. He was suddenly very aware of the position of his leg. Move it a fraction of an inch, and the tension on the trip wire would change. If it went slack, the bomb would detonate. If it were to be pulled free completely, as if by someone walking obliviously through it, it would detonate. He'd worked with enough similar explosives to understand that much…but Schwarz was the real whiz in that department.

Perversely, the muscle of his thigh began to twitch. Or it could have been his imagination. Was his leg moving? Dammit, he couldn't tell, not objectively. And Schwarz was sure to give him hell for—

"Somebody order a pizza?" Schwarz stuck his head into the little corridor.

"Careful," Lyons said, completely serious. "There may be more."

"On it," Schwarz said. All trace of humor had left his voice again.

The computer whiz, who was no slouch with just about anything technical, had seen his share of explosives, too. He knelt to examine the trip wire and the bomb to which it was attached.

Schwarz whistled.

"That's not helping," Lyons said.

"You've got a real doozy here, Ironman," Schwarz said. "I'm not certain but I think this might be Iranian. Not unlike some of the less sophisticated roadside bomb stuff they've recovered in Iraq and Afghanistan."

"Can you pull the trip wire?"

"Not without setting it off," Schwarz answered. "I'm going to have to go at it from the inside out." He removed a multitool from his web gear and began unscrewing the casing. "Try not to move."

"Yeah, I was about to tap-dance over here."

"That's the Carl I know."

Lyons waited for what seemed like an eternity. Finally Schwarz exhaled. "Okay," he announced. "You can move."

Lyons stepped back from the trip wire. Nothing happened.

"Thanks," he said simply.

"De nada." Schwarz grinned. "We had better sweep the rest of the building for traps."

"My thoughts exactly," Lyons said.

They began a careful search of the travel plaza building. Twice they found similar trip wires, each in different narrow corridors. There did not seem to be any rhyme or reason to the placement, other than physical convenience.

"They're not cutting off any specific avenues of escape," Gadgets said. "And they're not trying to hinder progress toward finding the bomb, because the trip wires aren't focused on one location. So what are they for?"

"Just chaos," Lyons said. The face of Karbuly Ghemenizov came to him, unbidden. "We're dealing with people who just like to see death and pain. They probably got their rocks off, knowing some first-responder would walk into a wire and blow himself to kingdom come."

"Guys." Blancanales's voice sounded in their ears. "I've got the bombs."

"Where are they?"

"Just outside, at the construction site. In a small mixer."

"A concrete mixer." Schwarz nodded. "Enough metal to foul the signal, for sure."

"Uh…guys," Blancanales said. "If I'm reading this right, these things are going to blow."

Schwarz and Lyons looked at each other. They ran.

Just before they hit the fire doors at the rear of the travel plaza, Lyons brought up the Daewoo and fired several slugs in the general direction of its hinges. Nothing blew, although by the time the big ex-cop hit the door, the door itself was ripped free and hit the pavement outside with a clanging like a gong.

Blancanales had leveled his M-16 one-handed at the door when the two Able Team members came through it.

"Ease down, Pol," Schwarz said. "Carl was just making sure."

"I'll say," he said. He turned back to the bombs nestled in the mixer. He was pointing the scanner at them and maintaining contact with the device, but he looked very worried.

"What's the problem?" Schwarz asked as he hurried to stand next to his teammate.

"It's not defusing." Blancanales shook his head. "The lights aren't changing."

"Very carefully," Schwarz directed, "I want you to give me the sensor, but with your finger on the button." Schwarz took the sensor unit and placed his own hand over his partner's, keeping his own finger on the button. When Blancanales withdrew his hand, Schwarz maintained his position. He watched the readings. "Oh, boy."

"Oh, boy?" Lyons asked. "Gadgets, it is never good when you say, 'Oh, boy.'"

"You know how you felt when you were standing against that trip wire?" Schwarz asked. "Well, we're all doing it now."

"And?" Lyons demanded.

"If Pol hadn't gotten here when he did with the sensor," Schwarz said, "these bombs would have exploded by now."

Lyons grabbed for his satellite phone. "Can you stop them?"

"No," Schwarz said. "The signal is holding them in check, but as soon as it's removed, everything blows."

"Delay?" Lyons asked.

"Maybe thirty seconds," Schwarz said. "And maybe not."

"Terrific," Lyons said. He snapped the phone to his ear and dialed the number for the Farm. "Barb," he said without preamble, "we are triple-red here. The bombs are going to blow. Repeat, the bombs are going to blow. Roll local hazardous materials response and inform the locals to maintain their cordon at all costs."

"Get out of there, Able," Price instructed.

"Already getting," Lyons said. "Out." He looked at Schwarz and Blancanales. "Go," he said.

The three men ran for their lives.

Lyons felt his muscles pumping as he charged, sprinting for the police barricades, estimating the distance. If they could make the cordon, they could just avoid the effective radius of the nerve toxin...unless he was misjudging the distance. He could see the wide eyes of the police watching them, see the few who brought up weapons, wondering if they were being attacked, see the fear written across the faces of the civilians who were gathered by one of the squad cars and being tended by a uniformed officer with a first-aid kit.

He felt the vibration before he heard the sound of the explosion from the rear of the travel plaza. The first concussion struck him, pushed him forward, urged him on—

The second explosion hammered him into the ground. He felt a wave of heat, as if a giant flaming fist was pressing him into the pavement. The sudden ringing in his ears gave the entire scene a surreal cast. He saw Blancanales, who had been farthest to the rear of Able Team's run, flying through the air, striking the side of one of the squad cars, leaving the passenger window spiderwebbed with cracks.

When Lyons opened his eyes again, he was lying on his back. Schwarz was leaning over him.

"Carl," Schwarz said. "Are you all right?"

"What happened?" Lyons asked. He sat up. His head hurt, but not badly. He felt himself for damage, found none that hadn't been inflicted on him by that damned giant, Karbuly Ghemenizov. "I'm fine. Stop fussing over me. You're making a habit of it."

"Sorry." Schwarz backed off.

"Where's Pol?"

"In the other ambulance," Schwarz answered. "He'll be okay, but he's got a slight concussion. The medics are going over him again to be on the safe side."

"How'd he get hurt? I thought I saw—"

"Yeah," Schwarz said. "Me, too. The bombs went off and set off the fuel tanks. Pol took the worst of it because he was closest. Picked him up and threw him. Damnedest thing I've ever seen. The medics said he was lucky."

"I don't feel lucky," Rosario Blancanales said as he walked over. He was rubbing the back of his head.

"Still feeling a little goggle-eyed?" Schwarz asked.

"It's a very mild concussion," Blancanales said.

"You okay to continue?" Lyons asked.

"Yes." Blancanales nodded. "You couldn't drag me off this one, Ironman."

Carl Lyons stood and gathered his shotgun, which had been placed next to him, probably by Schwarz. They watched the hazmat crews now on scene as their vehicles and protected personnel swarmed over the devastated travel plaza like plastic-clad ants. Lyons paused near one of the police cruisers. Its owner was nowhere in sight, but across the double-lane highway he could see Grimaldi's Chinook, waiting for them. Its rotors whirled slowly, beating a distant rhythm.

"Who's been talking to the Farm?" Lyons asked.

"Me," Schwarz said. "They're aware of the situation. Backup is being scrambled and Barb is coordinating the mop-up."

"Body count," Lyons said. "I want a body count."

"Just the two employees," Schwarz said quietly. "And one officer caught by shrapnel. Grimaldi offered to play mercy-flight but they took him by ambulance. I'm told by one of the locals he's expected to be okay."

Lyons watched smoke roil from the travel plaza. He stalked closer, stopping at the edge of the devastation, where a late-model import sedan had burned to a blackened hulk. With a burst of rage, Lyons put a fist into the front fender of the already destroyed vehicle.

As he marched off toward the Chinook, he pretended not to notice the look on Schwarz's face as the man surveyed the size of the dent Lyons had left in the car's fender.

CHAPTER ELEVEN

Tehran, Iran

McCarter seated the magazine of the Krinkov and racked the bolt. The Kalashnikov family were, as a lot, an ugly, brutish bunch of weapons. Purpose-built people-killers with no pretensions of being much use for anything else. What he would not give, he thought absently, for a nice FN FAL or even a Galil. Ah, well. Beggars could not be choosers, and all that.

The team sat in the diesel microbus Ghaem Ahmadi had procured. McCarter had to hand it to the Iranian intelligence agent. He hadn't wasted any time with re-criminations or indignant insistence that his poor feelings had been hurt. He'd understood the position he was in, understood the need for Phoenix Force to hold him in suspicion, and gone right ahead and proved they could rely on him. He'd done his best to outline what he understood of the CIA's network here in Tehran, although he had no idea where the leak might be. Deeply placed within IIS as he was, there was a certain distance between Ahmadi and the rest of the CIA's operatives. The fewer among them who knew each other, the better; there was less chance someone would crack or turn and reveal the works that way. It was a fairly standard espionage setup.

Ahmadi had also produced more Krinkovs, ammunition for their pistols, and appropriate gear to help them carry it. Each man of Phoenix Force now had a Krinkov and a bandolier to carry the magazines. All of them had plenty of full magazines for their pistols. With a strangely proud look on his face, Ahmadi had finally also produced a cloth bag containing what he considered a special prize: Jordanian military-issue combat knives. The curved blades of these elegant, clearly Middle Eastern–inspired service knives were razor-sharp. McCarter had been impressed by the knife's balance and ergonomics. Each team member now carried one.

With the element of surprise gone, McCarter welcomed the chance simply to "hit and git," as the saying went among his American compatriots. Yes, they were in more danger than ever. Yes, the political repercussions of their capture or exposure were greater than ever.

McCarter didn't rotting care, so long as they could get down to business. Those were only dangers if they got caught, and he wasn't about to allow that to happen.

He found himself wishing for a cigarette, which surprised him, as he only infrequently indulged the habit these health-conscious days. He wasn't as young as he used to be, either. Still, the prolonged inactivity of surveillance like this, anticipating violent action when the enemy finally appeared…that type of enforced boredom was bound to have a man craving all manner of vices. He could have done with a good can of Coke, too, but those were in short supply. Ahmadi had provided lunch, and he had to admit that the local fare was not bad. There was plentiful bottled water to wash it down, but it just wasn't the same.

McCarter sat in the passenger seat with Ahmadi behind the wheel. They were parked in a side street in the shade of some landscaped trees that looked heavily irrigated and quite out of place. The house itself was a grand stone affair with large windows, and was situated inside a heavy compound with a five-foot stone perimeter wall. There was no way to get closer than they now sat, on the street, nestled in among cars that were easily ten times as expensive as the vehicle in which they waited. The neighborhood was an affluent one, which stood to reason. Magham's most trusted personnel, his inner circle, would of course be the beneficiaries of their glorious leader's largesse. Wasn't that always the way with these strong-men dictators?

When things started to explode, it would be time for Phoenix Force to swing into action. They'd have precious little warning, but those were the breaks. A few of Magham's men would probably be killed. If Phoenix Force could take down the killers, however, they could deal a serious blow to Ovan's plans.

It was doubtful Magham himself would appreciate having his higher-ups sacrificed by Ovan's terrorists. To a dictator seeking to reaffirm his power, perhaps they would be considered acceptable losses. McCarter didn't like it. There was a good chance, if Ovan's people were operating so extensively in Tehran, that they were doing so with at least the tacit approval of the IIS. He supposed Magham could be moving his people around like pieces on a chess board, making it possible for Ovan's gunmen to do their work with a minimum of fuss, but still, the entire setup stank to high heaven.

They'd gotten out of Ahmadi's safehouse without incident. McCarter had expected the walls to close in at any minute. There had to be a leak within the CIA; that was the only explanation that made sense. But who and why? Could the Iranians have turned a CIA asset?

Or had they planted one of their own, just as Ahmadi had been turned and recruited?

A leak within the CIA wasn't a huge surprise, and had McCarter understood that Ahmadi was dutifully reporting their movements to his higher-ups all along, he would have insisted that cease before they got started. Intelligence networks were almost always porous.

What had been worrying McCarter was that they did not have a second step. Ahmadi, however, had made a positively top-notch suggestion, one that would not be possible without his local contacts.

"Dissident journalists," Ahmadi had said. "I will report to the CIA network that we intend to meet with them and expose the work of foreign terrorists in attempting to influence the Iranian presidential election."

"Will they buy that?" James had asked.

"I will tell them—" Ahmadi had grinned his lopsided grin "—that we have uncovered evidence so damning that I went dark to protect it, refusing to report in until we had secured the agreement of these reporters to bring our evidence to light."

"Bloody brilliant," McCarter had said. "Whoever's working in the CIA against us won't want that link exposed. He'll either act or he'll tip off some of Ovan's people. We get one or the other."

"There's a problem, David." Manning spoke up. "Dissident journalists are frequently the target of reprisals here in Iran. Whoever agrees to help us is essentially agreeing to hurt Magham publicly. Even if the reaction isn't immediate, it could be very bad for whomever we use as bait."

"This I understand," Ahmadi said. "I have relationships with many inside the dissident movement here in Iran. I know two, a man and a woman, who will agree to help us, despite the danger. They are brave people. Good people. We must do everything we can to safeguard them."

"And we will," McCarter told him. "It's a good plan, mate, and I've an idea or two with that. But first let's see if we can't give Ovan a good sock in the gob."

Ahmadi had blinked at that.

"Bloody nose, man," James had said.

"Ah." The Iranian had smiled more broadly. "Yes, of course."

So now they waited. The men of Phoenix Force were quietly checking their weapons. The night was warm but dry. McCarter could not hear any insects in the distance.

Ahmadi was loading a magazine for his own Glock 19. He dropped one of the rounds and, as he crouched to get it, lost it beneath the seat. Behind him, Calvin James leaned over to pick up the round, which had rolled between his feet.

The heavy rifle round that punched through the windshield cored a hole through Ahmadi's headrest and punched another in James's seat. Both holes were where each man's head had been a fraction of a second earlier.

"Go!" McCarter shouted.

Ahmadi, still crouching, hit the ignition and threw the microbus into gear. He hit the gas and the van backed into the car behind it. Metal shrieked. Ahmadi hit the shifter again and tromped the accelerator, pushing them forward, taking out the rear fender of the car in front of them as he swung onto the street.

The Phoenix Force commandos leaned out the open side windows, bringing their Krinkovs to bear. Armed men, all of them bearing Kalashnikovs, were advancing from both ends of the street.

"It's a bloody trap," McCarter pronounced. He looked left, then right. "Ghaem, lad, hard right, now!"

"But—" Ahmadi began.

"Now!" McCarter urged.

Ahmadi hauled the wheel hard over. The microbus smashed through the carefully tended landscape garden of an opulent home, sending bricks flying as it burst out the other side. The impact with two stone walls damaged something badly in the engine. Ahmadi cursed as they began to lose speed.

"They'll be on top of us any moment," Encizo warned from the rear of the van.

"Let's pile out, lads," McCarter ordered. "Give them hell. Ghaem, find us more transportation and meet us back…well, wherever the most bloody gunfire is."

Ahmadi nodded and disappeared into the night.

Bullets walked up the street as blood-curdling battle cries filled the air. Muzzle-flashes from the crowd of killers chasing them caused the gunmen's faces to strobe yellow and white in the reflected brilliance.

Calvin James crouched, took careful aim and shot a man neatly through the head.

The Stony Man operatives broke for cover to either side of the street, using the curbs and built-up yard frontings popular in this wealthy neighborhood.

"Two by two!" McCarter ordered. "Fall back down the street!"

The commandos covered each other in pairs, firing as each member fell back under the cover provided. They weren't so much falling back, really, as they were firing their way backward down the street, fighting a holding action to no particular goal. Until Ahmadi reappeared, they were on foot, and to be on foot would eventually be to die when facing so many shooters.

The gunmen didn't wear the uniforms of the Iranian Internal Security service, but that didn't necessarily mean they were Ovan's terrorists. Regardless, the trap that had walked into confirmed that someone or something was working against them. As he fought, some part of McCarter's mind analyzed the situation: Could Ahmadi have betrayed them? It didn't seem likely. That first bullet had been aimed to splatter the man's brains all over the inside of that bus. Luck had been with them at that moment. Stupid, to be so many sitting ducks waiting for a motivated foe to pounce on them…but then, there was something to be said for being lucky rather than smart.

Well, he'd know in short order if Ahmadi had been playing a long con on them after all, for if the man didn't show up again, they'd die here on the street knowing full well whose side the Iranian had been helping.

GARY MANNING FIRED OUT his Krinkov and dropped the magazine, automatically reaching for another. He blasted a man who was encroaching on his position, then another and then a third. Too late, he realized they were flowing over his position like water, heedless of their own safety, gripped with a fanatical zeal to destroy the men against whom they were pitted. Manning hunkered down, bracing himself behind the stone planter he was using for cover, from which the plastic fronds of a fake plant jutted.

A gunman vaulted the planter and Manning put a ham-like fist into the man's gut, doubling him over. Manning then rammed the man's head into the planter, took his weapon and kicked him out into the street. He emptied the magazine in the AK-47 in the direction of his enemies and was rewarded with several hits.

Beyond the crowd, urging the gunmen on, Manning saw Ebrahim Ghemenizov. He looked exactly like his briefing photos, and he was firing a pair of Skorpion machine pistols. Manning tried to track the terrorist leader but lost him amid the sea of shooters advancing up the street.

It was time for Manning to fall back as Encizo covered him. He did so, then took up position, allowing Encizo to leapfrog back with him. James and Hawkins were doing the same, alternating with McCarter directing. They continued to move as the entire neighborhood erupted in small-arms fire. War had come to the streets of Iran, a covert war whose truth would, if Phoenix Force did their jobs properly, be revealed to expose Magham's machinations. But would they be able to do so, and would they be able to make the public believe it?

Manning continued to watch for Ghemenizov. The gaunt man reemerged at the far side of the advancing line of terrorist gunmen. Manning laid down a fusillade with his Krinkov, holding the trigger back, spraying out an entire magazine in one long burst. As the line of shooters reacted, pulling back to avoid his gout of bullets, Manning dived for his chance. He shouted his intentions for the benefit of the Phoenix Force men listening, but had no idea if they could hear him over the noise of the battle.

He also wondered, as he ran, when the Iranians would respond to the battle. A full-scale shooting war in one of their richest neighborhoods would attract police, security, military, *something*. Phoenix Force would not have much of a window of opportunity. At the very least, however, they were drawing the attack away from the Magham conference. Although, as he considered the way the battle had opened and how it had progressed, it seemed unlikely that the terrorists had ever intended to hit Magham's people. If Phoenix Force was the target, that meant someone knew the Stony Man operatives were here and that the mission itself was potentially compromised. For an enemy to know to target them, that enemy would have to know that they existed and have an idea before the fact what they were after.

The others would already have put that together. Manning made a note to bring it up once things got a little less hot…if they did.

He crossed the street, bullets nipping at the heels of his combat boots, and slapped a new magazine into his Krinkov. Shooting ahead of himself, he shattered the plate-glass windows of the large house facing him.

He found himself bulling his way through a well-appointed sitting room. Glass crunched under his boots as he shoved aside an interior door and found himself in an anteroom. He went for the door, couldn't find the door bolt, and simply lowered his shoulder, smashing his way out the other side.

And there was Ebrahim Ghemenizov.

The terrorist leader, shooting down the street, didn't see Manning appear at his flank. The big Canadian raised his weapon—

Several terrorist shooters turned and fired, seeing the threat before their leader could. Manning threw himself back and down. The bullets raked the air above his head as he bore the impact on his shoulders and upper back. He splayed his legs and fired between them, then rolled, pushing himself inside the house he had just invaded.

He just hoped no one was home.

Bullets destroyed the facade of the house, punching hole after hole into the walls and hallway above and beyond Manning. The big Stony Man operator had no choice but to crawl back the way he had come. He would need to work his way around the building again.

"I lost him," he reported, not knowing if the others could hear him. "Repeat. I had a chance at Ebrahim, but I lost him."

"Circle back, mate." McCarter's voice came back. "We're continuing down the—" there was a pause and a distant burst of gunfire "—street."

"On my way," Manning said.

RAFAEL ENCIZO FELT LIKE he was back home, in a way. The Cuban-born guerilla fighter was no stranger to gun battles like this one. As hot lead burned the air all around him, destroying everything and anything in sight, it was hard for a man not to feel more alive than at any other time in his life. Encizo had been playing the gunfight game for a long time, longer than most, and he knew how to check that type of self-deception. A man could become combat-drunk, and after that happened, it wasn't long before he lost all sense of reality. It could turn a man dangerous, even self-destructive. Encizo had seen it before.

He saw Manning burst into the building to his left and heard him announce he had a shot at Ghemenizov. Encizo did his best to cover the big man, but there was so much lead in the air he could barely move. A car parked on the far side of the street exploded, spraying hot metal everywhere. Just what had detonated it, Encizo did not know, but he was suddenly worried the terrorists were lobbing grenades or RPGs into the mix.

He ran dry and crouched behind a property wall to

change magazines. One of the terrorists was on top of him, then, and grabbing at him before he had a chance to reload. His right arm was pinned, and as he went for his Glock with his left hand, the terrorist hit him with a powerful head-butt. The blow missed the bridge of his nose, but it stung.

The two men hit the pavement and began to roll onto and off of each other. Encizo managed to get a grip on his knife, the Jordanian blade Ahmadi had provided them. He shoved it between the man's ribs, up and in, twisting it as far as he could. The terrorist squalled and started to clench up. Encizo pushed him off, grabbed up his Krinkov, reloaded and dispatched the wounded man with a mercy shot. Then he knelt, cleaned his knife on the dead man's clothes and resheathed it.

He was up and fighting again, continuing the strategic movement that was the team's only play.

It was all in a day's work.

CALVIN JAMES SAW first Manning, then Encizo go down in turn, grappling with and dispatching enemies. He was suddenly glad of the big knife in his belt, which reminded him of the old days.

The targets were starting to thin now as James fired them down in turn. The aimed fire of Phoenix Force was taking its toll against the wild spray-and-pray tactics of the enemy. These turkeys so seldom bothered with anything resembling fire discipline or trigger control, it was a wonder the world's armies kept on doing what they did. James would have laughed at the thought, if he hadn't been busy shooting.

He ducked behind a car that he could swear was a Bentley. Bullets walked up its hood, shattered its front windshield and perforated its roof. All of its tires went flat. James, who could admire a fine automobile as well as the next man, said a silent prayer asking forgiveness of the automotive gods for the sin he was committing in letting such a fine set of wheels get blown to hell. Better it than him, he figured.

"David!" he shouted over the din. "Where are we going, man?"

"That way," McCarter shouted back.

James saw then the most beautiful sight he'd seen in a while. It was Ghaem Ahmadi, driving a Cadillac Escalade SUV. Just what one was doing in the middle of Tehran he didn't know, but the beautifully waxed black truck came plowing down the street with all the reckless abandon the Iranian operative could muster. He hit the brakes and the steering wheel at the same time, burning rubber and pulling the rear end around to present the back of the SUV to the Stony Man team.

"Don't have to tell me twice," James said to himself. He jumped for the back of the truck and continued shooting, covering the other members of Phoenix Force as they started to converge on the vehicle.

"Nice ride!" James shouted at Ahmadi, who was leaning out the driver's side window to fire his Glock.

"Go, go, go," McCarter ordered as he reached the vehicle. He was the last one in.

Manning and Encizo helped pull the Phoenix Force leader up and into the truck bed as Ahmadi sent them wheeling down the street, leaving behind far fewer armed terrorists than had started the day.

McCarter thought he caught a glimpse of Ghemenizov, gathering up what was left of his force and withdrawing in the opposite direction. They'd given Ovan's boys a bloody nose; that much was for sure. Though he had to wonder how Ovan's people had known they'd be here and why they showed up gunning for Phoenix Force.

Only after a few blocks did Ahmadi slow down. James, feeling suddenly weary from the adrenaline dump of the firefight, slumped in the back of the SUV, enjoying the wind in his hair. He could hear McCarter shouting back to Ahmadi, who nodded and said something in response; he gathered they were figuring out where next to hide, for they stuck out like a handful of sore thumbs in the bullet-scarred truck carrying automatic weapons and looking anything but Iranian.

CHAPTER TWELVE

Binghamton, New York

The Chinook raised a small tornado of litter and grit as the big chopper landed in the parking lot. Loaded for bear, the black-clad, combat-booted men of Able Team wasted no time piling out of the chopper, weapons ready.

They had watched the news feeds transmitted to their phones by Stony Man Farm as the chopper carried them to their destination. No sooner had they gotten back to the Chinook than Grimaldi was telling them to stand by for an important update from Price. The terrorists who had hit the travel plaza had been seen leaving north, and Binghamton stood on a direct route north up the highway from the Pennsylvania border. The gunmen had wasted no time seizing the city hall.

Somehow the jackals in the news media had gotten wind of the attack. Kurtzman's team had tracked down at least one anonymous phone call to a local television station, intercepted from a wireless phone tower in the area. They had run the accent through voice analysis and come up with Turkmen, possibly even Karbuly Ghemenizov himself. The terrorists wanted media coverage, and they were stepping up the pace and ferocity of their attacks.

The television footage showed ski-mask-wearing

terrorists moving around the exterior of city hall. They carried Kalashnikovs and had executed at least one city employee to show they meant business. The news footage also showed the terrorists moving in and around iron-work trash receptacles dotting the perimeter of the building. Lyons was willing to bet they were placing bombs.

In their position, he would take and hold the building long enough to give the television cameras a hostage drama, bug out...then sit back to wait for the carnage when the bombs exploded hours, days or weeks after the fact. If they worked as they were programmed and designed to do, the bombs would theoretically sit there for any amount of time until they were disturbed or until they had plenty of victims within the range of their sensors.

One particularly large figure in a ski mask that looked lumpy and misshapen over his face strutted with a gait Carl Lyons recognized. It was Karbuly Ghemenizov himself, leading the attack. Lyons could almost taste how badly he wanted a rematch with that big son of a bitch.

"What I don't get," Blancanales had said as they rode in the chopper, looking a little green around the gills thanks to his concussion, "is why they're hitting so many small towns. Why not concentrate their efforts on a higher-profile target?"

"Bigger targets have better security," Schwarz had said. "New York City, for example, has a big target painted on it, and everybody knows it. You wouldn't get anywhere near any of its bigger prizes, not without somebody blowing the whistle. It's the same reason it's so hard to hijack a plane these days. Everybody on a plane knows what the stakes are, and citizens are taking down shoe bombers and would-be hijackers because they know that compliance will get them killed. Terrorism has made hard targets of the biggest target sites."

"A small town," Lyons said. "Think about it like a terrorist, Pol. Plenty of innocent people. A slower-paced lifestyle. People don't expect the outside world to hit them in the face or shoot them in the chest. These little municipalities they're striking aren't equipped to deal with serious terror."

"Yes," Blancanales said. "Of course." He nodded and then looked as if he regretted it.

"You sure you're okay?" Lyons had asked.

"I'll be fine, Carl," Blancanales had said. "I want some payback as much as you."

Lyons nodded. He doubted Blancanales or Schwarz would understand if he explained just how badly he wanted Ghemenizov, but he understood Blancanales's desire to stay in the action. He'd have to keep a close eye on the man. The Stony Man Farm commandos had been through countless missions together, and he knew each one of them would perform well beyond his capacity if he thought the circumstances required it. Lyons wasn't about to let his teammates get killed simply out of either man's overdeveloped sense of duty. He knew that sense of duty well; he had it himself, and in Blancanales's position, he knew that he would damned well have his brains slosh out of his head before he'd admit that he couldn't continue with the mission.

Now they were on the ground and ready for action. The local police had set up a perimeter around city hall and the Farm had run interference for Able Team from the outset. The locals would be expecting a federal troubleshooting team. They had also been instructed to stay out of the way unless asked to render assistance.

Lyons didn't give a good damn about jurisdictional territories right now. He just wanted to get his hands around Karbuly Ghemenizov's throat.

They had discussed, on the Chinook, exactly what the plan was to be. Schematics of city hall had revealed a very large hole in the terrorists' plans. There was a pedestrian tunnel, newly installed and not yet completed in an attempt to modernize the city, that ran directly under city hall. It would not be in any public plans of the building; such plans were not yet updated, but of course the Farm had access to the latest tentative updates. The terrorists should be unaware of it. Lyons would use that tunnel to get into the building to free the hostages that Ghemenizov and his goons were holding. With the terrorists distracted by a wolf in their midst, Schwarz would defuse the bombs. Blancanales would cover him, as he would be vulnerable each time he stopped to neutralize one of the devices.

"Ready?" Lyons asked as Able Team paused just behind the line of squad cars.

"Ready," Schwarz said. Blancanales nodded, his brow furrowing as he did so.

"Then let's hit 'em," Lyons said.

He nodded and then jogged for the far end of the cordon, where a building stood open and waiting with a police guard at either side. He passed through the double doors of the structure—it looked like the sort of place where you'd find a nest of ambulance-chasing lawyers and insurance salesmen renting space—and followed the gesture of the uniformed cop standing inside. The local gave him an odd look, staring at the USAS-12 and then at Lyons's face. Lyons ignored him.

He took the stairs leading down, tore past some sagging caution tape and found himself in a darkened hallway that smelled of fresh drywall. There was plastic draped over the entrance to the tunnel, which connected this building to city hall and presumably a couple of others on the other side. Lyons snapped open the folding tactical knife clipped to his pocket and slashed the plastic open, stepping through.

He moved carefully along the corridor. Ovan's killers had already demonstrated a fondness for booby traps, and if something had gone wrong and they knew about this route into city hall, they might well have mined it to prevent any sudden guests. He saw nothing, however, and reached the far end without difficulty.

He found himself in front of a pair of metal fire doors that had been chained together with heavy steel links. A large padlock secured the chains. Making sure a round was not chambered in the USAS-12, he brought the heavy stock down on the padlock. It took three more strikes before he managed to bash the lock apart. When he removed what remained, the chains slipped free.

The whole point was to make noise, so he kicked in the doors and let the chains rattle to the floor. Jacking home a shotgun shell in the USAS-12, he told himself that Karbuly Ghemenizov was inside, and Karbuly Ghemenizov was going to pay.

The tunnel opened into an anteroom with a small elevator and some stairs leading up. He ignored the elevator and took the stairs, doing his best to stomp heavily up them. He could have started yelling, he supposed, but that would have been a little too much. He didn't want to get his head shot off the moment he stuck it out there.

He reached the top of the stairs. Mindful of trip wires or other explosive surprises, he eased the door open. He was in a basement level, at one end of an L-shaped corridor dotted with narrow wooden doorways marked as storage and maintenance accesses.

A man walked past.

He wore American-pattern camouflage BDUs, probably purchased at any of countless military surplus stores in the area. He was also wearing a ski mask and carrying an AK-47. Lyons let the door slam loudly shut behind him.

The guard whirled.

Lyons shot him through the face with a 12-gauge slug. The blast echoed through the corridor as Lyons broke into a run, charging around the corner and hitting the next fire door for the stairs leading up. A ski-masked terrorist was sitting inside, smoking a cigarette. The door hit him in the face and sent him sprawling. He clawed for a weapon in a shoulder holster.

Lyons tripped a double-blast from the shotgun and kept him on the steps for the rest of his life.

As the big ex-cop took the stairs two at a time leading upward, he could hear shouts from the level above. The terrorists had heard the commotion and were finally reacting to it. If he did them enough damage, they'd be too occupied with the firefight he was about to give them to bother with Schwarz and Blancanales running around outside.

The typical rules of engagement for hostage situations were completely out the window here. Ovan's killers didn't have demands they wanted met; they wanted to use the hostage situation to cover the fact that they had seeded their Iranian smart bombs around city hall. That way, after it was all over, when the bombs sensed plenty of victims nearby, they would create an incident far worse than the circus that was the seizing of this building by armed men. The lives of the hostages were forfeit; only direct action would save them.

The aftermath of this action was going to be bad enough. Such a high-profile attack on a government building in an upstate New York town was going to be all over the news. The cable networks would have a field day with it, chewing at it twenty-four hours a day, bringing in idiot commentators who knew nothing about the incident but would fill time by jawing about it. The idea was enough to make him sick. He despised the way that sort of thing was done. Bunch of jackals picking at the corpses of innocent men, women and children, just so they could shove cameras where they didn't need to be, pick at wounds that should be left to heal over.

As he always did, he channeled the cold fury ignited inside him by the thought of the injustices Ovan and his gunners had perpetrated. When he hit the first floor, he slammed the door aside and walked right into an armed guard, who had been reaching for the handle with one hand while balancing a Kalashnikov in the other.

Lyons kneed the terrorist in the crotch, doubling him over. He drove a hard elbow into the back of the man's neck, which put the gunman on the polished floor. The he simply stepped over the shooter and leveled his automatic shotgun.

They came like ants, piling out of the adjacent rooms on the first floor, their weapons spitting bullets. Lyons crouched and moved left, spraying out the magazine in the USAS-12, stitching first one man and then another. The thunder of the powerful weapon immediately made his ears ring and drowned out all other sounds. The shouting of the terrorists became a distant background hum as he focused on acquiring targets and punching them down in rapid succession.

Dropping the empty shotgun magazine, he slapped in another, this one loaded with double-aught buck. He slapped the cocking lever of the shotgun and brought the weapon on target again, blasting one man before he could bring a pistol to bear.

He had to clear the first floor. There was no way to know exactly where the hostages would be or how spread out. He would simply fight his way through, level to level, and when he found the city hall employees, he would free them. The attack itself could bring reprisals, but he was counting on the terrorists' sense of self-preservation coupled with their desire to execute their mission. They were vicious but they weren't stupid.

The hostages were the only leverage they had, the only thing stopping the cops surrounding the building from unleashing everything they had. Ghemenizov and his men were well armed, but they were vastly outnumbered by the army in law-enforcement uniforms outside. The hostages were their exit strategy. In their position, Lyons would pull the usual safe-passage-for-hostages'-lives routine, taking some of the hostages to use as shields. If they did that, Ghemenizov and his goons would doubtless murder whomever they took with them. It was the sort of play that bearded giant would get off on, Lyons had decided.

He went door by door, kicking in each with a solid plant of his combat boot, each strike a Shotokan front kick that would break bone in a human target. Quickly acquiring and discarding targets—he stopped himself from blasting a coatrack in one of the small offices—he made sure there was no one hiding on the first floor before he hit the stairwell to ascend to the second.

"Carl, this is Gadgets." Schwarz's voice came through

his earpiece. "We have the first bomb and we are defusing."

"Copy that," Lyons said. "Keep on it. Resistance?"

"Light," Schwarz said. "Pol shot two who tried to snipe us from in the building. They're keeping their heads down now dealing with an internal problem. Seems they've got a madman in the building."

"I've heard that, too," Lyons said. "Out."

No sooner had he opened the door to the second-floor stairwell than bullets rained down, blasting apart the concrete of the stairs themselves and raising a choking dust cloud. Lyons waited patiently for the gunners to burn through their magazines. Smart shooters would stagger their fire, but from the cacophony, it was obvious several men with Kalashnikovs were spraying and praying simultaneously.

When the pause came, he sent a long burst of double-aught buck rattling up the stairwell, where the ricochets would give the gunmen something to think about. Then he plucked a stun grenade off his web gear, popped the pin, let the spoon spring free and chucked the steel egg upward. He watched it bounce off the wall at the perfect angle to send it careening through the doorway off the second-floor landing.

He closed his eyes tightly, turned away and shrugged his ear into his shoulder, covering the other ear with his free hand. The blast echoed down the stairwell and almost staggered him despite the fact that he was ready for it. With actinic blobs still floating in his vision from the flash visible through his eyelids, he pushed his way to the stairwell and through the door, following the business end of the shotgun.

Ski-masked gunmen were writhing in the floor, some of them still clutching weapons. Lyons had only a moment before they regained their senses and fired on him. He aimed, fired, turned, aimed and fired again, repeating the process, walking his way through each of the stunned shooters, ending their lives before they could continue with their murderous intentions.

A conference room dominated the second floor. Lyons reached for the door handle and heard a bolt being pulled back. He ducked aside just as full-auto assault rifle fire chewed up the heavy wooden door from the other side. He waited, but the fire continued and was joined by a second, then a third rifle. The door began to disintegrate as he held himself against the wall, hoping that luck would be with him and a bullet would not pass through the wall itself to perforate him.

At the first lull in the firing, he dived low, smashing aside the kindling that was all that was left of the door. As he plowed through the wreckage of the barrier, he fired beneath the level of the conference table, using the buckshot in his USAS-12 to chop his enemies down at the knees. The terrorists were dressed in military surplus fatigues and wearing combat boots, easy to discern from the civilians who were seated at the conference table among them.

The shotgun was empty. He left it on the floor, ripping his Python from its holster and standing to draw down on the wounded shooters. One of them started to reach for a civilian seated next to his position—they had been standing, dotted around the conference table, waiting as their hostages sat immobile and tied with duct tape to chairs pushed up to the table—and Lyons beat him to it, putting a .357 Magnum round through his throat. In the time it took Lyons to empty his revolver, the threat to the hostages was over.

One woman began screaming. A man next to her,

wearing a rumpled suit and with his tie at half-mast, began yelling at her to shut up. Lyons bellowed at him to be quiet. He paused to shuck the empty brass from his revolver, reload it with a speedloader from his web gear and reholster it. Then he retrieved his shotgun and reloaded that, as well. Finally, he went from chair to chair and used his knife to free each of the half dozen hostages.

"Anybody here know how to use a gun?" Lyons asked.

Two of the hostages, one man and one woman, tentatively raised their hands. Lyons gave each of them a Kalashnikov and showed them how to set it to single shot.

"Keep it there," he warned. "No full-auto Rambo stuff. Now wait here until somebody gives you the all-clear. And for God's sake, don't answer the door with those guns in your hand if the cops come through the building." He was rewarded with wide-eyed nods. He could have asked where they'd gotten their experience with guns, but he didn't care. Frankly, he thought of it as a crying shame that among six Americans, he'd found only two who could handle a gun…and it was a worse shame that he counted himself lucky the percentage was that high.

"Sir." The woman who spoke up was an attractive middle-aged brunette who looked like she had held a rifle more than once. "There's one more. Kayli Appleton. She's on the third floor. They took her."

"You're it?" Lyons asked. "No more hostages in the building?"

"No, sir." The woman shook her head. "But they took Kayli. She's one of the receptionist staff. A big man with a beard grabbed her and said he was taking her upstairs."

"I'll get her," Lyons said grimly. "Stay here. Watch your asses."

"Carl," Schwarz reported again as Lyons made his way to the third floor landing, once more through the stairwell. "We have defused four units. I'm checking the last of the planters, but the signal is dying off. I think we've got them all."

"Check," Lyons said. "Coordinate with the locals. I've cleared the first two floors and the sublevel, but I can't guarantee nobody's slipped around me to backfill. Tell the locals they can proceed into the building, but to do so cautiously. There are hostages with weapons, repeat, armed hostages with liberated terrorist weapons, in a conference room on the second floor. Inform them to tread carefully."

"Will do, Carl," Schwarz said. "What is your status?"

"I have an unconfirmed report of another hostage still in danger. I've got unfinished business on the third floor. Out."

The third floor housed executive offices, from the gilded lettering on the doors. Lyons came out of the stairwell full barrel, expecting to meet heavy resistance. No one greeted him. He hit first one office, then another, but again, there were no targets. When he reached the last door, he paused. He heard voices within.

Stepping back, he fired a kick near the sweet spot just beside the door handle. The door blew aside and hit the wall within, rebounding, but Lyons was already through. He had the USAS-12 to his shoulder and his finger was tightening on the trigger.

There were three shooters in the outer room of the

office. They had turned over a desk and were crouched behind it. Lyons lowered the shotgun and simply raked it across the face of the desk on full-automatic, blowing the gunmen away before they knew what hit them. He vaulted the desk, leaving the now empty shotgun on the floor, yanking his Python once more from its shoulder holster. There was no time to reload, no time to do anything but bring the big pistol up as he hit the inner door and burst into the office beyond...

Karbuly Ghemenizov stood there with a young woman in a headlock. Her blond hair spilled out over his gigantic forearm. He had removed his ski mask and stood, grinning, his teeth bright and white as his smile split his craggy face. A Makarov pistol was gripped in his fist, dwarfed by his thick fingers.

"So!" he bellowed. "It is you!"

"Ghemenizov—"

"I had thought it unlikely," the giant sneered, "but here you are. I am so very pleased to see you again, my friend!" He laughed again, and then something changed in his eyes.

Lyons started to squeeze the Python's trigger.

The shot that rang out was muffled by the woman's hair. Ghemenizov put a round through her brain and shoved her body forward, directly at Lyons, turning and throwing himself bodily through the plate-glass window behind him. It was only as the terror-master leaped that Lyons saw the wireless phone in his fist.

The next few seconds passed as if in slow motion. Lyons caught the dead girl, easing her to the floor, and stepped over her lifeless body with the Python tight in his grip. He reached the shattered window in time to see Ghemenizov land heavily on the roof of a navy blue cargo van that had burst through the police cordon. Two gunmen with assault rifles were crouched on the roof, firing one-handed as they helped grab Ghemenizov to keep him from rolling off the top of the still-moving vehicle. Men inside the van were trading fire with police on that side of the building. Lyons saw at least two officers down.

"Ghemenizov!" he roared, thumbing back the hammer of the Python and shoving his arm out to full extension. The terrorist leader turned to look up at him, and Lyons pressed the trigger to send a single Magnum round burning on its way.

Karbuly Ghemenizov, still grinning, grabbed the terrorist closest to him and hugged him just as Lyons fired. The hollowpoint bullet took the human shield in the head and exited, but Ghemenizov was crouching behind the body of the hapless thug. As the van burned rubber and carried the terrorist leader away from the police cordon, bullets sparked and pinged from its flanks and chewed up the pavement behind it. A tire went flat, causing the van to swerve, but the driver corrected and simply floored the accelerator, pushing the damaged vehicle onward. As the van wheeled widely around the next corner, the police at the cordon were in disarray.

Just before he disappeared from view, Karbuly Ghemenizov threw the body of his dead man aside, raising his fists to the sky in victory.

Carl Lyons stood framed by the shattered window, hate burning in his eyes.

CHAPTER THIRTEEN

Tehran, Iran

The parking garage, several levels underground, was pleasantly cool compared to the heat at street level. What McCarter found disconcerting, by contrast, was the presence of so many white-painted IIS security vehicles. Ghaem Ahmadi had arranged the meeting with his dissident journalist friends in the most outlandish place possible: a motor pool used by the IIS, one to which he had access thanks to his position within that agency.

McCarter had earlier asked Ahmadi how it was that he had so much time to move around the city freely. Weren't his IIS bosses going to miss him? Ahmadi had explained that very few among the IIS who were not the uniformed enforcement arm were seen in the office on anything resembling a regular basis. Such men were expected to be out mingling with the Iranian public, ferreting out dissenters, seditionists and revolutionaries, the secret and always watchful police whom the Iranian people could always suspect were in their midst. The whole thing sounded fairly diabolical. McCarter again had to give Ahmadi credit for seeing the lack of merit in such a system and choosing to work with the CIA.

Not that the CIA was perfect, given the rat they seemed to have in their pantry. The more he had thought about it, the more he had decided that Ahmadi's movements must have been anticipated by someone who knew him—someone from within the Central Intelligence Agency network in Tehran. He hadn't reported the stakeout at the Magham conference, no, but it was the only logical move available to them at the time. Whoever was targeting Ahmadi and thus Phoenix Force would know that, too.

If McCarter was any judge of character, the little bit of theater in which they were about to engage would at least get Ebrahim Ghemenizov off their backs. In Ghemenizov's position, having led such a superior force to take out a small armed team, and having lost so completely, he'd want blood. He'd personally want to lead the mission to take out the quarry he'd so frustratingly missed. Ahmadi had followed through with his plan, filing a status update with the CIA that explained where he had gotten to and why he had done it. He had outlined his meeting with the dissident journalists, explaining that he was conducting it in the one place no one from the IIS would think to look.

The fact that it was a nice, isolated spot away from civilians with plenty of "combat stretch," of course, would not be covered in that report. McCarter liked it. There was enough cover for him and his team, but plenty of open space in which to trap Ebrahim Ghemenizov and his men when they came calling.

It was possible that IIS itself would be called down on them, as their "friend" in the CIA had used, and warned, both Ovan's terrorists and IIS personnel. But which was the more likely tip? He had run it through in his head. All Ahmadi had reported was that information was being brokered to dissident journalists. Their CIA mole would know that wherever Ahmadi was, Phoenix Force was likely to be, and he could share that information with Ebrahim Ghemenizov knowing full well that the Turkmen terrorist would come in shooting. Trying to sell the same story to IIS would raise more questions than it solved. An efficient use of resources would be to use the simplest method to remove Phoenix Force from the chessboard. That would be Ovan's gunmen, who were already working in less than aboveboard circumstances.

Ahmadi had more than done his part to facilitate the operation. He had stolen yet another Iranian-made passenger truck—the man was a one-man crime spree— and placed it prominently in the center of the parking level. He'd hung some towels from the overhand straps in what was, in the dim light, a reasonable approximation of figures inside the vehicle. The towels and the truck were the stand-ins for Phoenix.

His two dissident journalist friends were standing with Ahmadi near the elevator. The journalists had re-hearsed as much as time allowed. When the shooting started, they were to run with Ahmadi to the far end of the parking level, where the ramp to the next lower level awaited them. They were to go down the ramp, hide behind the closest concrete columns and wait out the battle until Phoenix Force came to collect them or until the battle was drawn away. Presuming that they themselves were the target, just as outside Magham's conference, Phoenix Force would move up and away from the journalists, if necessary, leading the firefight to the upper level. In the process, they would be cut-ting off the terrorists' only reliable means of escape, for Ahmadi had the lock-out code for the elevators and had programmed it in. Once they came in, Ovan's terrorists would be boxed in as Phoenix Force manipulated the firefight to keep them pinned.

The rest was a killing box, with Ebrahim Ghemenizov in the center.

McCarter checked his wristwatch as he leaned up against the column that was his cover. From his position, he could see Calvin James across the way. The other members of Phoenix Force were similarly concealed, but he would not be able to see them until the shooting began and they broke cover to take aim at their quarry.

He checked the fit of his earpiece. "Almost showtime, lads. Check."

"Calvin, check."

"Gary, check."

"Rafe, check."

"T.J., check."

McCarter nodded as each man's voice sounded in his ear. He checked his watch again.

The sound of a vehicle moving slowly from the upper level echoed down the concrete ramp. McCarter checked his Krinkov, pulling the bolt back just far enough to verify that a round was chambered. He did not need to check the Browning. It was cocked and locked and ready inside his waistband in its clip-on holster.

The truck was of local manufacture, a make and model McCarter didn't recognize. It consisted of a forward cab and an open cargo bed covered with a canvas canopy. As it approached, the two journalists bolted with Ahmadi leading them. The truck rolled to a stop slowly, as if Ahmadi and his two charges did not exist.

The canvas cover was ripped back.

At least a dozen men stood crouched in the bed of the truck. Three more men in the cab moved around, reaching for what could only be weapons. Two of them poked the snouts of Russian-made machine pistols through the windows, while the men in the truck bed raised a forest of AK-47s, Skorpions and what looked to McCarter like at least one old World War II grease gun.

One of the men in the truck's cab was Ebrahim Ghemenizov.

"Steady, lads," McCarter said quietly. "Wait for it."

The parking lot exploded in strobing, flashing, flaming muzzle-blasts.

The deafening firestorm tore into the decoy vehicle, punching out every last square inch of auto glass, ripping holes in the sheet metal and puncturing the tires. Bullets walked up and across the decoy truck's metal skin. The mirrors shattered. Under the onslaught, the front bumper detached on one side. Something popped in the undercarriage. In the cloud of high-velocity lead, the stolen truck disintegrated in front of McCarter's eyes.

The roar of multiple automatic weapons gave way suddenly to the sounds of metal on metal as the men in the truck struggled to reload their weapons.

"Now!" McCarter yelled. He brought up his Krinkov, the folding stock extended, and took careful aim, choosing a gunman at random. Then he squeezed the trigger, milking a 3-shot burst from the Krinkov's full-auto setting.

The bullets walked up the doomed man from the neck to the bridge of his nose. Whatever he'd been thinking, McCarter mused, was now splashed all over the face of the man next to him. The sudden death of McCarter's target was met by three more terminations, one of those an unfortunate gunman whom two of the Phoenix Force commandos had targeted simultaneously by coincidence. The rear of the shooter's truck had turned into an abattoir in less time than it took for McCarter to think of the word, radically changing whatever plan the gunmen had been holding in their minds.

That was what a successful engagement was all about, McCarter thought as he chased a target in the sights of his Krinkov. You took the enemy's visual picture, his expectations, and you turned them sideways, upside down and backward. You robbed him of the initiative, of the momentum. You pressed him. You overwhelmed him. You denied him any attempt to catch his breath, to steady his mind, to do anything but freeze, cower and die in the shower of your sudden and superior force.

Bloody simple, really.

The terrorists—with Ebrahim Ghemenizov in their midst there was no doubt that these men were Ovan's operatives—had spilled out of the truck and scattered for the corners of the parking garage like so many roaches. McCarter liked the comparison. Insects they were, and like insects they would be ground under Phoenix Force's boots. There was only one way to deal with an infestation, he mused, stroking the Krinkov's trigger and hitting a fleeing terrorist in the center of the back of his head.

You exterminated it.

An enemy shooter took a blast to the torso that folded him backward. His Kalashnikov sprayed the ceiling of the parking level, showering his corpse with pieces of concrete. Another terrorist was laid out on top of him as he tried to flee. That man's rifle clattered to the asphalt.

The resistance faded. Soon the only shots fired were those from the Krinkovs carried by Phoenix Force, distinctive in their higher pitch. These quickly died down when there were no targets to track. Stony Man operatives did not waste ammunition firing blindly.

The voices of his team echoed in his ear as each man confirmed that he was still operational. There had been little chance of a casualty, really, given the scenario they had put in place. Ghemenizov and his team of ghouls had walked right into it. Unless there was a second contingent of terrorists waiting to spring the trap already sprung, well...McCarter didn't believe in fairies, the Easter bunny or Santa Claus, either.

But a certain someone was not accounted for—

He saw him then. He caught a glimpse of Ghemenizov through the pall of smoke that was all that remained of the gun battle. A gout of Krinkov fire joined his own as one of his team—Calvin James, judging by the position—ripped up the asphalt of the parking garage's floor chasing the terrorist leader as he made a break for it.

"He's going for the lower level." James's voice was urgent.

"I'm on him," McCarter said. "Mop up here, mates. If any of Ovan's men are alive, see what you can get from them. Make sure none of them is shamming. Calvin, back me up."

"Right behind you."

McCarter moved. He would have liked to go after Ghemenizov man-to-man, but of course that was just so much macho nonsense. They were here to achieve an objective, and as long as he had the resources to make doubly sure of success, he would use them. But damn, he wished he had a cigarette about now. He laughed at himself. The Briton had always been the team hothead, and now that he was in charge, he was thinking like a responsible grown-up. The idea made him chuckle under his breath.

As he ran down the ramp he heard pistol shots.

Ahmadi was firing away from the protection of a column, shielding the two journalists with his body. McCarter assessed the angle of the gunfire and easily picked out the column across the level where Ghemenizov must be hiding...or where Ahmadi, at least, thought he was. The Briton crept into position and stationed himself behind a concrete support column of his own.

The Krinkov was awkward against the concrete pillar, so McCarter laid it gently by his feet with the safety engaged. He drew the Browning Hi-Power. While well-worn, the pistol was accurate and its sights were true. He had used it to great effect so far this mission and had learned he could trust it. Extending his arm, he hugged half of the column, framing Ghemenizov's cover as he took careful aim.

Ahmadi was giving as good as any member of Phoenix Force might have, methodically chugging away with his Glock 19. McCarter could spare him only the briefest of glances, but the Agency or the IIS had taught the Iranian well. His weapon ran empty and he retracted his arm, ripping free a magazine and slamming home a fresh one with only a moment's hesitation. Then he racked the slide, pushed the gun forward, and started firing again. His shots had a pacing, a rhythm, that was unhurried but also unpredictable, which prevented his enemy from picking the holes between bullets.

James came up behind him. McCarter whispered into his earpiece for his teammate's benefit. "Work around, mate, and see if you can flank him at an angle opposite. We'll have him in a nice little cross fire then."

"What about Iranian security?" Manning's voice cut in over the line. "David, do we have the time for this?"

"I'm betting," the Briton said, "that the Iranian

officials have been warned well clear of this site by the same means they've been mysteriously absent whenever Ovan's bully boys have gone to work."

James's voice came back to him. "In position."

If Ahmadi had noticed the Phoenix Force men gliding through the shadows of the parking garage, he had given no sign of it. He emptied what was apparently the last of his magazines and then grabbed the two journalists, pushing them farther toward the asphalt and literally lying over top of them. McCarter saw that and shook his head. That man had brass balls on him, and that was a fact.

Ghemenizov stuck his head up, sensing the opening. He had a pistol of some kind in his hand, from which he released a steady stream of full-auto fire that lasted about a second. A Stetchkin APS, if McCarter wasn't mistaken. The terrorist leader started to bring his weapon up, aiming at Ahmadi's position.

Well, that wouldn't do.

McCarter's pistol, rock-steady in his experienced hands, barked once, then again. Ghemenizov shrieked and fell back, losing the Stetchkin. It burped a few remaining rounds when it struck the pavement, ricochets whining into the underground darkness.

"Calvin," McCarter instructed. "I've lost him. My angle's bad."

"I've got him," James reported. "He's covered."

McCarter reholstered his pistol and retrieved his Krinkov. He circled around to where Ahmadi was practically crushing the two Iranian reporters. "You can get up now, mate," he said. "All clear, provisionally. Though I wouldn't want to dawdle here any longer than we have to. I wouldn't want to take on faith that the Internal Security forces will keep ignoring this place for too much longer."

Ahmadi, from his position, opened one eye and looked at McCarter. "It is safe?"

"Safe as it's going to be." McCarter nodded. He offered Ahmadi his free hand and pulled the man up, then helped the other two to their feet. For their part, the two reporters looked shaken but no worse for wear.

"We heard the shots," the woman said. McCarter had never gotten her name and, truth be told, it was better that Phoenix Force know as close to nothing about the pair as possible. If anything went wrong, there was no need to drag these two down with them, on the distant chance that they were interrogated to the point of breaking and then questioned about this part of the mission.

"It sounded," said the man, "like a war." Both of the journalists had very good English, but the male had almost no accent at all.

"It is a war," McCarter said. "And it's not over yet. Ahmadi, keep an eye on them. We'll be rolling out of here in just a moment."

Ahmadi nodded.

McCarter found James standing over Ebrahim Ghemenizov. The fanatical look in the terrorist leader's eyes had never been more intense. He gazed at the two Phoenix Force operatives with burning hatred.

"So you are Americans," the terrorist leader said weakly. His gaze bored into James, who shrugged.

"Speak for yourself," McCarter said.

James held his Krinkov on Ghemenizov, who held his stomach while kneeling in an awkward half crouch. Blood was soaking through the terrorist's shirt and he was very pale. His hands were shaking as he tried to hold himself together. McCarter had seen wounds like that before. Ghemenizov was a dead man. There would be no saving him.

"You…you look on me and laugh," Ghemenizov said bitterly. "But I gladly die…knowing that I have killed many of your kind." He tried to spit and couldn't manage it. Instead he collapsed onto his back. His legs flopped at odd angles; he probably couldn't feel them at all. The pool of blood beneath him was spreading.

McCarter waved James back. He handed his teammate his Krinkov and drew his Hi-Power once more, press-checking it unnecessarily to make sure there was a round in the chamber. The gesture would be clear enough to a gunman like Ghemenizov.

The terrorist leader coughed, then his body racked with great, convulsive heaves that made his back arch. Blood trickled from his mouth. The light was rapidly leaving his eyes. He could, however, linger that way for some time. Suffering, even in a monster like Ebrahim Ghemenizov, was not something McCarter would tolerate. He bent, checking Ghemenizov for weapons, finding only a spare magazine for the Stetchkin and a satellite phone. He handed the phone to James.

Ghemenizov looked up at McCarter. "I wish…a moment."

"It's more than you've given anyone, you blackhearted bastard," McCarter said. "But take your moment."

James was looking through the satellite phone. If Ghemenizov noticed or cared, he didn't hint at it. Finally the Phoenix Force operator handed the phone to Ghaem Ahmadi, who had walked up with a weary expression on his face.

"Where'd the reporters go, man?" James asked.

"I have sent them on their way," Ahmadi said. "They have agreed to help us."

"Help us what?" McCarter said. "Haven't they already?"

"You know as well as I do," Ghaem said, "that your country cannot truly move against Ovan or Magham without broad political support. The key to such support will be exposing what is happening here in Iran. If we can do so from within, we stand a very good chance of changing it. My two friends have agreed to help us spread whatever we task them with disseminating. No matter what it is. No matter the danger."

"They understand the danger?" McCarter asked.

"None could know it better." Ahmadi nodded. "Those attempting to tell the truth in the news, to 'speak it to power,' as I think you say…many have been punished. Tortured. Killed. It is one of the many reasons Magham must be stopped."

"Very well, then." McCarter nodded. "Then we'll—"

"I know this number," Ahmadi said. He was staring at the satellite phone's screen.

"What? How?" James asked.

"I have it memorized," Ahmadi said. "It is a phone used by… I…"

"Well, man," McCarter said. "Spit it out."

"This…this phone is used by Garret Aimler. He is the head of the CIA network in Tehran."

"Aimler as in the man to whom any status report from you would be available," McCarter said flatly.

"Yes." Ahmadi nodded slowly. "But…Mr. Aimler has been in the Agency for years. He was one of the men who recruited me originally. He is no Iranian spy."

"Whatever the reason," McCarter said, "it looks like we've found the mouse in your house."

Ahmadi said nothing. He looked bewildered.

"You have anything to say about that?" McCarter gestured to the phone with his off hand before mating it with his gun hand, emphasizing his words by extending the Hi-Power fully. He toed Ghemenizov with one shoe, wondering if perhaps the man had lost consciousness. He was rapidly running out of blood, from the look of him.

Ghemenizov, eyes closed, managed a laugh. It was not a pleasant laugh. It was the reed-dry laugh of a mummified corpse, the humorless cackle of an evil man who knows he is staring his final moments in the eye and wants to make someone suffer as he goes.

"You will be destroyed…from within." Ghemenizov laughed softly to himself. "My brother…he will make you pay. He is already among you."

"Wake up," McCarter said harshly. He kicked Ghemenizov's foot. "Open your eyes." The terrorist's eyes came open slowly, but open they did. He stared at McCarter, all of his feigned humor gone now. Smoldering hate and something like insanity met the Briton's gaze.

"Tell me about Garret Aimler," McCarter ordered.

"I…will not…help you," Ghemenizov shook his head limply.

"Suit yourself, mate." McCarter shrugged. "A wound like that could take an awful long time to kill you, finally. Well. An awful long time in the relative sense. You don't really have much time. Be a shame to go that way all the same."

"I…wish to make…a statement," Ghemenizov breathed. "I will speak of the decadent West. I will—" he paused, coughing blood that he did not bother to wipe from his mouth "—make you understand…why it is that we must…

destroy you. And after I have said my final words…you will send me on my way."

McCarter shook his head, the barrel of the Hi-Power never wavering. "I'll send you on your way," he said quietly, "but I'll be bloody well damned if I'll listen to a lot of prattle from the likes of you."

"Then…kill me…"

McCarter pulled the trigger.

CHAPTER FOURTEEN

Outside Schenectady, New York

Karbuly Ghemenizov sat alone in the van, hunkered in the passenger seat with his satellite phone clenched in one huge fist. He spoke haltingly, with uncharacteristic deference. He was easily a hundred pounds heavier than the man to whom he spoke, but he feared no man on Earth save this one. He was speaking to Nikolo Ovan, President for Life of the newly re-formed nation of Turkmenistan.

He was speaking to his father.

"I am waiting," Ovan said over the line. He sounded peevish and disappointed, a tone with which Ghemenizov was only too familiar. In speaking with his master—for never was there any doubt in the mind of Karbuly Ghemenizov that Ovan was his master—he felt he was once more a child, eager for approval and terrified that nothing he did was good enough. These emotions made so much more difficult the task before him, which was to explain why so many of the planned bombing sites had become killing fields for Ghemenizov's men. The forces he had brought with him, the security operatives and trained killers who formed the backbone of Ovan's offensive network here in the United States, were very large, for a coordinated series of attacks such as this one required a great deal of manpower. It would not be inaccurate to say, in Ghemenizov's assessment, that this operation, and its end goal of securing a steady supply of high-tech weaponry from the Magham administration, represented the culmination of Ovan's life's work.

His father was a complicated man in that way. Ghemenizov knew what Turkmenistan's own dissident movement had to say about Ovan, and he had personally crushed the skulls of more than a few of these fools. The nation's feeble resistance, which was kept feeble by the work of Ovan's guard and his other enforcement agencies, saw Ovan as a stony-faced, implacable, intractable dictator who would not rest until he held the entire nation under his iron grip, presumably simply for the love of controlling others. This was nonsense. Nikolo Ovan may well have been stony-faced, though, glancing at himself in the side mirror of the van, Karbuly Ghemenizov was hardly in a position to criticize. Implacable, he surely was. Intractable, he could sometimes be. But these were the traits of a man accustomed to power, a man who understood that it takes strength to rule. Karbuly Ghemenizov was no stranger to strength. He understood what it could and couldn't do. He understood how versatile it could be. He understood how necessary it was.

He and his brother, Ebrahim, had known neither their father nor each other during their formative years. Karbuly knew that Ebrahim had grown up the child of privilege, for his mother had been married to a person of some wealth in Iran. Just what the arrangement was between Ovan and Ebrahim's mother, or between Ovan and the man Ovan had cuckolded, Karbuly did not know and had never cared to ask. Karbuly, for that matter, had never known his mother and had never asked about her, either. The circumstances of his birth were irrelevant.

Karbuly had grown up on the streets of Ashgabat in Turkmenistan. While homeless and poor, he had never thought of himself as disadvantaged. He was, however, hungry, always hungry, and his earliest memories were of beating other street children to take what food or money they had to fill his belly directly or indirectly. In so doing he learned, even as he grew head and shoulders taller than children his own age, that he enjoyed beating them. He enjoyed the feeling of their bodies gripped in his fists, the tension in his opponents' muscles going slack as he choked them into unconsciousness. The first time he accidentally killed a boy, by twisting his neck just a little too hard, the warm sensation that filled him with what he could only call joy truly surprised him. It became widely known in the wretched neighborhood Karbuly called his territory that to cross paths with the Large One, as they called him, was to take your life in your hands.

He began running small errands for the local criminal underground when he reached his early teens, and by his midteens he carried a knife and would accept even the most paltry of sums in exchange for his services as an assassin. He was just beginning to contemplate killing his employer and seizing what few assets the man commanded when an emissary from Nikolo Ovan's brutally nationalist political machine found Karbuly Ghemenizov in an alley. Would Ghemenizov like to make a few more coins than he normally did in a day, the emissary had asked, and in the next few seconds Ghemenizov had closed the distance between them, his big fist on the hilt of his *kindjal* knife, prepared to slay the man for wrongfully assuming that Ghemenizov was a street prostitute. The terrified little man had quickly explained that he had meant no offense; he only wished to transport Ghemenizov for an audience with his here-tofore long-lost father.

Ghemenizov remembered feeling nothing special about the invitation. He knew that other children had families, that they had mothers or fathers or both, with whom they lived and for whom they worked. He had always assumed that it was simply his lot in life to have neither the advantages nor the obligations of such an ar-rangement. He had never felt as if he had been wronged by circumstance or chance. He had never felt as if he was lucky. He had never really felt *anything* about it, for Ghemenizov took what was simply as it came, dealt with it by crushing it between his massive palms and lived as he wished to live by taking what he desired.

He had said as much to Nikolo Ovan, whom he even then understood to be a political figure of some impor-tance. Ghemenizov understood wealth and power, and knew that the guards standing at either side of Ovan held firearms against which his size and his strength were of little value. The guards stood far enough back that he could not reach them to rend them limb from limb if this Ovan ordered it. Thus it was that he spoke candidly but with respect. He told no lies and he asked for nothing. This Ovan had wished to see him; this Ovan claimed to be Ghemenizov's father; this Ovan said it had been a relatively easy thing to track the boy he was now claiming as his own.

Ghemenizov hadn't asked why he had been left to his own devices for so many years. He didn't care. He had wished to advance, to command more power, to prosper as a man of action. Now, on the cusp of making a decision at a much lower level, he was being offered the chance to assume a place in a much more important hierarchy of Turkmen power. Who but a fool would refuse? Who but a fool would disrespect Nikolo Ovan by making demands or asking a bunch of stupid, pointless questions? Whining did not change the past. It was weak.

Ovan had asked Ghemenizov if he had such questions, perhaps as a test. Ghemenizov had said proudly that if he did, he would be neither so stupid nor so weak as to utter them. The answer had pleased Ovan. The older man did not hug Ghemenizov, but something in his eyes implied that the impulse was there. Ghemenizov had shrugged. Was there work to do? he had asked. Could he begin immediately? That, too, had pleased Ovan.

Ovan had introduced Karbuly then to the skinny, sallow youth whom he named as Ebrahim. The two were both Ovan's sons. Karbuly accepted this without comment, nodding to Ebrahim and expecting no response. Agitated and always in motion, Ebrahim had been difficult to tolerate at first. Karbuly learned to accept that, too. Blood was blood.

In comparing notes, both boys learned that they had, now in their late teens, been plucked from their respective existences in Turkmenistan and Iran without warning. What prompted Ovan's action, neither of them would ever learn. The half brothers were placed in the household of Inram Ghemenizov, a trusted bodyguard to the then up-and-coming Ovan. Inram was a security specialist and had previously been a special forces operative. But he was first and foremost a torturer, an interrogator.

It was Inram who had taught both young men the value of breaking an enemy, and the joy of so doing. Inram—old, beloved, stern Inram—taught them everything they would need to know to be useful to Ovan as leaders in the regime the man was building. Inram taught them weapons, taught them fighting, taught them how to deal with and dominate people. But he also taught them much more important things. He taught them to read. He taught them to understand the news and to grasp the subtle shades of political meaning that were so often conveyed in the media. He taught them to lead. He taught them that they would be the hands that would enforce the will of their father. In seeing to it that Nikolo Ovan's word was law, they would come to know themselves and to value themselves, to reach their full potential. In the years that he worked with them, Inram Ghemenizov was more father to them than Nikolo Ovan had ever been in practical terms, and both young men came to love the grizzled old soldier for it.

Karbuly and Ebrahim were issued identification and official credentials. For simplicity's sake and to avoid the appearance of impropriety, they took Inram Ghemenizov's surname. It was a final tribute to the old man who had taught them so much; he died of a heart attack in the garden of the Ashgabat estate where the half brothers lived during their training. Karbuly had dug the grave himself in that very garden. Ebrahim had said a few words, choosing to read from the Koran for no reason Karbuly understood or cared to question. Inram was not a particularly religious man, nor was Ebrahim, and until that moment Karbuly had never even seen the Koran. But it had seemed appropriate. It had satisfied Karbuly Ghemenizov.

Coming to know his brother had been more difficult. Even during the time they trained under Inram, it would not be true to say Karbuly knew Ebrahim as a person. Working through Ovan in the years that followed, this improved somewhat. Karbuly could say, eventually, that he honestly liked his brother. Ebrahim, for all his petty weaknesses and annoying character tics, was indeed his father's son. He shared Karbuly's hatred for all things that Ovan hated: weakness, the West and those who opposed Nikolo Ovan. In working as part of Ovan's terrorist network, first in Turkmenistan and then in Iran during the early stages of establishing the operation, Karbuly had learned that Ebrahim could be counted on to get things done. He was able, he was capable, he was vicious and he was persistent. These qualities Karbuly Ghemenizov could respect.

These were also the keys to understanding a man like his father. When Ovan had tasked Ebrahim and Karbuly with setting up the terrorist network in Iran, Karbuly had enjoyed his work and wished to make his father proud. When he had been dispatched to take charge of the covert operations that would soon become overt acts of war against his father's most hated foe, the United States, he had leaped at the chance.

And now he had to explain to his father why he was not succeeding. The first part of every such phone call with his father, meaning calls in which Karbuly reported less than total success, was an oration by Ovan in which he reiterated his goals. Karbuly could recite these speeches from memory and sometimes wondered if his father realized that they sounded like campaign rhetoric. He would never mention it, however. He might be physically stronger than his father by a fluke of birth, but no man was more brutal and no man was more given to sudden, violent action than was Nikolo Ovan. Displeasing such a man was unwise. Doing so repeatedly was dangerous to one's health.

Karbuly had no illusions that his relationship to Ovan by birth would afford him any protection should his failures mount so greatly as to warrant his death. His heritage might earn him Ovan's personal attention rather than the knife blade or the bullet of some stranger assassin. That was all. If he wanted to continue to breathe, he had to persuade Ovan that all was not lost, and that his failures were not total. His fist clenched around the phone so tightly that he heard the plastic casing creak. He let his hand go slack quickly, for it would not do to break the phone and make Ovan believe he had hung up.

"I therefore wish to know, Karbuly," Ovan was saying, his tone shaking Karbuly from his reverie and signaling that a response would be expected soon, "why it is that you report such extensive losses in personnel, and why so few of the bombs I have purchased at tremendous expense from the Iranians have been used for their intended purpose. I do not need to remind you that the operation in the United States serves two purposes. It deals a blow to the Satan worshippers, the sexual perverts, the fat, lazy American scum by showing them they are not safe behind the porous borders of what they laughingly believe to be the greatest nation on Earth. But it also demonstrates to the Iranians that should they choose to supply *me,* Nikolo Ovan, with the weapons at no small risk to themselves politically, those weapons will be used to hurt a common foe. Every weapon that does not kill Americans is a waste of time, effort and money that could have been used otherwise. Every weapon that does not detonate becomes evidence that can be used against us, but also against our Iranian allies. Magham is already in a precarious political position, a position our operation is supposed to be improving. Your failures are hurting that position, now or later, directly or indirectly."

The sudden silence on the line caused Karbuly Ghemenizov to yank the satellite phone from his ear and stare at its lighted face to make sure they were still connected. Obviously that was his cue to reply to the accusations leveled by his father, many of which he would be hard-pressed to argue. He had no choice but to try.

"I understand, Father," he said, his tone most humble and respectful. "It is true we have encountered unexpected resistance. The Americans have a counterterrorism team of some sort, and they have sent this team to root out our bombings and in some cases prevent them. I do not know how they have anticipated our movements, but from the moment I learned they had been pitted against us, I have stepped up our timetable and vigorously increased the pace of my efforts to compensate. We have taken bold moves against the Americans." He cleared his throat. This type of high-minded speechmaking did not come naturally to him, but it was the sort of formal response he had come to learn that Ovan expected.

"Explain to me," Ovan said sternly, "exactly what it is you think you have accomplished."

Here it was, Ghemenizov knew. This was the test. His response would set the tone for Ovan's reaction. Either his father would forgive him and send him on his way, warning him to work harder, or he would become suddenly gentle and understanding, suggesting that perhaps Ghemenizov need no longer risk himself personally. If the summons to Turkmenistan came, it would be the sentence of his death, for the moment he set foot in Ovan's presence after such an order, he could expect a bullet in the brain.

"It is true that the Americans have interfered with

several detonations," he said carefully. Lying or soft-pedaling these problems would only enrage Ovan, and he could not afford to do that. "But the primary purpose of our campaign is to hurt the Americans. The threat of the bombs is, in that capacity, almost as dangerous as the bombs themselves. Americans fall to pieces the moment they believe a little boy has floated away in a balloon or fallen down a well. Their cable news networks are at this moment full of hysterical shrieking over the many deaths that *could* have occurred. We have killed some of them, and we have detonated some of the bombs, which makes the threat of the others that more real. Their people see the targets we have devastated and they picture the unexploded bombs ripping through their loved ones.

"But the Iranians still must accept that many of their bombs will be recovered and analyzed by American authorities.

"If the Iranians actually expect you to believe their activities are not already known to America—" Ghemenizov took a calculated risk in being so bold "—then they are bigger fools than they presume you to be. Iran is well-known to be supplying roadside bombs and other explosives to enemies of the West in Iraq and Afghanistan. The American intelligence agencies must already possess extensive knowledge of the bombs themselves, for how else would they be deactivating them? For that matter, if they did not know about the Iranian devices and our deployment of them, they would not be able to anticipate our movements as they have been doing. Only my initiative has saved us from aborting the operation, for the Americans have known what we were trying to do almost before we thought of it."

"I see."

Ghemenizov did not know how to react to this. Ovan was not normally given to neutral observations of this type; he usually made his demands or pronounced his judgments. Was he expected to respond? He was not sure. He opted to remain silent, feeling the moments tick by.

"I will…persist in my efforts," he said finally, when he could bear it no longer. "We will continue with the operation."

"You will do so," Ovan said, "in the spirit of revenge."

"Father?"

"Your brother. Ebrahim. He is dead." Ovan's tone was flat. It betrayed neither sorrow nor anger, nor did it reveal the lack of either.

Karbuly blinked. He did not know what he would be expected to feel in such an instance. He had liked Ebrahim Ghemenizov, even respected him. He did not feel close to the man. He did not feel angry that Ebrahim was dead, for if he had died, he must have failed, and the price of failure was always death. But it did bother him that Ebrahim was necessary to his father's plans in Iran. It stood to reason that if Ebrahim had failed and been killed, some part of his father's plan was in danger. That angered him. It angered him very much.

"I will avenge Ebrahim Ghemenizov," he said hotly. "Do you require me to come home or to travel to Iran, Father?" There, he had said it. He had as much given his father the option to retask him…or to recall him to his execution. He had decided that if his life was forfeit, he would face that fact without fear, as he had always faced his life.

There was a long pause. Finally, Ovan said quietly,

"No. No, you are needed there. I presume you are in Vermont?"

"We are near the border," Karbuly said. "Retracing our route from the earlier Albany operation."

"Then do what you must do," Ovan said. "Exert my will. And, Karbuly…"

"Yes, Father?"

"Make them pay. Make them pay for Ebrahim."

"Yes, Father."

NIKOLO OVAN, seated in his fortified presidential palace in Turkmenistan, ended the satellite phone transmission with a press of his thumb. He took the phone from his ear and stared at it for a moment, the expression on his face blank. Slowly, his brow furrowed. On the armrest of his ornate antique chair, his left fist clenched, the knuckles turning white.

With great force of will he managed to exert control over himself once more. A blind rage would do him no good. He wanted to stand and begin tearing apart his own office. He wanted to smash the phone. He wanted to shatter the mirror in the gilded brass frame on the wall. He wanted to throw his chair through the window, take up the pistol in his desk drawer and shoot the first man who responded to the commotion. He stared at the double doors to his office, as if by force of will alone he could cause one of his aides to blunder through them and take a bullet.

No. He would be calm.

Such rage was weakness, and he would not give in to it. Ovan despised weakness in all forms. He would not become what he hated.

Ovan stood and went to the window, which afforded him a view of the once beautiful grounds of the now fortified presidential palace grounds. He clasped his hands behind his back and willed himself to appear calm. To look calm was to be calm. It had always been and ever would be so.

He felt the flush recede from his cheeks, felt the killing madness dissipate, felt his swollen brain begin to cool as he regained his ability to reason. Above all, he must not be weak.

The West was weak. It was why he had always wished to destroy it so. It was not envy on his part, for there were other wealthy nations that did not suffer from the depravity, from the laziness, from the utter, contemptible softness that was the United States. The Americans were the ultimate hypocrites, sitting in judgment over the rest of the world simply because the power of their military allowed them to dominate the planet.

Well, Nikolo Ovan had always known he would fight that weakness, that hypocrisy. Even as he built his political network and worked his way to the position of power he now held, he had not done so out of a desire to control Turkmenistan. This country, his country, was but the first step to a reordering of power on the world stage that would begin with destroying the West. To destroy America, to deal it a thousand killing blows that would destabilize it and cause its people to lose faith—that alone was to empower the rest of the world. Any injury done to America would help to root out the cancer that was the hated, lazy, weakling West.

He had thought so even as a young boy, when his own parents' wealth had enabled him to take to politics and to lay the groundwork for the many years of campaigning that lay ahead. His earliest memories were of his desire to amass power so that he could correct the wrongs of the world. When he learned of the extent to which the West was wrong, he had known that hurting the Americans would be the lynchpin of his plan to change the face of the Earth.

So much could be done with power, with strength. It was a lesson his bastard son Karbuly understood. It was a lesson that his other bastard son, Ebrahim, had understood.

He grieved, in his own way, for the loss of Ebrahim. He had thought himself beyond the need for filial ties, but when his spies had alerted him to the fact that two of his offspring were alive and well into their teenage years, he had determined to make use of both men. He had not been disappointed.

Until now.

Ebrahim's death was very inconvenient. It was the inconvenience, the possible conflict with his operation, that made Ovan so angry, for he had worked too hard to see his plans endangered now. Hopefully, Karbuly could bring about results in America despite the interference in the Magham election. As for the Iranian situation, that was more difficult.

He would need to figure out what to do. He needed time to think, and to plan. This was recoverable. This was not the end. He would see to it. He was President for Life Nikolo Ovan, and he was going to change the world.

CHAPTER FIFTEEN

Tehran, Iran

The Range Rover sped through the streets of Tehran. McCarter, who had always been a skilled driver and who, truth be told, often found it difficult to give the wheel to anyone else, enjoyed the feeling of power. Where Ghaem Ahmadi had found yet another of the British vehicles in Tehran, McCarter didn't know. Apparently the imports were popular among the city's wealthier power brokers. The truck had been equipped with license tags provided through Ahmadi's contacts in Iranian Internal Security itself, ensuring that they would trigger no official scrutiny simply from being seen on the road.

After seeing the two dissident journalists to relative safety, Phoenix Force had accompanied Ahmadi to his own home in Tehran. This was extremely risky, and they had gone in hot, expecting at any moment to encounter still more Ovan operatives. They were blown, with the head of the CIA's network in Iran calling the shots and walking enemy fire right onto them. Aimler would know Ahmadi was acting as Phoenix Force's liaison. Aimler would know where to find the Iranian intelligence agent. Even without status updates, any safehouse Ahmadi chose to use would be a point of potential vulnerability, for Aimler would know which sites were logical choices and which sites were accessible to the Iranian double agent.

They had rearmed themselves from the personal cache Ahmadi kept under the floorboards of the second story of his home. Ahmadi had also retrieved what had brought them here: his encrypted laptop, which had a small satellite interface used for making uploads and receiving downloads to and from the CIA network. Ahmadi had been muttering something about "VPN access" and "terminal emulation" since he had first recognized Garret Aimler's phone number in Ebrahim Ghemenizov's satellite phone. He had been uncharacteristically subdued since that time, and understandably so. The man had been in position and regarded as a valuable Company asset for some years now. Finding out he was being betrayed by the man in charge of the CIA here would have been a blow to his sense of health and well-being, and then some. Frankly, the Briton gave Ahmadi all the credit in the world for not going to pieces the moment he learned of it.

They had no specific destination in mind, for which McCarter was grateful, being completely unfamiliar with the city and its challenging traffic patterns. Still, he took pleasure in piloting the truck. He dodged a French subcompact and took a hard right to get them out of a particularly congested stream of vehicles. The traffic down this new street was still heavy, but he was able to increase their pace from a slow crawl to something more like a rapid clip again.

Ahmadi was typing on his laptop, and typing faster than McCarter was driving. The Phoenix Force leader looked over as James leaned forward from the rear seat to get a better look. Manning, Hawkins and Encizo, meanwhile, were playing lookout to the sides and the rear, making sure nobody on the street or in traffic became unduly interested in the Range Rover.

Ahmadi finally stopped typing. "I have it," he announced. "I am in."

"You've accessed Garret Aimler's private files?" James asked.

"Yes." Ahmadi nodded. "There are certain files I cannot access directly from this computer," he explained, "but we can at least see the file names and their locations. Aimler has partitioned a portion of the network for his private use."

"Wasn't that encrypted or protected or something?" Manning asked from where he sat.

"It was," Ahmadi said. "But all CIA operatives can access the network using their passwords, if they know where to look. The partition is visible only if you enter several subdirectories in Aimler's network space. One must believe one's employer has something to hide in order to confirm that he is hiding it." His face split in an echo of his lopsided grin before his expression became serious again. "In the morning, the file access tags will update. If Aimler looks, he will know I was snooping in his files. He may be very angry. But it is worth it. I believe you will find this interesting."

McCarter suddenly regretted being behind the wheel of the Rover.

James leaned closer and whistled. "David," he said. "This guy... If these file names are correct, he's got what must be hundreds of MP3 and AVI files, all of them tagged with Magham's or Ovan's names. There are time and date stamps, too."

"Video and audio," McCarter interpreted. "Of what?"

"He is using the same file conventions we normally use in cataloging our surveillance recordings," Ahmadi said. "But I have never seen these files. I am not aware of their existence. I should know these exist, for they bear directly on my own work here in Tehran. Aimler has been keeping these separate, a secret. Which means…"

"Which means," McCarter said when Ahmadi trailed off, "that he's got hundreds of tapes of Magham and Ovan talking about who knows what. And whatever that is, he doesn't want anybody to know about it."

"David," James said, "this could be precisely the information we need to make sure gets spread around to the public."

"Indeed it could, mate." McCarter nodded. "And I just bet Ghaem knows a couple of people who would be willing to make sure it gets into the papers."

Ahmadi grinned again. "There is something else," the Iranian said as he scrolled through the list. "I cannot open the video or audio files, but text files I can access. There is a… I… Oh, no. I do not believe this."

"What is it?" James asked.

"Aimler." Ahmadi shook his head. "Aimler…he has been concealing the location of the Iranian weapons lab."

"The lab," McCarter repeated. "The laboratory where they make the smart bombs? That lab?"

"Yes," Ahmadi said. "This is so… It is beyond reckless. It is… It is a betrayal of such magnitude that I…" Ahmadi stopped, apparently unable to speak.

"What can you tell us about this laboratory?" McCarter asked.

"I can give you its exact location," Ahmadi said. "It is listed here, as well as notations indicating that it possesses heavy armed security in the form of an IIS presence on-site. The odds will be overwhelming."

"Hell, man," James said. "Overwhelming odds are our specialty."

McCarter found a suitable location and pulled over. He motioned for Ahmadi to take the wheel. "Enough fun, then," he announced. "Ghaem, how quickly can you get us there from here?"

"Not more than half an hour, I should think," the Iranian operative said.

"Then don't waste time telling me about it." McCarter smiled. He pointed, and Ahmadi dropped the truck in gear and stomped the pedal.

He made it in almost half that time.

The laboratory was not visible from the street level. A narrow alley ended at a half flight of concrete steps leading down to a subterranean doorway. There were no guards in the alley itself, but Ahmadi warned that they were most likely under video surveillance from the moment the Range Rover turned into the alleyway.

The Iranian operative parked the Rover some distance from the doorway. He and Manning stayed with the vehicle to guard the rear, while McCarter and the rest of Phoenix Force went for the doorway.

"Commo check," McCarter said quietly.

Ahmadi and Manning responded first; Hawkins, James and Encizo chimed in after. McCarter was first down the stairs to the locked steel door to the laboratory. He couldn't see any cameras, but that didn't mean they weren't there.

He tried the knob. It didn't move. The door was solid to the touch, with no play even in the knob itself. He found himself wishing for some plastic explosive, but there wasn't any. Then he had an idea.

"Ghaem," he said. "Is there a tow strap in the Rover?"

"I will check." Ahmadi's voice was tinny in his ear, but audible. There was a pause and then he said, "Yes. There is."

"Drive up here," McCarter instructed. "Rafe, T.J., Calvin, at the ready, lads. Smart money says they know we're out here already."

Ahmadi brought up the Range Rover, while Manning, walking alongside it, secured the yellow tow strap to the brush bar covering the Rover's grille. The bar was really an extension of the heavy steel aftermarket bumper, which was in turn anchored to the Rover's frame to allow for towing and pulling. The only thing the Rover lacked was a winch, but that was just as well. McCarter had seen plenty of would-be off-road aficionados affix winches to their vehicles that were too small to pull them free. To those amateurs, the winch was an accessory they bolted on to look cool. Such people rarely left the asphalt anyway.

McCarter took the slack in the tow strap as Manning tossed it down, over the railing that protected the concrete pit surrounding the doorway. He wrapped the strap around the heavy steel knob and knotted it twice. With any luck, the knob was as heavy as it looked.

James checked his end of the alley, while Encizo checked the opposite. "We're clear," Encizo announced.

James echoed, "All set."

"Go." McCarter raised his arm and let it fall.

The Rover slowly backed down the alley, pulling the tow strap taut. There was a creak of metal straining, and McCarter suddenly worried that the steel doorknob would become a flying missile. He braced himself to react…but was rewarded with the high-pitched pop of something inside the door lock mechanism giving way. The door did not leave its hinges, but something about it looked askew as it slammed aside, rebounding off the concrete face of the building into which it was set.

Automatic gunfire, unaimed and uncontrolled, spouted from the doorway, raising showers of concrete debris and striking sparks from the metal railing. One of the joints of the railing popped free. Ahmadi's Rover took several hits, and before he could pull back farther, a metal cylinder came flying up from within the lab. It bounced off the pavement and rolled under the Range Rover.

"Grenade!" McCarter shouted. The men of Phoenix Force scattered. "Ghaem! You've got to—"

The grenade detonated. Rather than blowing apart the nose of the Rover and shredding Ahmadi's body in a shower of metal fragments, it flashed and burned with blinding intensity, showering the nose of the vehicle with liquid flame. The incendiary round had taken Ahmadi by surprise, but it hadn't dampened his spirit or his nerve, nor caused him to take leave of his senses. With the driver's side door opened, he realized the danger the burning vehicle represented, and instead climbed back into the vehicle. Then he hit the accelerator while the engine was still operational and sent the burning Range Rover flying backward down the alleyway.

Manning went after Ahmadi, no doubt understanding that the spectacle would soon attract attention. The burning Range Rover struck the building opposite the alley mouth and slewed around as Ahmadi turned the wheel, pushing the mortally wounded truck to get it away from the site of the laboratory.

Brass balls, McCarter thought again. Brass balls and an iron nerve on that one. Well, Manning would see to it his friend stayed out of trouble if it was at all possible. In the meantime, they had to strike before the Iranian security forces dug in and got their heads around the fact that they were being attacked.

McCarter stood to the side of the doorway with his Krinkov and aimed the weapon around the corner, firing blind, hoping to put whoever was hurling firebombs on the defensive. James, Encizo and Hawkins recovered and converged on his location, taking up strategic positions outside the doorway. McCarter made eye contact with each of them, slapped the receiver of the Krinkov and then loosed another volley around the corner, emptying the weapon. When his Krinkov went dry, James took the lead and fired a stream of fully automatic fire through the opening, allowing McCarter to reload.

"Ready, lads," McCarter said when James had finished. "On me, each by each, cover and move. Go!"

They went. McCarter went in first and crouched low, his fully reloaded Krinkov leading the way, with the three Phoenix Force team members backing him up at his flanks and over his head. They found themselves in a narrow, dark hallway lit only by bare lightbulbs set in the walls, with open corridors leading off to the left and right, as well as far ahead. From a room-clearing standpoint, it was an urban-warfare nightmare.

The men of Phoenix Force had seen its like countless times before.

Moving without speaking, knowing from long familiarity what each team member would do almost before he did it, they moved slowly down the hallway. The key in clearing a hostile, hot location like this was to stay mobile but not to rush, always maintaining a pace that would keep one ahead of the enemy but prevent becoming careless or missing a hidden foe. McCarter kept his weapon trained forward, trusting his teammates to cover the sides and the rear. Each time they came to a corridor, they were prepared to unleash hell, but they did not fire when they could not see targets. This was supposed to be a manufacturing facility with weapons of mass destruction. Such places did not respond well to errant gunfire.

They heard footsteps as they got farther down the corridor. That, McCarter thought, was almost certain to be their fire-chucker. He pressed the Krinkov's open folding stock tighter to the sweet spot between his shoulder and his pectoral muscle, watching over the sights with cool detachment.

When the man showed himself, he was wearing the paramilitary uniform of the IIS and carrying what looked like a satchel. If that was a satchel charge and he was intent on blowing them all to kingdom come, there wouldn't be much McCarter's bullet could do to stop it, but he took the shot anyway. The ugly, stubby Krinkov barked, spitting an empty brass casing up and across his field of vision, an aberration that this particular rifle produced sometimes. McCarter ignored it; the occasional hot casing down the neck of his shirt might burn him, but it wouldn't really hurt him, whereas a lapse in concentration over it could kill him.

The high-velocity bullet struck the man in the chest, causing him to turn. McCarter's follow-up shot took him under the armpit and proceeded through his torso. He fell to the ground, dead on the way down. The Briton mentally braced himself for the explosion that would rip through the hallway, sweeping Phoenix Force down the corridor in a bloom of expanding flame.

The explosion never came.

Incendiary grenades, their pins still in place, spilled out of the satchel and rolled across the grimy floor. McCarter gestured and Encizo picked them up, a wicked grin on his face. "Can't see carrying any of these back out of here," the guerilla warfare expert said as he held up the bag. "Wouldn't want to hurt myself hauling them."

"I'm inclined to agree, mate," McCarter nodded.

The hallway began to open up, and as it widened, it became cleaner, cooler and better lit. McCarter realized that they were walking on a slight grade, which meant the facility was deeper underground the farther they walked. Twice IIS men took aim at them with AK-47s, and once they faced a man who emptied a Glock G18 machine pistol at them. In each case, the Phoenix Force shooters took down their enemies with little difficulty, sending them on their way with well-placed shots from their compact Kalashnikov variants.

"This isn't the overwhelming odds I thought we were going to face," James said. He checked himself then, as movement caught his eye to his right, and he brought the Krinkov up just in time to put a bullet through the head of an IIS man who had come running out of the darkness holding a shovel.

"An entrenching tool?" Hawkins drawled. "Are you kidding me? They run out of guns, or what?"

"We've put a pretty big dent in their numbers," Encizo said. "They might have pulled personnel from other positions to cover where they think they're needed most. Magham might be using them to safeguard his own location, wherever that is."

"Joke's on him, then," James said.

Before they were done in Tehran, McCarter thought, the IIS was going to need to engage in a serious recruiting drive. "Can the chatter, lads," he said. "Looks like we've come to it."

At the end of the hallway they faced a double set

of doors plastered with warnings in Farsi. There were pictorial warnings, too, which pointed to the presence of dangerous and explosive components within. McCarter reached out and placed his splayed fingers experimentally against the right-hand door, which was dominated by a reinforced-glass window. The glass was fogged and translucent. A press of his fingertips showed some give to the doors.

"Right, then," he said. "Let's waste no time." With that, he reared back and planted a whipping kick in the door to the right just over the crash bar, slamming the doorway inward and clearing the way for his team.

They came in hard and fast, weapons up and prepared for aimed fire, sweeping in each direction like the well-oiled unit they were. Men in white lab coats scattered from workbenches that were spaced around the perimeter walls. Enough high-tech electronics to make Gadgets Schwarz jealous were piled on the benches, too, with several digital readouts and laptop computers running amid the piles of wires, leads and specialty tools that the Briton didn't immediately recognize. McCarter also caught a glimpse of the metal spheres that were the explosive cores of the smart bombs, set in racks at two of these workbenches.

A pistol cracked. One of the lab workers had a Makarov and was firing haphazardly while hiding halfway behind a rolling metal cart that couldn't have been much more than a pair of wheels with a sheet-metal skin. McCarter lowered the barrel of his weapon and triggered a blast through the cart. The Krinkov's 5.45 mm rounds effortlessly punched through the cart and the man behind it, leaving holes and a spray of blood on the wall opposite him.

The death galvanized the other Iranian workers. They

must have been wearing holstered pistols, for each one of them managed to produce a weapon of his own without first scrambling for an armory of some kind. That surprised McCarter; he would have thought such personnel would be guarded by the IIS, rather than ranking weapons among their ilk. It emphasized to the Phoenix Force leader just how thoroughly intertwined the Iranian government and this little bomb-and-terror-works buried in the heart of the city were.

The high-pitched, hollow-metal clatter of the Krinkovs cut short the Iranian workers before they could score even a lucky shot, although a stubby Makarov bullet here or there did manage to put some of the equipment out of commission. McCarter didn't think a bullet strike would set off either the smart bomb components or the nerve gas they contained…but he was not precisely sure. He looked to either side and behind him, checking his immediate area of operation, making sure there were no more hostiles he had missed.

"Clear," he announced.

"Clear," Hawkins echoed. His voice was joined by James and Encizo.

"Calvin," McCarter said, peering at the nearest workbench. "You and Rafe, use your phones. Get photos of everything on the benches.

"T.J., take video. We want a record of everything in this little chamber of horrors. I'll see to the dead."

With that, McCarter removed his secure satellite phone and activated its camera feature. Making sure the flash was on automatic, he moved from dead body to dead body, toeing over those on their stomachs to get images of each face. They would upload these digital photos to the Farm, where Kurtzman and his team would run them through face-recognition software and compare them to both official and black-operations intelligence databases. Likely at least some of them were on record somewhere as being the types of scientists and technicians who specialized in weapons of mass destruction. The infamous "Dr. Germ," Rihab Rashid Taha, sprang to mind. The England-educated Iraqi microbiologist was notorious among UN weapons inspectors for her role in developing weapons-grade anthrax and botulinum for Saddam Hussein's biological WMD program.

"Move quickly, lads," McCarter said as he finished his photos. "They'll be on us quickly enough, if they're not moving already." There was no telling how many reinforcements might be poised to respond to a breach of the lab. McCarter gazed around at the smart bombs that were the cause of so much strife, so much danger, so much potential death.

"David," Rafael Encizo said, "are you thinking what I'm thinking?"

"I surely am," McCarter said. "I surely am. Mind you, share now." He held out his free hand, and Encizo placed an incendiary grenade in it.

They used all of the grenades and then ran like hell. The heat from the overlapping detonations was lapping at their backs as they made their way through the corridors, weapons once again at the ready, and finally hit the street level. Manning, with a slightly scorched Ahmadi in the driver's seat, was waiting in a Peugot sedan just large enough to seat them all. Ahmadi threw the Peugot in Drive and got them out of there before the last of the team members had closed their doors. He knew what was coming.

"Street crime's gonna go down about a thousand percent when you stop boosting us rides," James commented to Ahmadi.

"I suspect the incidence of gun violence will drop precipitously once you leave the city, as well," the Iranian retorted, deadpan.

"Touché," Manning said softly.

James started laughing. Soon Encizo, Hawkins and even the usually stoic Manning were joining the laughter while Ahmadi looked satisfied at having scored a direct hit.

When the explosion behind them rattled windowpanes for a block up the street, McCarter allowed himself a satisfied smile, as well.

CHAPTER SIXTEEN

Bennington, Vermont

Carl Lyons, flanked by Schwarz and Blancanales, surveyed the grounds outside the Bennington Battle Monument. Schwarz carried his scanner-jammer, and Blancanales toted his M-16. The USAS-12 was cradled in Lyons's fists as he swept his hard gaze over the field dominated by the three-hundred-foot stone monument itself. Behind them, the rotors of the Chinook helicopter whirled, creating a windstorm that whipped grit at the backs of their heads and sent the smarter monument visitors running. The ones who weren't quite as smart just stopped and stared, looking on as if to ask what interesting, exciting thing might be imminent. Lyons mentally urged them to take the hint and get moving. He looked up at the stone obelisk, which rose more than three hundred feet in the air, and wondered what they would find inside it.

The monument, built in the late 1800s, commemorated events in 1777, when British General Burgoyne attempted to capture a cache of supplies kept in Bennington to prevent American revolutionary colonists from using them. The monument housed an elevator used to take visitors to an observation floor that offered a commanding view of parts of Vermont, New York and Massachusetts. If Iranian smart bombs were detonated in and around the battle monument, the death toll could conceivably be very high. Bennington was a popular tourist destination for travelers from all three contiguous states.

Lyons had scanned the tourist information and other briefing data sent by Stony Man Farm when the Warlock network had identified strangely erratic signals from this location. As targets went, it was perfectly logical. There would be plenty of innocent people on hand at such a site, and of course the tie to America's history would help intensify the damage of the attack. It would signal that nothing about America was safe, not even its heritage, and it sent the message that the terrorists held such history in contempt.

A snarl curled Lyons's lip. Yeah, well. He had some contempt of his own for his enemies.

"I'm getting a really strange signal close by," Schwarz said. "I think it's coming from the monument itself."

That was not a surprise. Lyons urged the trio on. They approached with speed, but cautiously, waiting for enemy bullets they knew could come at any second.

As they approached the monument, a sign on the walkway to the entrance caught his eye. It apologized in large block letters, proclaiming the monument closed for maintenance. But the dates listed in fine print on the sign were wrong; they were from six months ago. Lyons reached out as he passed the sign and ran his finger along the top edge of it.

His fingers came back covered in dust. He looked at his teammates showing them his fingertips. Both men nodded. The sign had been dragged out of storage somewhere; Lyons would bet his next cup of coffee on it. He brought up the shotgun.

They hit the entrance behind Lyons's brutal front

kick, Schwarz and Blancanales flanking Able Team's
leader. A shotgun blasted, and it wasn't Lyons's Daewoo.
The pump gun held by the shooter had been sawed back
to the magazine tube. The man holding it screamed
something in the language Lyons had learned to recognize as Turkmen. Well, that figured; these were Ovan's
killers, after all, just as they had been each time Able
Team had squared off against them.

Please, Lyons thought, let that bastard Ghemenizov
be here. The big ex-cop had been spoiling for a rematch
with the terror-master before Binghamton, but now it
was personal. To murder that woman in front of Lyons's
eyes, so needlessly, then to use his own men to shield
his escape... Lyons would be damned if he would let
Karbuly Ghemenizov walk away from another encounter with Able Team.

Lyons cut off the terrorist's scream with a shotgun
blast of his own. He swept the small area inside the base
of the battle monument, finding no other resistance, as
Blancanales and Schwarz guarded the door and the entrance to the elevator respectively. Opposite the entrance
to the elevator, he found a dead man.

"Got a corpse here," he said. He checked the man's
name tag. He was a tour guide of some kind. His name
had been Lewis. He had been shot through the head.

"Anything else?" Schwarz asked.

"No," Lyons answered, circling back. "But that elevator isn't down here," he said, pointing. "I don't like it.
Pol, hit the switch. Gadgets, watch the entrance."

The call unit looked newer than the rest of the equipment surrounding it, as if it had only been updated recently. An access key was in the lock and had been
turned. A key chain attached to the key read, simply,
Lewis. Well, that answered that. The tour brochures had

promised a guided elevator trip to the observation deck. Today had been Lewis's last day on the job.

Lyons waited for the elevator to descend, taking too long as it did so. His fingers clenched around the USAS-12 while he waited.

The door opened.

Lyons almost triggered a fully automatic stream of 12-gauge rounds. A man was crouched in the elevator, and on the floor next to him was a folding-stock Kalashnikov rifle. This one had the wooden foregrip common to some Romanian models. The man beside it looked up, his eyes wide with terror. He was holding himself in that awkward crouch with one hand pressed to the floor of the elevator.

His other hand was pressing a button on an Iranian smart bomb.

"Don't move!" Lyons bellowed. "Get your hand off that bomb or I'll spray you across that elevator!"

"Wait!" the man cried at the same moment. "You do not understand!"

Lyons could feel his finger tightening on the trigger. Engaging an armed enemy in conversation was a sure way to get dead. Cagey opponents would try to distract you by giving you a question to answer, then draw down on you and take your life.

"What's the frequency, Kenneth?" A famous television news anchor had been asked that just before he was punched in the face and mugged. Some time after that a group of dope-smoking hippy musicians wrote a song about it, if Lyons remembered correctly. It was a valuable lesson: don't talk to the bad guys.

Something about the man's look of flop-sweating terror stayed Lyons's hand. As the Stony Man operative looked closer, he saw that the man's finger was white with the pressure he was exerting. He was stabbing the button on the bomb's control panel with all his might.

"Carl!" Schwarz cried from the doorway. "I've got hostiles coming in from two directions! On our nine and at our two o'clock!"

"Pol." Lyons jerked his chin toward the door. "Cover our backsides."

The first bullets began to pepper the outside of the heavy stone obelisk. Lyons was grateful for the protection as he poked the snout of the USAS-12 up under the crouching terrorist's chin. A blast of automatic fire behind him, lighter than the Kalashnikovs in the hands of the men now assaulting their position, was Schwarz's 93-R deployed in 3-round burst. Blancanales's M-16 stuttered, as well, adding to the din.

A handheld CB radio was clipped to the terrorist's belt. It was turned up loud enough that Lyons could hear snatches of conversation, also in Turkmen, coming from it. He knelt to lift the terrorist up by the barrel of his shotgun, causing the man to crane awkwardly to maintain his hold on the bomb's button.

"Care to tell me just what the hell you're doing?" he asked.

"The bomb," the terrorist said. "There was a…a malfunction." His English was thickly accented, but Lyons could understand him. "It started to go through the detonation sequence while I was arming it."

"And that button?"

"I am preventing the explosion," he told Lyons.

"Well, now," Lyons said.

He made no effort to move, keeping the terrorist off balance. Sweat streamed down the man's face, hitting the floor of the elevator in fat droplets. Lyons was disgusted. He knew how Ghemenizov's mind worked by now. He thought he knew just what had been in the minds of these killers when they set up this attack.

"Let me guess," he said, his finger still tight on the trigger of the USAS-12. "You and your murdering filth waltzed in here and took out whomever you chose. Maybe we'll even find some more dead staff hidden on the grounds. Then you came up here after planting that closed sign so you wouldn't be disturbed. I bet you were going to take it with you, give the tourists a chance to start circulating again after the tragic accident here. And now—" Lyons ducked as a shot punched through the top edge of the doorway and whined off the steel frame of the elevator cage "—you've called your buddies back because you needed help when your bomb tried to blow up in your face. Am I about right?"

The terrorist nodded furiously. "Yes! It is as you say. Please. If the bomb explodes, we all die here and now! Please, we must find a way to deactivate it."

"Gadgets," Lyons said quietly, trusting his earbud transceiver to relay his words. "You get all that?"

"I did, Carl," the Stony Man technical expert said. "We've kind of got our hands full here. Pol and I have waxed several tangos each, but they're not exactly in short supply."

"Switch with me," Lyons said. He turned to the terrorist. "Stay here. Don't move." The man stared after him blankly.

"Making new friends, Carl?" Schwarz asked as he passed the Able Team leader.

"Yeah," Lyons said. "He's a real conversationalist. Bet he'd be great fun at parties."

Lyons took up Schwarz's position at the doorway. The terrorists were using a couple of outbuildings for cover, appearing around the corners of the structures and taking potshots. They had automatic assault rifles and pistols. Lyons swapped out the magazine in his shotgun from buckshot to slugs, needing the additional range of the slugs for the distance to the target. Blancanales was doing quite well with his M-16, meanwhile, squeezing off short bursts and single shots and winnowing the ranks of the oncoming terrorists.

Lyons heard the crackle of small-arms fire from low and to his left. He looked to see a pair of civilians in the parking lot, a man and a woman, firing what appeared to be .45-caliber 1911-pattern pistols into the ranks of the terrorists clustered behind the nearest outbuilding. The angle was perfect for the civilians. They caught the gunmen unaware and dropped them, as the corner of the building prevented Lyons and Blancanales from getting good shots at the would-be killers.

"Hey, Carl!" Blancanales shouted above the gunfire. "You see that?"

"Yeah," Lyons nodded, grinning despite himself. "That's Vermont for you!" Vermont had no laws governing the possession or carrying of pistols at the state level. That had always made sense to Lyons. He saw no reason a man should be left helpless by the law, his right to self-defense restricted to some bureaucrat's whims.

Lyons took careful aim. His shotgun slugs split the head of one terrorist and splattered the brains of another across the corpse of the first. Then he saw a particularly large figure with a rifle moving behind the ranks of the foremost gunman.

That could be him. That could be Karbuly Ghemenizov. The size was about right, or at least seemed so at this distance. Lyons waited for a clean shot as Blancanales started picking off the men to either side. Blancanales apparently had seen what Lyons had seen and knew what the big ex-cop intended to do.

"All clear," he said when he had finished shooting. "He's yours, Carl."

Lyons let out half a breath and held the rest, squeezing the USAS-12's trigger. The shotgun slug rocketed toward its target and struck home. The big man with the AK-47 collapsed where he had stood, never to rise again.

"Got it," Schwarz said behind them. "Bomb deactivated."

"We've got another problem," Blancanales said.

Lyons turned back. "Yeah?"

"I've got several of them flanking us, moving around behind the building—"

The snout of an AK-47 was suddenly being shoved into the doorway by someone standing outside and against the door opening. Lyons grabbed the barrel and pushed it down, into the ground and away from Blancanales, feeling the barrel grow hot as the gunman pulled the trigger on full-automatic. Suddenly he was fighting a live bullet hose that writhed in his fist like a snake. Bullets chopped up the floor at his feet, narrowly missing his toes, showering him with debris that choked him and got into his eyes. He flinched and squeezed his eyes, dropping his shotgun to the floor and forcing the barrel of the AK into the side of the wall.

At this angle he didn't have the leverage to wrench the weapon free, nor could Blancanales line up a shot on the attacker. Lyons instead drew his Colt Python. He shoved the long barrel of the revolver out the door, bent his wrist, and squeezed off first one round, then another.

The AK was suddenly empty and free. The force of

his push slapped the assault rifle into the door frame. He let it go, throwing himself through the doorway. A second man with a rifle had been backing up the first, and he turned at the movement. Lyons put a .357 Magnum bullet through the terrorist's throat in a hasty snap-shot. He checked left, then right, looking for more targets, but the sudden and relative silence signaled the end of the gun battle.

The two civilians were running up to him. Lyons braced them with his Python low but ready. "Federal agent!" he yelled. "Do not aim your weapons at me!" He did not want any ugly misunderstandings.

"We understand," the man said. He was already holstering his pistol. The woman, Lyons was amused to note, was wearing a T-shirt that marked her as a member of a popular firearms discussion website. Lyons took one look at the wedding bands on each person's hand, which showed the same scrollwork pattern, and decided they were a married couple. "Sir, we just want to help."

Lyons bit back a hurried retort. This, he thought, was what he was fighting for. These were the types of people, like those brave shooters in Binghamton, who were part of the solution rather than the problem. "Thank you," he said simply. "Please keep your weapons holstered unless another threat occurs. There are going to be police and emergency personnel on-site soon, and we wouldn't want any misunderstandings."

"They're terrorists, right?" the woman asked. "Like 9/11?" She was shaking. The adrenaline dump, and possibly a realization of what she'd done, were taking hold.

"Something like that." Lyons nodded. "I want to thank you, sir," he said to the man. "Your wife may be going into shock. I want you to find a place to sit

down and see if you can keep her calm. Tell the para-
medics, when first response arrives, what happened.
Do not under any circumstances draw your weapons in
the presence of law enforcement unless they ask. You
folks helped me and my men. You did the right thing. I
appreciate it. Tell the truth about what you saw and did.
You're good Americans. Keep it that way."

"Yes, sir."

He approached the fallen terrorists at the corner of
the outbuilding. It was some sort of souvenir shop, he
saw. He checked through the dead men quickly, making
sure of each one. A single shamming terrorist could
take up a rifle and mow down countless people before
he was stopped. Lyons was not going to permit that.

He reached the biggest of the corpses, finally. The
dead man was turned on his side, his head twisted
at an odd angle, but now, close enough to really see
him, Lyons could tell that this man was not Karbuly
Ghemenizov.

Dammit.

He took his secure satellite phone from his web gear
and speed-dialed the Farm. Barbara Price answered.

"Lyons here," he said gruffly. "Bennington Battle
Monument is secured, repeat, Bennington Battle Monument is secured. We found one terrorist with a bomb
that was ready to explode. Schwarz has deactivated it.
I need you to roll police, fire and medical personnel in
case we've missed anything."

"Affirmative," Price said. "The Warlock network
shows no additional signals in your immediate area."

"We'll do a visual sweep," Lyons said. "Just to be
sure. We await further intelligence on next target."

"Understood," Price said. "We are currently tracking
multiple signals. Warlock is trying to resolve the overlap

and isolate a geographic location, but Kurtzman's team is having trouble. This could be big, Carl. Aaron says the signal overlap is caused by a huge concentration of smart bombs running concurrently."

It was Lyons's turn to say, "Understood." He signed off and replaced the phone, then made his way back to the battle monument.

From the parking lot, sitting on a bench at the edge of the asphalt, the married couple whose names he had never gotten watched him with something like awe. Lyons wished he could tell them that the feeling was mutual. The country needed more men and women willing to take decisive action in the face of terror, no matter how badly they thought they might suffer for it. He wondered who might sue them. He made a mental note to check with Price and the Farm when this was all over, make sure nobody got punished for helping Able Team to head off mass murder.

It just burned him that he had to think of it at all.

"This is Lyons," he said as he approached the entrance. "I'm coming in. Don't shoot me."

"We read you," Blancanales said. He appeared in the doorway. "Come on in."

"Watch the door again, Pol," he said as he moved past Blancanales. "I want to have a little chat with our new friend."

"You got it." Blancanales nodded and smiled.

"How's the head?"

"Thick as ever." Blancanales chuckled. He still looked a little pale, but he was more like himself than he had been. Lyons nodded.

Schwarz stood from the crouch he had been holding. He holstered his 93-R as the Able Team leader entered the elevator.

"Come here," Lyons said, grabbing the terrorist by the lapels of the oversize Hawaiian shirt he wore. What was it with terrorists and bad fashion sense? This one obviously thought he was blending in.

"I have helped you!" said the terrorist. "I want immunity! I will testify!"

"Been watching some cop shows, have you?" Lyons said. He threw the terrorist roughly to the ground and planted a heavy knee in the small of the man's back. He was rewarded with a pained groan. "You stupid bastards think you can come in here and commit mass murder, kill women and children and whoever else gets in your way, and then make a mockery of our courts?"

"But I helped you! I help you!"

"You didn't help anybody," Lyons said as he roughly searched the man for weapons, "except yourself. Couldn't stomach the thought of getting blown into scraps of meat like your victims, could you, tough guy?" He found a small hideout pistol taped to the man's ankle. Only the fact that it was taped there with fabric tape, rather than carried in a holster, had stopped the man from drawing it at some point, Lyons would bet. He shoved the tiny pistol, an old Raven Arms .25 ACP, into his pocket. "And what were you gonna do with that? Negotiate with your court-appointed attorney? What's on your other leg?"

"Please, I want to—" The terrorist suddenly wrenched himself sideways, bringing up his other leg. He ripped something from around his ankle and was suddenly on his feet. The cloud of vapor that suddenly spewed from his fist bore the distinct spicy tang that Lyons recognized: pepper spray. A heavy kick to the face stunned him as the murderer made a break for it.

The pepper spray added to the stunning affect, but

it wasn't too bad. Lyons had long ago stopped thinking of it as much of a deterrent, but Blancanales caught a face full of it as the man went rabbit. The terrorist snatched at Blancanales's M-16 as he ran into and over the startled Stony Man operative. Then he was on the lawn and charging for the parking lot.

Lyons willed his eyes to open fully. They were watering, but his vision was not badly affected. He knew enough to rub at them with his hands. Blancanales was already covering, drawing the Beretta M-9 from his holster, preparing to pursue.

Lyons simply brushed past him. The Python, an extension of his arm, was still held firmly in his grip. He thumbed the hammer back and raised his arm to full extension.

The man was running, moving at roughly a forty-five-degree angle. He was a clear and present threat to all he encountered. He was armed. He was dangerous. He had very nearly murdered countless civilians. And all because his master, Ovan, hated America and wanted to hurt it.

Standing on ground where a monument had commemorated American willingness to fight for freedom for well over a hundred years, Lyons watched the terrorist flee. He settled the sights of his Colt Python on the running killer, led him and let out a relaxed, patient breath.

He pulled the trigger. The bullet punched through the back of the running man's skull and pitched him forward, onto his face.

As Blancanales watched, Carl Lyons holstered his Python and walked back to the waiting chopper without so much as a word.

CHAPTER SEVENTEEN

Tehran, Iran

The office building, tucked away in a congested corner of Tehran, looked no different than office buildings in a dozen countries that David McCarter had visited. This building, however, was the personal lair of Garret Aimler, at least according to Ahmadi's description of it. There could be any number of booby traps, deadfalls, secret passages…basically, any ridiculous spy gadget that a Central Intelligence Agent could think up, especially after years of covert occupancy behind hostile territory. It was, therefore, a surprise to McCarter when Phoenix Force managed to penetrate the building without incident.

Once they had reached the site, they had done something McCarter was none too happy about but was necessary under the circumstances. They had notified the Farm about their findings and announced their intentions to raid Aimler's headquarters.

The operation carried a great deal of risk. A firefight at the location would expose the CIA network in Tehran, or at the very least this arm of it. According to Ahmadi, there were other facilities in play, and there were plans in place to fall back to these contingency facilities should the main headquarters be exposed. The problem was that the fallback plans all included the destruction of

the primary CIA network in the building, which they
needed to access before it was lost to them. If Aimler's
operatives became aware of the threat of their building's
breach, they would initiate their flight protocol and clear
the building.

The other problem was that most of the men in the
building were loyal CIA operatives. At least, McCarter
assumed as much. It was likely Aimler had loyalists
among them, and perhaps he had even chosen to bring
some of them into his confidence. Maybe he even thought
he had a compelling reason for betraying Ahmadi and
Phoenix Force. The latter he would know only as outside
government agents operating on his territory under his
auspices. Whatever the reason, Phoenix Force could
not simply assault the building and kill any and all opposition, for many of the operatives within its walls
doubtless thought they were simply doing their jobs.

They therefore coordinated with the Farm. Price and
her people arranged through channels to notify the CIA
operatives on the premises, using Central Intelligence's
knowledge of the satellite phones, emails, and other
means of contact for their personnel of record. The message was coded, the intent clear, and it translated to
this: "Facility compromised. U.S. government agents
on-site to raid building. Offer no resistance. Fall back
per arrangements. As ordered under the authority of the
President of the United States."

With that signal given, the men of Phoenix Force,
with Ahmadi backing them up, came on in force. They
attacked multiple entrances, splitting their force to
account for every possible avenue of escape. Garret
Aimler, according to Ahmadi, was to be found in that
building if he was to be found anywhere. While he occasionally left the safety of his private lair, he was still a

highly placed intelligence operative, and the more time he spent on the streets of Tehran, the more vulnerable he became. Aimler had not reached the longevity of career he now enjoyed, especially playing the dangerous game he played, by being unnecessarily vulnerable.

McCarter had opted for the frontal approach, possibly the most risky of them. Manning and Ahmadi were taking the rear west corner, while Encizo and Hawkins were covering the outside of the building in case anyone slipped through. James was entering through an access corridor on the east side of the building. The building was reasonably large but not high, which meant the ground floor was the only target zone that meant anything. They were coming at Aimler from all possible directions, squeezing from the outside to the center, trapping him within. Their paths would herd all opposition, if any was encountered, toward the rear center of the building, where Aimler's office was located.

When the first gunshot rang out, he knew that Aimler must have turned at least some of the staff available to him—or brought in hired goons to help him. Either way, there was armed resistance afoot. It was time to put an end to Aimler's dirty business once and for all.

He caught a glimpse of a man in street clothes, with blond hair and pale skin, ducking across the hallway ahead. McCarter triggered a blast from the Krinkov that laid waste to both side walls and the floor between, not expecting to achieve a hit. He simply wanted to drive the gunman into cover so he would have some room to move. Fighting inside, in urban, built-up areas, was about denying freedom of movement to the enemy while moving from point of cover to point of cover yourself.

He owed the agent at least the chance to surrender. "Federal agent!" he shouted. "I am duly authorized by the United States government to seize this facility!" He did not mention Aimler's name. Aimler would, himself, understand what was happening, as soon as he knew the building was under assault. He saw no reason to reveal his intent to anyone who might not already possess the notion.

McCarter simply hoped they would have time to reach Aimler before the man realized their true goal. Ahmadi had explained that after initiating the purge protocol, the CIA computers connected to the covert network would begin to delete their contents. This data was, in theory, recoverable…provided he could get to Aimler's computer and initiate the unwipe before the delete process was initiated…or before it was complete. They had a very narrow window of opportunity.

His enemy tried to use the doorway on the left for cover, extending his gun hand across the wall and firing several shots wide of McCarter's position. The Briton walked a stream of lead from the Krinkov into the wall next to the doorway, blasting the molding apart and driving the gunner away from the opening. Another short burst caught the man in the sternum and walked up to his face, splitting him open and putting him down forever.

McCarter hurried on. In his earpiece he could hear the check-ins from the other members of Phoenix Force in the building. A man down here. Another man down there. Moderate resistance being met. Small-arms fire was being taken from multiple locations. Every shot, every echo, was one that would be heard by those in adjacent buildings, reported to authorities. The full might of the Iranian Internal Security forces would rain down on them before it was over, for the Iranians were not stupid. Phoenix Force had caused countless firefights in the city in the short time it had been present. In each of those firefights, forces loyal to Magham or forces colluding with Magham had been dealt serious blows. Many killers had themselves been killed. By now the news would be on the street, and Ahmadi had said that his dissident journalist friends were already receiving news of rumors: resistance to Magham's tyranny, true resistance, was building.

Each bullet fired by Phoenix Force was a blow to the iron-fisted rule that was Magham's ruthless control of the nation. Each time the people of Iran saw that it was possible to stand up to Magham and those helping him, freedom stood a greater chance of taking hold in this oppressed land.

But first things first. Those high-minded ideals were all fine and good, but first McCarter and his team had to get to Aimler's computer…and to the evidence he had so thoroughly accumulated.

McCarter entered an oblong room full of dusty desks, each of them equipped with an ancient computer. The desks themselves were piled with papers. He paused, crouching behind one of the desks, and picked up a sheaf of paper. The writing was Farsi. It could have been grocery lists or damning confessions by every member of the agency co-opted by Aimler; McCarter would have no way of knowing which.

He heard the scrape of a shoe at the other end of the room.

McCarter crouched, making sure no part of him was visible behind the desk. He reached up and, finding what had to be the world's most ancient stapler, threw the heavy metal accessory into the corner of the room.

Submachine gun fire tore through the room, blasting apart first one monitor, then another. Showers of sparks surprised him; they accompanied the storm of plastic and glass as each monitor in turn was shot to fragments. The bullets tore up the surfaces of the desks, walking across the papers and turning them into confetti.

McCarter hit the floor. He extended the Krinkov sideways, allowing himself to get the weapon flat with the ejection port and bolt pointing up. Then he took careful aim at the two sets of feet he saw at the other end of the room and pulled the trigger, walking the weapon from left to right.

The spray of bullets chopped his opponents off at the ankles, folding them over. A submachine gun—a folding-stock, full-size Uzi, appropriate enough for Company personnel—released what was left of its magazine into the ceiling. McCarter, cautious of the dangerous, wounded animals he had just created, pushed back to his feet in a combat crouch and threaded his way through the desks to the other end of the room, where short bursts from the Krinkov ended the lives of the gunners before they could fight through the pain and trauma to bring weapons to bear on him.

He came through the other side, caught movement and found himself face to face with Calvin James. There was little danger he would kill his teammate; the men of Phoenix Force did not shoot blindly. The two men, veterans who had fought together time and time again, exchanged nods as they continued on down the corridor. From the description of the simple floor plan that Ahmadi had shared with them on the way to the target site, they knew they were approaching Garret Aimler's office. The plain wooden door, which bore no markings of any kind, waited for them.

"Calvin," McCarter said, "left or right?"

"Left." James nodded.

"Right for me," McCarter said.

The two men pressed themselves against the door to either side, then moved two half paces farther away from it.

James reached out with one lanky arm and tapped the door very lightly. "Candygram," he said softly.

Shotgun blasts cored the door in the middle as automatic gunfire punched holes in the light drywall at either side of the door, in the exact position both men had been standing before stepping sideways. McCarter allowed himself a wry smile of self-satisfaction.

James and McCarter stepped back at forty-five-degree angles and fired their Krinkovs from the hip, blasting through the door in a short-range cross fire. They emptied their magazines, changed them, and emptied them again. As they made their withering assault, Ahmadi and Manning approached cautiously from either side, having obviously separated and come around to bracket the source of the furious battle.

"Gary." James nodded casually, turning over his smoking Krinkov to seat a full magazine.

"Calvin." Manning nodded back. McCarter had to suppress a genuine smile. Ahmadi, for his part, looked worried, and no doubt that was because he understood the timetable with which they were dealing.

"Gary, if you would lend me your tree-trunk leg for a moment." James nodded to the bullet-shredded doorway. Manning made his way cautiously over and tried to put his foot into the door, only to go through it and stumble through the opening in a shower of slivers and fragments.

The Phoenix Force man was up with his gun in front of him almost as if he had planned it…and given the condition of the doorway, he very well might have. Calvin James and David McCarter were right behind him.

There was movement to their left as they swept into the room in formation, with Ahmadi bringing up the rear wielding his Glock. It was Manning who triggered a short burst from his stubby Krinkov, killing the Uzi-wielding operative before the man on the floor could get off a shot. McCarter could only assume the man was yet another of Aimler's loyalists; he didn't look like an Iranian and he dressed like a Company man. What these idiots thought they were proving by dressing like American spies while hiding in the middle of Tehran was a mystery to McCarter, but arrogance and overconfidence were a danger inherent to the type of long-term, deep-cover operation Aimler was running. No doubt the mental strain of running such an operation was also at least partly responsible for Aimler turning traitor. It was all speculation, at this point.

Garret Aimler was seated behind his desk.

"Well," Aimler said as the Phoenix Force operatives approached with Ghaem Ahmadi in tow. "Ghaem. I have to admit you've surprised me. I knew you were a good operative. I didn't realize you were this good."

"Yeah, yeah, yeah," Calvin James said. He approached, keeping his weapon aimed at the CIA man, and yanked him roughly from the chair. "You get yourself up against that wall, man," he said, "and don't move a muscle. You twitch, I drill you."

"Charming," Aimler said. He put his hands behind his head and stood by the rear wall. "These must be the mercenaries our government sent in to show me how it's done."

"Mercenaries?" McCarter said. "Mate, you have no idea what you're talking about."

"British?" Aimler asked. "Curiouser and curiouser. I guarantee your well-mannered friend—" he jerked his chin at Calvin James "—doesn't spend a lot of time in London."

Ahmadi seated himself behind Aimler's desk. He began tapping keys on Aimler's computer.

"You're wasting your time," Aimler said. "As soon as I heard the first shot, I initiated the purge protocol."

"Your personnel taught me more about this network than you think they did," Ahmadi said. His fingers flew over the keys. Then he produced, from his pocket, a memory stick. He connected this to the laptop and began transferring files as McCarter looked over his shoulder. All the while, the Briton kept an eye on Aimler, who was far too cool for a man whose entire little empire had just been dashed.

"Will it take long?" he asked Ahmadi. "The IIS or the Iranian military could be here at any moment."

"I know, Mr. David," Ahmadi said politely. "The files are transferring." He clicked one of the files in the queue and brought up a media player automatically. The file had no video, and displayed only the sine waves of the audio track it contained. The voices were discussing Magham's election woes and the use of armed men to make it appear as if Khan were attacking Magham's supporters.

"I know that voice," Ahmadi said. "That is Magham himself."

"And the other voice," McCarter said, "will be Nikolo Ovan, I'm willing to bet. The file is tagged with his name."

"Indeed," Ahmadi said. He began sifting through the other files. "It is as we suspected. He has been stockpiling private, unlogged surveillance. He has the entire plot here." Ahmadi began reading through the notes and summaries he had not been able to access remotely, due to what McCarter assumed must be limitations in the remote access file transfer process. Anybody knew that computers were bloody uncooperative whenever you asked anything particularly useful of them.

"What is it?" McCarter asked. Ahmadi had gone red in the face.

"Verification," Ahmadi said. "According to this, Magham is actively conspiring with Ovan. He is fully complicit in the attacks on his people. It is part of his attempt to manipulate the election. There is also ample ancillary evidence…admissions by Ovan of his use of terror tactics on targets in the United States."

"Well," McCarter said, "color me unsurprised."

"You're undoing everything!" Aimler said. "You fools. I had all of this planned. Everything was running smoothly until you blundered into all of this. The key to Iranian stability is a strong leader in Magham. Only after that's secured can we arrange peace on our terms. I have all the leverage we'll ever need to make Magham the willing puppet of the United States government."

"And you know better than everybody else," Manning rumbled. "No matter how many Americans the smart bombs kill."

"Everybody knows the Iranians are selling weapons on the world market to be used against the United States," Aimler shot back. "What will this prove?"

Manning said nothing. He simply stared at Aimler as if the man was a bug on the wall—a bug to be smashed.

"The surveillance files are copied," Ahmadi said. "There is just one more file. This computer says Aimler accessed it only minutes before initiating the purge I have undone."

"What the bloody hell…" McCarter murmured, reading over Ahmadi's shoulder. "Is this a novel?"

"No," Ahmadi said. "It is his memoirs." Ahmadi began reading out loud from the page he had opened. Aimler turned red as the men of Phoenix Force turned toward him, their faces hard with disgust.

"Conspiracy nut fodder," James pronounced. "Wrapped in a bright bow that says, 'I hate America.'"

"I love my country!" Aimler said. "I simply hate my government. The torture! The secret prisons! Assassination squads! America is the source of all that is evil in the world—"

McCarter realized too late what Aimler was doing. He was using the old trick of engaging the enemy in conversation, as his hands, clasped behind his neck, suddenly went for something at the small his back. The knife that came out in Aimler's hand might well have landed in Calvin James's throat before James could pull the trigger.

But three shots rang out.

Ahmadi had drawn his Glock from behind the desk and punched the shots into the center of Garret Aimler's chest in less time than it took for the Phoenix Force leader to realize what had happened. Then Aimler, rolling and reeling from the shots, suddenly threw himself out the window.

"Stop him!" McCarter shouted.

Aimler hit the ground and was up running, clutching at his chest.

"He must be wearing a vest," James said.

"Rafe, T.J., he's out the back window!"

"I've got him." Encizo's voice came back. "He's got a car parked here."

"I want that bastard alive," McCarter said.

"I'm taking the tires—" Encizo started to respond.

The blast, when it came, slapped the back of the building with a wall of heat, light and sound that rattled the remaining window in its pane and sent objects on Aimler's desk shaking off of it. Ahmadi and the Phoenix Force commandos hit the deck. McCarter's first thought was that the IIS had found them and were using RPG launchers against the building.

A pall of smoke wafted through the broken-out window. Flames could be heard roaring and crackling on the other side of the wall. Cautiously, McCarter raised his head to look out the window, his Krinkov ready.

The car in the alley behind the office was wreathed in flame. The passenger compartment had been blown apart from within. Garret Aimler had been reduced to an oily spot in the center of the charred frame.

"Smell that?" James said. "Almonds."

"What happened?" Ahmadi asked.

"If I'm to guess," McCarter said, "I imagine one side or the other, either the IIS and Magham's people, or Ovan's terrorist network, decided that they weren't overly happy with Aimler's interference. If he was tipping off one, the other or both, and I'm betting we'll find all the proof we need to verify that he was in his computer files—" he pointed to the memory card in Ahmadi's fist "—they must have decided to thank him with Semtex."

"Say it with plastic explosives," James intoned, as if reading ad copy for a florist.

"Let's get out of here, mates," McCarter said. "We've no time to spare."

"I am reinitiating the memory purge," Ahmadi said. "And I am formatting this computer's hard drive." Then he took the still-formatting laptop, raised it above his head and threw it forcefully to the floor. The hard drive made a noise not unlike a garbage disposal chewing up an egg beater.

They hit the street in the Peugot just in time. As they left the formerly covert CIA headquarters behind them, they heard the braying-donkey sirens of the IIS approaching. Ahmadi was careful to stick to side streets and maintain a reasonable speed, attracting no attention to them, as he put block after block between Phoenix Force and the approaching Iranian Internal Security operatives.

All in the vehicle were silent for a time. Finally, Ahmadi said, "I assume you have arrangements in place to leave my country."

McCarter nodded. Ahmadi didn't know the details. In a predetermined locker in the Iranian airport, intelligence contacts that led, in a roundabout way, back to what some called No Such Agency would have left travel documents, passports and fresh identities for Phoenix Force. They would depart on separate commercial flights and eventually make their way to Pakistan, near the Afghan border. A U.S. military base in Afghanistan would provide them with air transportation to their next target: Turkmenistan and Ovan himself. Ahmadi was going to make the next phase of their mission possible.

"You've got the evidence," he said to the Iranian.

"As do you." Ahmadi grinned, and this time his smile

was ratcheted up to full intensity. He handed a flash memory stick to McCarter. "I made two copies."

McCarter blinked. "Well, I'll be damned."

"I hope not, Mr. David. I hope not."

"Your friends can get the word out here?" James asked.

"They can, and they will," Ahmadi said. "I will do my best to help reconstitute the CIA network in Tehran. It will not be easy. But with Aimler a traitor and his supporters dead with him, someone must see to it that our work continues, and I am the senior agent now."

"Funny thing, that," McCarter said. "Local boy makes good, eh?"

"I sincerely hope so. I trust you will see to it that news of Magham's and Ovan's crimes reaches the free media of the West?"

"We will, mate."

"Then I will say my goodbyes to you now." He nodded. "It would not do to raise a scene at the airport."

"And here I was going to have you pull up to the front entrance and see us all off." McCarter grinned. "So long, mate." He offered his hand to the Iranian double agent. "You're a good man, Ghaem, and I'm proud to have worked with you."

"The pride is mine," Ahmadi said. "Go with God, Mr. David, and all of you. The work you do...it is what we need. It is what we hope."

Those words would stay with David McCarter for a long time.

It was what he hoped, too.

CHAPTER EIGHTEEN

Upstate New York

"Stand on it, Gadgets!" Lyons yelled.

The rental SUV, a Ford Explorer, roared and whined in protest. With the passenger's side window open, Carl Lyons leaned out, holding the door frame with one hand and bracing the Daewoo USAS-12 against the side of his body. A new day was dawning, promising to be hot and bright, and the rising sun was behind the men of Able Team as they chased the pair of cargo vans that carried their quarry.

The Warlock network, Price had explained, was having trouble making sense of the signals clustered around this particular region of upstate New York. Lyons had no doubt that they were in roughly the right target neighborhood, given the sites that Karbuly Ghemenizov and his ghouls had hit thus far. They had stuck close to this area and they hadn't had enough time to get very far, nor was it necessary to travel any distance to find another juicy target. The only thing that would warn them off would be Lyons and his team, but he was betting that the giant would press on. Any cautious man would have aborted the operation as soon as it became obvious that a government team was working to stop it, but Ghemenizov hadn't done that. Instead he'd changed his tactics, becoming bolder, even taunting his enemies, while persisting despite the fact that Able Team was intercepting him in many cases before he could complete his work. Cowardice, Lyons reflected, was not among the terror-master's faults.

Grimaldi had landed at the nearest airport, a cramped little strip that barely had room for a few Cessnas. From there, Able Team had taken the rental truck delivered to them by a Stony Man courier. They had driven into the nearest town and begun searching street by street, with Schwarz using the sensor-jammer as a kind of divining wand.

They had been looking through the gray rays of first light and into the early morning when they spotted the two vans traveling together at a distance. Schwarz had pointed the sensor and immediately gotten a response. There was no telling how many shooters might be squeezed into the vehicles, but some part of Lyons's combat instincts told him they were definitely on the right track. He just *knew*. He couldn't explain how.

The righteous anger that had been building in him since the start of the mission ramped even higher when he saw the target the terrorists had picked: it was an elementary school. As Lyons and his team neared in their SUV, he could see the writing on the lead van. It was a uniform-and-floor-mat service.

It made perfect sense. How many businesses used such a service? Nobody paid any attention to the floor-mat guy, after all. The terrorists could use that cover to bring their explosives into the building, wrapped in mats or in bags supposedly holding uniforms—could children attending a public elementary school be wearing uniforms from a service? No, he decided, it had to be floor mats—and nobody would give them a second glance.

A damned elementary school building. Right then and there, Carl Lyons made a decision.

Lyons watched as the first van rolled to a stop in front of the service entrance to the elementary school. He saw a man getting out of the rear of the van with a floor mat over his shoulder. That mat looked heavy. The sensor in Schwarz's fist, which he was bracing on top of the steering wheel, immediately went wild. More importantly, in the rear of the van, Lyons caught a glimpse of armed men waiting on benches along either side of the vehicle's interior.

"Gadgets," Lyons said. "Speed up. Ram the lead van."

Schwarz hadn't hesitated. He hit the gas and took them on a course that resulted in a glancing blow to the front right fender of the van. As they sideswiped it, jolting the van and no doubt sending the men inside spilling to the floor, Lyons pushed his shotgun out his window and triggered a blast of double-aught buckshot that had flattened the man with the floor mat, dropping him and his wrapped bomb to the pavement.

"Out," Lyons directed. "Pol, ride shotgun."

As Schwarz dived out the driver's side, Lyons took the wheel and slid over. He would deactivate the bomb. Lyons dragged the steering wheel hand over hand, bringing their Ford between the van and Schwarz, protecting the Able Team commando from their gunfire. Watching in the rearview mirror, Lyons sprayed the flank of the lead van with heavy shot, peppering its flank with holes the size of individual light-caliber bullets.

Blancanales tripped the rear door of the SUV from inside and Schwarz had piled in, bringing the deactivated smart bomb with him for safekeeping. The lead van was already rolling again, and the other van fell in behind it as Lyons harassed them, turning the grille of the Ford to a gap-toothed ruin as he hit them again and again.

All of that had been moments ago. Now they were chasing the vans through the streets, taking the initiative, making the terrorists the victims, hunting the predators. Lyons had switched with Schwarz on the move once more so that he could quite literally ride shotgun, bringing his heavy weapon to bear on the vehicles. Now he was tearing apart the van he had shot up earlier, as the two terrorist vehicles jockeyed for position and switched places.

"Blow up a school, huh?" Lyons roared. He fired repeatedly, taking great pleasure in watching pieces of the van fall away. "Gadgets," he yelled. "Can you tell if there are more bombs in that vehicle or its partner?"

"I'm not getting any, Carl," Schwarz said, juggling the scanner and the steering wheel as Blancanales looked on and occasionally fired at the already heavily perforated van. The real beauty of this, Lyons thought to himself, was going to be when the plan they were working came together.

He glanced back at Blancanales, who was on his satellite phone again, talking to the Farm as Price and her team coordinated with the local authorities. He almost let out a yelp of victory when the parking lot of the vacant grocery and hardware store plaza came into view. Empty retail space was everywhere in upstate New York, and a vast plaza like this one was just what the men of Able Team needed. The local police department was standing by to close the jaws of the trap.

The two vans moved into the center of the plaza with Able Team shooting at them from behind, urging them forward. Once Able Team's SUV was past the mouth of the trap, the police needed no prompting to close their cordon. Their vehicles closed in, front bumper to rear bumper, forming a roadblock made up of state and local police cruisers.

The vans slowed to a stop side by side at the center of the net. The terrorists, perhaps knowing they couldn't escape, chose to go out fighting.

Lyons didn't mind that at all. He chose to stay mobile, however. "Gadgets!" he shouted. "Circle 'em!"

Schwarz pushed the SUV for all it was worth, fighting at the very edge of its maneuverability, a one-truck siege weapon that made a burning rubber track around the two terrorist vans. Lyons fired again and again, not caring when bullets struck close to him.

The terrorists were bewildered by the assault. First one, then another went down under the buckshot and then slugs that Lyons laid down in fully automatic bursts from his 20-round drum magazines. Ovan's killers wanted to go out in a blaze of glory, did they? Well, he'd give the murdering bastards as much glory as they could handle. He'd give them so much glory they could choke on it.

They were coming around for another pass when the RPG launcher appeared in the passenger window of one of the vans.

Schwarz saw the nose of the rocket and tried to compensate. He whipped the wheel around, changing their course, almost putting them up on two wheels to do it. Lyons was thrown from the vehicle and rolled to a stop on the pavement, cradling the USAS-12 to him, riding out the rough-and-tumble stop. He rolled over and got his eyes back on the enemy just in time to see the RPG move as if in slow motion. The rocket-propelled grenade floated on a tail of white smoke, touching the very rear of the SUV as it struck the asphalt beneath the rear bumper.

Schwarz and Blancanales were jumping clear of the doomed vehicle as the RPG hit. Lyons saw them rolling, saw the explosion, felt the heat and the concussion slap him in the face. He didn't hear the blast; it washed over him but he never noticed. He was watching Schwarz come up in a combat crouch and level his Beretta 93-R, firing 3-round bursts, and Lyons watched Rosario Blancanales hit the pavement headfirst.

Lyons was up and running then. Schwarz was moving forward, toward the vans, as deadly accurate as any fighter who had fought the years-long antiterror war that was Stony Man's mission. Lyons trusted his friend to end the waning resistance from within the terrorist vehicles, hoping that there were no more rocket-propelled surprises in store.

He reached Blancanales and put his body between his partner and the enemy. He didn't want to move the man, but there was little to be done; he needed to assess Blancanales's condition and couldn't simply leave him to catch a stray bullet. At first glance, the outlook was not good. Blancanales was staring heavy-lidded and unresponsive, his pupils blown, one noticeably larger than the other. He'd struck his head again on top of the earlier head injury, which could mean he was in very grave danger.

"G-Force," Lyons called. He pressed his finger to his ear. "Able to G-Force. Come in."

Jack Grimaldi's voice was full of static but audible. "G-Force here. Come in."

"Jack, I need you, right now, for a medevac." He checked his secure satellite phone; it was operational. Grimaldi would be able to home right in on it. "Bring the chopper in here right now. We've got you a nice big landing zone. There's no time to waste. Pol's injured and we need to get him to the nearest hospital."

"On my way." Grimaldi's voice was perfectly serious, all traces of levity gone. The Stony Man pilot had been in the game as long as any of them. He was all business when the life of a teammate was on the line.

Schwarz was approaching, reloading his 93-R with a fresh 20-round magazine, when Lyons placed the emergency call to the Farm. He informed them of what had happened to Blancanales and requested the Farm's support in coordinating the fastest possible medical attention. As he did so, Blancanales regained consciousness, after a fashion, and started speaking nonsense words.

"I need that treatment arranged at the closest hospital," Lyons repeated. "Pol's all kinds of screwed up."

"We can do that," Price said. "But, Carl, there's something you need to know."

"Go ahead."

"The signals we've been tracking. Warlock has managed to sort them out. It took some extra processing time…but, Carl, we're looking at the worst one."

"Worst one what?"

"Multiple bombs," Price said. "More than you've yet seen. All of them in the vicinity of the New Nine Mile Nuclear Power Plant. It's exactly thirty miles northwest of your position, off Interstate 81."

"Nuclear power plant," Lyons repeated. "Understood. Please transmit all relevant data to my phone."

"Carl," Schwarz said. "How bad?"

"Bad," Lyons said, replacing his phone in its pouch on his web gear. "Gadgets, give me the sensor."

The Stony Man technician handed over the unit. "Why, Carl?"

"Because Pol's hit hard," Lyons said. "He's going to need one of us with him. If he gets delirious and starts talking about the Farm, we can't have that. I want a teammate with him. And he needs one of us. That's going to be you."

"Okay, Carl, but you're not thinking of—"

"Gadgets," Lyons said flatly. "Don't. Don't test me on this. Pol needs one of us. And I need to see this through."

"Carl, we all—" Schwarz stopped as he saw the look on his teammate's face. "All right, Carl. I'll look after him."

The heavy thrum of the Chinook's rotors was audible in the distance now. Lyons looked up and found a smoke canister on his web gear. He popped it and threw it some distance from their position, giving Grimaldi something to home in on. "I am popping green smoke," he said for Grimaldi's benefit. "Repeat, green smoke. You may land and accept one passenger and one escort for immediate medevac."

"Immediate medevac, one passenger and one escort, over," Grimaldi acknowledged.

Lyons hefted his shotgun and stood, starting for the police cordon.

"Carl!" Schwarz shouted.

Lyons looked back. "Yeah?"

"Go get 'em!"

Lyons nodded grimly.

He reached the police cordon in what seemed like only a few broad strides, his need to make justice for his friends and for the victims of Ovan's terrorists fueling the cold, righteous rage that was smoldering in the pit of his stomach. He figured he might as well give Brognola yet another thing to worry about, as if the big Fed didn't already have his hands full fielding phone calls about multiple shooting wars breaking out all across the Northeast.

He approached the nearest cop, a member of one of the responding local departments. "Officer," he said, "I need your car."

"Sir?"

"Federal agent," Lyons said. He gave his Justice Department credentials a workout, waving them under the officer's nose. "I don't have time to argue with you. You got a 12-gauge in there?"

"In the rack in the front."

"Locked?"

"Yes, sir."

"Key," Lyons demanded. He held out his hand and the officer detached the key from his ring and handed it over. "And 12-gauge shells?"

"Plastic shell box in the trunk, sir."

"Good," Lyons said.

He pulled the car door open. The keys were in the ignition and the LED lightbar was going full blast, though thankfully the siren wasn't howling.

Lyons threw the powerful cruiser in gear and hit the accelerator, pushing it for all it was worth, hearing the big rear-wheel-drive car, the last of a breed of interceptors, roar throatily in response to his heavy foot.

Major nuclear facilities were included in the standard briefings at Stony Man Farm. His secure satellite phone began to vibrate, no doubt signaling the receipt of updated briefing files and schematics from the Farm. He would check these, but he already knew the broad strokes: the New Nine Mile nuclear generating station was a two-unit nuclear power plant on the shore of Lake Ontario. The nine-hundred-acre facility, built in the late

1980s, consisted of a pair of General Electric boiling water reactors, producing an average annual power yield of more than a dozen gigawatt hours between the two units.

Whatever Ovan's murderers were planning, it was big, possibly the grand finale to this opening salvo of Ovan's terrorist campaign against the United States. He checked the coordinates being sent to him from the Farm to his phone, then compared that to the device's GPS locator.

He had never really been a loner. Even in the earliest days of the war all Stony Man personnel fought, when he had spent his time hunting for a certain famous vigilante only to be recruited, eventually, by the very man he had once pursued, he had been part of a team, a task force. He had logged more time with the men of Able Team than any one warrior ought to be able to recount. Even now, he was not truly alone, for the Farm could track him through his phone and would be there to provide him with support every step of the way.

What the Farm couldn't do, however, was walk in his boots for him. There were no other assets in the immediate vicinity. In the time it would take to scramble backup, even a team of blacksuits from the Farm, it would be too late. Schwarz was protecting Blancanales, and Grimaldi was the critical transportation link; Lyons would not entrust his teammate's fate to anyone else.

That left Carl Lyons.

To be a part of Stony Man meant being willing to take action. It meant being willing to put it all on the line when you were required to step in. It meant being willing to fight and die because there was nobody else who would do the job for you. What was it that famous writer had said? The American people slept safely in their beds at night because rough men and women, like the personnel of Stony Man, stood ready to do violence on their behalf.

Lyons took no pleasure in violence. He did, however, have a duty to use the most direct, overwhelming force necessary to end threats to innocent American citizens. Ovan and Karbuly Ghemenizov. As he thought of Ghemenizov, he thought of that woman in Binghamton. What was her name? Kayli. That woman was dead because predators like Ghemenizov existed, because they walked the Earth breathing the same air as decent people, fouling it with their inhuman touch and with their evil stink.

Before this was over, Carl Lyons was going to see to it that Karbuly Ghemenizov stopped breathing that air forever.

CHAPTER NINETEEN

Turkmen Airspace

Garret Aimler was on fire. The flames crawled up his back, across his neck. They danced on his face, crawling across his cheeks with a thousand tiny stinging pin-pricks, shredding the flesh of his body, turning him into a charred ruin. Garret Aimler knew then that what he felt was the eternity of burning hell that awaited him for his many crimes, his many sins, the many lives for which he and his horrific nation were responsible for taking in the name of American security—

Garret Aimler awoke, screaming.

He was on the plane. He reminded himself of it again and again. He was on the plane.

He looked out the window, wondering if they were close to Ashgabat. He could not tell from the terrain.

He shifted in his seat. His back still pained him very badly. He removed the bottle of painkillers from his pocket and swallowed two more dry.

The military transport was not long on comfort, and the men around him were already staring at him. The Iranian assassins glared at him, betraying none of their thoughts except perhaps irritation at his outburst. He did his best to avoid meeting their gaze. It would not do to antagonize such men. He was surprised they had even permitted him among them. He had thought that his summary execution was as likely as their cooperation, and some part of him did not care.

Everything he had worked for was gone. Just like that, gone, thanks to that damned Ghaem Ahmadi and those meddling corporate mercenaries. He had seen their faces, though, and in seeing them, he had known them for what they were. They were the type of hunter-killer squad he had long believed the United States employed. Lawless killers like that, all of them probably plausibly denied and long officially dead, were sent around the world by the U.S. government on kill missions to extend the illegal domination of the United States over the remainder of the world.

In looking at them, in seeing the evil behind their eyes, he had finally understood precisely what they were doing and what they were truly after.

Ahmadi must have figured out how to breach the network security somehow. He had discovered the files and the surveillance footage Aimler was keeping. In conducting his killers around Tehran, he had helped them prevent attacks on Magham's people, but that was a holding action only. Of course! Why hadn't he seen it? In their position, from the view of the powers that were in the United States, saving Magham's supporters was not going to stop the issue of Ovan's interference in the presidential election. The United States, in its never-ending quest to meddle, obviously wanted the moderate Khan installed in the presidency.

The preferable course of action would be to stage yet another illegal war. Such wars were very useful back home; they helped desensitize the American people to torture and murder in the name of American security while distracting that same public from their real problems. The government always used such wars to cover its indiscretions, for everyone knew the only truly good war was one in which the nation had no true national interest, one in which it could spread goodwill and gain respect by performing acts of global altruism. Why nobody else could see the evil his country perpetrated, Aimler didn't know. But suddenly everything was clear to him.

Instead of simply murdering him outright, the mercenaries had used Ahmadi to access Aimler's computer files. His logical mind had, even as he stood in his office ostensibly a prisoner, gone to work on the problem. Obviously they needed the evidence Aimler had accumulated, evidence they had discovered somehow. They had come with Ahmadi to recover it because they wanted to publicly expose Magham and Ovan. It was the perfect justification for a shooting war, or more accurately, one of the many undeclared police actions that the United States was so fond of employing. It meant those in power could do whatever they pleased without answering to the American public, all in the name of saving that public from terrorism.

The murder team that had invaded his office and almost taken his life was a good example of how that sort of thing worked.

He couldn't believe their smug look. Murdering brigands. How dare they sit in judgment over him after pointing their guns in his face, after killing the men whose loyalties he had so painstakingly cultivated?

As for his manuscript itself, his life's work, he was upset about the loss of the most updated file, but the bulk of his work was not gone. A few hours' work from memory would restore it. He had uploaded his latest draft to an internet file-sharing site under password protection only a few days before. It would be waiting for him when he finally chose to complete it. He would find a publisher willing to tell the truth, and he would reveal to the world exactly how evil his nation truly was. If he got rich and famous in the process, so be it. Why, perhaps when he was done exposing the ruinous empire that was the United States government and its security machinations, he could turn to more pleasant pursuits. He was certain his experience in the CIA could yield more than a few interesting novels. A man who hit it big as a novelist…why, with his books in every grocery store in the nation, he was sure to attract women. There might be groupies in store for him yet.

He congratulated himself for effecting his escape from so hardened a team of assassins, whom the Company or the NSA or some other black-ops organization had probably charged with eliminating Aimler from the outset. It was possible he had missed something. It was more and more likely, as he thought about it, that those mercenaries had been sent with killing Garret Aimler in mind all along, using the operations with Ahmadi against Ovan's terrorists and Magham's IIS as a smoke screen. Aimler was a highly placed operative whom his superiors knew could not easily be fooled. They would not be above mounting the larger operation just to catch him by surprise. They certainly had done that much.

If not for taking the time to prepare for even these catastrophic contingencies, Aimler might never have gotten away or, had he escaped, he would have had nowhere to go. The car he kept in the alley was functional, yes, but it was also rigged with enough Semtex to blow it and anyone in it to cinders. It had a hatch in the floor of the passenger seat that connected to a spider hole concealed in the ground beneath the vehicle. Knowing that trying to drive away would be pointless, especially when he saw the gunmen stationed to prevent escape from the back of the building, Aimler had opted for faking his own death.

The only problem was that he had miscalculated, and badly, in rigging the charge. He had used too much explosive and not enough heat shielding. The fire that had burned above him had scorched his skin, leaving him practically parboiled when he finally judged it safe to emerge from hiding.

At least he was alive, he reminded himself.

The bug-out bag he had stashed in a nearby dummy transformer box contained everything he would need to survive in the event of catastrophic failure: passports and other identifying documents under the name Terry Beasler, an H&K USP in .45 ACP and ammunition for it, a Glock fixed-blade combat knife, a multitool, some power bars and rations and a medical kit. It also contained an untraceable satellite phone that he periodically updated using a remote wireless interface. The interface confirmed that the phone was charged and ready, and he was able to keep all of his vital contacts in it up-to-date that way.

It was using that satellite phone that Aimler had put the next phase of his plan in motion. His only goal, at this point, was revenge. He had never considered himself one for revenge, but the way those mercenaries had treated him, the way they had judged him, the way they had dared to try to take away everything he had…he could not live with that. He could not go on to live his life under his new identity, publishing his book under a pseudonym, knowing those soulless killers were out there somewhere, walking around breathing his air and laughing at the memory of the CIA operative they had so humiliated.

If they were going to expose Magham and Ovan, it stood to reason that their next step would be to take direct action against Ovan himself. If he was one of the military minds of the United States, he would use overwhelming force only if absolutely necessary. He would use a kill team such as the men Ahmadi had assisted to take out Ovan covertly, and then he would cook up some unconvincing explanation for the military junta or democratic revolutionary coup that eventually toppled the government of Turkmenistan. Ovan had seized the country by force, after all. He could be removed as easily, either in reality or as part of a broader narrative composed after the fact.

The way was clear to Garret Aimler. If he wanted revenge, he needed to get to Ovan. If the CIA or the NSA or whoever else was responsible for the attacks on Tehran chose to send a different mercenary team, he would gladly kill them, just on principle, or better yet, see to it that they were killed. But he didn't think that would be the case. Such men as he had met today were rare. They were not commonly found even in intelligence circles. Such a team, after spending so much time and effort thwarting Ovan and exposing Magham's complicity in Ovan's scheme to manipulate the Iranian presidential election, would not then leave the covert removal of Magham to others…not when they were already close to striking distance of Turkmenistan. It was simply sound intelligence doctrine to use assets already in position, or close to it, to accomplish goals those assets had proved they were capable of tackling.

Aimler congratulated himself for reasoning it out and for thinking objectively despite the pain he felt. He looked around and was sorry he had done so, for a handful of the Iranian assassins were still glaring at him. He quickly looked away.

Getting on this plane had been perhaps his greatest feat. Using his satellite phone, he had placed a call to no less than Ovan himself. He had surprised Ovan, who almost did not believe a truly anonymous individual could have contacted him so brazenly, by telling Ovan every detail he had learned of the plan Ovan and Magham had cooked up. Intrigued, then enraged and finally bewildered by the amount of information Aimler had on him, Ovan had relented. Yes, he said, he could use men of talent, men who had proved their worth as part of intelligence services. Yes, Ovan had admitted, his anonymous contact truly did have intimate knowledge of Ovan's operation. Would Ovan be willing to receive a visitor by way of his friend and ally Magham, if the caller was able to arrange it? Yes, Ovan would be.

Aimler's next call had been to Magham, who did not yet know the amount of danger he was in. Garret had explained as succinctly as he could that he was an intelligence operative who believed Iran's best interests lay in keeping Magham in power. He had conveniently skipped the various machinations he had originally planned. Using the same techniques he had used to gain Ovan's curiosity if not his confidence, he deftly manipulated Magham into believing Aimler was a person of some value. If Magham wanted to make the men pay who had endangered his chance at reelection, and provided he had the resources to hand, Aimler had smoothed the way for Magham to dispatch a team of men to Turkmenistan to assist his would-be ally and like-minded leader.

Magham had agreed to meet with Aimler. It had been a near thing; the CIA man had expected to be murdered at any moment. Magham had proved surprisingly trac-table, however. He phoned Ovan as Aimler watched, and the two men reached an understanding in English that allowed for their mutual benefactor to come calling in the company of Magham's team of assassins. Those assassins would assist Ovan in rooting out whatever threat was coming to his door. Ovan was grateful for the assistance, and Magham, probably wrongly, seemed to think that attacking the men who had worked against him would help him prevent losing the election. Aimler, quite without evidence, had sworn up and down that the same team who had run amok in Tehran would be the death squad assigned to murder Ovan in Ashgabat. Before it was over, the Iranian dictator would be lucky not find himself in front of an international human rights tribunal…but Aimler was not about to tell him so.

If his plan, which was reckless and hanging by a thread, did not yield the opportunity for revenge that he wanted—if he could never again find the mercenaries, including the Englishman, the black American, and the others—he could at least make a temporary home for himself with Ovan. A cunning intelligence operative could always turn a dictator of that type to good use. Such men valued ability and were vulnerable to flattery. Aimler had plenty of both to offer. To have a pet rogue CIA operative was no small thing. Aimler was willing to bet that no matter what happened, if he just kept his wits about him and stayed flexible, he could come out ahead of this thing, alive and poised to get even.

Ultimately, once he was a bit more stable he hoped to be able to settle things with Ghaem Ahmadi. He had nothing against the operative, but Ahmadi knew the extent to which Aimler had been used and humiliated. Just as he could not abide the thought of those smug, arrogant mercenaries living with the knowledge of what they had done to him, Aimler could not bear the thought of a man subordinate to him knowing how Aimler had been disgraced.

Around him in their seats, the assassins were checking automatic weapons. If Aimler understood correctly, there was an airstrip in Ashgabat they would use, and from there they would be transported directly to Ovan's militarized presidential palace. Just what the killers whose company he now kept had been told about the foreigner in their midst, Aimler couldn't guess. He had managed to persuade Magham that he and he alone was the best insurance against rooting out the mercenaries and making sure Magham's assassins or Ovan's men discovered and killed them. He wasn't sure that was even a lie, for he had seen them, talked to them, interacted with them for those brief moments. The faces of those killers were burned into his brain.

In the retelling of the highly censored, highly rewritten tale, it was possible he had exaggerated the length, tenor and context of his interaction with the mercenaries. Ovan and Magham thought he was some sort of freelance spy who hated the West and wanted to keep both men in power for the good of the region. Well, that was substantially true. There was no point confusing either world leader with distracting and irrelevant details.

It occurred to Aimler, as he squirmed in his seat and fought the pain on his back, that he was in the company of truly bloodthirsty murderers. These men radiated a cold menace that even the Agency kill team in his office had not. Those men who had humiliated Garret Aimler obviously thought themselves in the right. They had believed what they were doing to be morally correct, and that was what had been so insufferable about them.

These assassins of Magham's, whether secret police, military or some other contingent, these men did not believe what they were doing was right, if Aimler was any guess of a man's demeanor and carriage. These men simply moved, walked and quietly talked among themselves like professional killers. They were mechanisms.

They were death on two legs, each and every one of them.

Aimler just hoped he would get a crack at the mercenaries before these implacable killers finished them.

CHAPTER TWENTY

New Nine Mile Nuclear Power Plant, New York

Carl Lyons's borrowed squad car barreled at full speed through the gates of the nuclear power generating station. By rights, security personnel from one of the respected contract companies—whose men were in their own right special operators—should have been opening up on him as soon as he smashed through the gates, police car or no. The fact that no gunfire was forthcoming simply verified to him what he had feared: that the density of signals identified by Warlock here at the plant meant that Ghemenizov and his ghouls were in control of the facility.

As he brought the cruiser to a fast stop in front of the main entrance to the power plant, before an imposing set of concrete steps, he saw one of the guards. The man's head was bent at an impossible angle and he had been shoved into a stand of landscaping shrubs in a planter on one side of the steps.

Lyons had taken advantage of the cruiser's ammo supply to rearm himself. With the USAS-12 at port arms, he stepped carefully from the vehicle and ascended the steps.

The security station just within the doors was unmanned—or it appeared to be. Lyons caught the motion in his peripheral vision before the head of the hostile poked up in the opening behind the bullet-resistant glass. He pushed the USAS-12 out in front of him, bracing the stock against his shoulder, and triggered a single 12-gauge slug that threaded the needle that was the opening in the security station. The gunman's brains splattered against the wall behind him as the slug left a hole the size of a quarter in the drywall at the center of the mess.

Well, so much for the element of surprise.

He checked the sensor and took note of the readings it displayed. God help him, but the stupid thing was starting to make sense to him. He had a general idea of the direction in which the concentration of bombs would most likely be found. He simply went in that direction without subterfuge and without a clever plan.

He did have a plan, of sorts. He was going to shoot everybody. He was Carl Lyons, and woe to anyone who tried to get in his way.

Three terrorists hiding behind an alcove at the end of the screening corridor were waiting for him, having heard the shot that had announced his presence. He aimed the Daewoo, flicked the selector to full-automatic and braced the heavy weapon against his shoulder as he emptied the drum magazine. The fire hose of 12-gauge slugs punched fist-size craters from the tiled wall to either side of the alcove, penetrating the walls and blowing the men apart who hid behind them. The sound of multiple corpses flopping to the polished floor was a wet, dead-meat sound unlike any other.

"Let the bodies hit the floor," Lyons hummed to himself, hearing the popular death-metal song in his head.

He found the first bomb on the other side of the screening station. He was going to bet, based on the schematics he had reviewed, that the terrorists were lazy and would plant their smart bombs in the office areas of the plant. The more technical areas of the plant were harder to access and had multiple hard barriers that would have been automatically engaged when plant security was breached. The terrorists would be counting on the fact that their bombs didn't need to go off at the center of a cooling tower to damage the plant and cause a panic—if not actual radioactive fallout. Enough bombs could create an explosion powerful enough to create another Chernobyl, this time on American soil. The thought of a vast swath of upstate New York rendered an uninhabitable cancer zone, with fallout and weather disruptions affecting the rest of the nation and even the world in time, was not one Lyons could accept. He would prevent that from happening at all costs.

He blew through the complex, firing his shotgun through each doorway as he verified his targets, not so much shooting the enemy as punching them down in place with the brute force of his heavy automatic weapon.

He wasn't even looking at it and he felt the scanner start to go off in his hand as he reached a small, circular amphitheater-like room he imagined was used for press conferences and addresses to the staff.

The room was full of men and bombs.

Lyons was absolutely baffled as to how they could look so surprised. Maybe they had thought no one could possibly get through the ranks of their own to reach them here, where they were obviously arming at least ten of the smart bombs. Picturing all that potential destruction, Carl Lyons felt his righteous anger kick in again. He snapped the barrel of the USAS-12 up and on target and squeezed the trigger on full-auto, practically blowing the nearest man in two.

The reaction was instantaneous and chaotic. Some men continued frantically with the bombs, perhaps afraid to abort what they were doing in the middle of the procedure. In the back of his mind, Lyons realized that if any of the bombs did not function as designed, as some of them had shown a tendency to do, he might well be blown up quite unintentionally along with Ghemenizov's men.

If he was going to go, he was going to make sure as many of them as possible went first.

He shoved the barrel of the shotgun into the face of an attacking terrorist, who held a large fixed-blade knife. The blast from the USAS-12 at close range emptied the weapon and practically shattered the knife-wielding man's head. Lyons brought the Daewoo down and back, ignoring the blood streaming from its barrel, and slammed the heavy butt into the side of another man's head. The terrorist's eyes rolled up and he dropped, dead limp with a crack in his skull.

There were gunshots, but Lyons didn't really hear them. One of the terrorists went down, shot by his fellow killer at close quarters. Lyons fought like a man berserk, the bloody shotgun a bludgeon, an ax, a sword in his hands, smashing it down again and again on the mass of murdering terrorist operatives surrounding him. He crushed a face with the butt of the shotgun. He smashed the barrel across the teeth of another. He snapped a man's knee with a vicious front kick, drove his toe into the bladder of another with shocking force and, as several men tried to bull him to the ground, he released the shotgun and used his thumbs to press into the eye sockets of the unlucky man on top of him.

The inhuman shriek of agony that came from the blinded terrorist's mouth was matched by that of the next man when Lyons reached out, grabbed the man's testicles and pulled and twisted with all his might. A horizontal elbow-smash drove the castrated man into the floor and a stomp of Lyons's combat boot kept him there for the rest of his life.

Lyons roared.

It was a bellow of animal fury. He drew his Colt Python and began pulling the trigger, shooting first one man, then another, then another. He fired all six shots and was rewarded with a total of six bodies on the floor.

And then there were no more.

Lyons stopped. Almost numbly, he went to the first smart bomb and used the sensor as Schwarz had shown him. He then went to each of the bombs in turn, waiting neither patiently nor impatiently. With each deactivation, he ticked off the threat in his mind. He felt nothing; he was simply aware, a warrior who held the power of life and death in his hands and in his guns and in his feet.

His Shotokan instructors had called it *zanshin,* the "remaining mind," that relaxed state of alertness in which a man could fight without consciously thinking of the components of the fight itself. He had felt it before; he was no stranger to combat and no stranger to experiencing the edge between precious life and eternal death.

The men who lay broken and dead at his feet would feel nothing more, ever.

He glanced down at the sensor. It gave a clear, singular reading; there was one more bomb somewhere. He would have to search the facility and find it. Spatters of blood not his own dripped from his fists.

He picked up the USAS-12 and checked it. It was bloody but undamaged, but as he checked his web gear, he realized he had used all of his shotgun shells. He placed the weapon carefully on the deck again. Then he checked his Python, reloading it from one of his speedloaders and replacing it in his shoulder holster.

He felt tired. The feeling hit him suddenly, and he realized he was crashing from the adrenaline dump of the battle he had just waged. There was no time to stop and rest now, though. Even one bomb, depending on its placement in the plant, could unleash devastation from which the state and perhaps the nation might not recover.

He took the smaller of two doors leading off from the amphitheater and found himself in a small cafeteria. There were several rows of tables with attached benches, somewhere the plant staff would have lunch. A kitchen behind a serving line was decked out in institutional stainless steel. Lyons made his way slowly through the cafeteria, checking the scanner. The room was only dimly lit. His combat boot crunched on something and he looked down to see piles of broken white glass and fine white powder on the floor. Looking up, he saw that the fluorescent tubes in the overhead lights had been broken out, one after another. But why would anybody do that unless—

The terrorists were hiding under one of the low tables. Two sets of hands shot out to drag him off his feet, and as he went down, he cracked the back of his head painfully against the edge of one of the tables. The two terrorists who immediately jumped on top of him wore camouflage fatigues and ski masks. Lyons bit back a witty comment about their fashion sense; he didn't have the breath to make it.

The killers punched at him, most of their blows ineffectual, but a few of them bruising his ribs and finding other vulnerable points. He covered up, protecting his head, pulling his chin in and making sure they couldn't claw at his eyes or punch him out with a flailing, lucky shot. He tried to go for his Python, but it was clawed from his grip and skittered across the floor.

The men on top of him were fighting with animal fury. Both wore Marakov pistols in holsters on their belts, but neither was making any attempt to use them. Lyons had seen it before. Something about combat, about the fight-or-flight reflex of a real battle, made some men revert to their most atavistic. They forgot their tools, forgot their strategies, forgot their advantages, opting instead for simple brute force and gross motor action. The pressure of fighting for their lives, of coming to terms with the fact that another human being in close proximity meant to do them harm, was more than their minds could grasp, and so they had become their most primitive in response.

The urge to turn animal was with us all, and Lyons knew that any man or woman, no matter how strong his or her will, could fall prey to it. These animals, however, were not going to take him down without a fight.

He surged to his feet, using every ounce of his considerable strength to launch himself like a rocket up and through the gap between his two attackers. As he did so, he gathered each man in half a bear hug, squeezing with all his might and actually succeeding in knocking their heads together. As they reeled, he pulled them close, still squeezing, and reached out with both hands to grab the butts of their Makarovs.

He brought the pistols up and double-actioned them both. One of them was on safe and did not fire, but the other sent a bullet through the skull of the man on the right. Lyons whipped the gun to the left and triggered a second shot, blowing the other man's brains out through a hole that started at his left eye socket.

Lyons glanced down at the pistols he held. The unfired weapon he placed in his waistband. The other one had a few shots left in it. He ripped the magazine free and tossed it aside before racking the slide on the pistol and throwing it in the other direction. Then he repeated the process for the other weapon. He saw no need to carry them but refused to leave a live, functional weapon behind him if he could help it.

He heard a noise in the kitchen and crouched low, duckwalking to where his Python still lay. He picked it up and checked it.

The terrorist in the kitchen apparently thought an unconventional approach would save his life and win the day. Instead of entering through the door to the kitchen, the threw himself over the serving line. Lyons saw him coming and thrust the Python to full extension. The .357 Magnum round cored a hole through the hostile's chest. It stopped the man's clock before he had finished his dive. The body rolled off the serving line and toppled onto the floor of the cafeteria.

Lyons found a door at the rear of the cafeteria, which he opened cautiously. The Python was ready against his flank, where he could fire from retention if necessary. The room beyond was a storage pantry, off of which he found the stainless-steel door of a walk-in cooler. As he pointed the scanner, it lit up.

A closed metal door. One last bomb within. There was something just a little too convenient about that. Lyons reached out to grip the handle. Once it was in his grip, he would rip it open and shoot however many enemies were lying in wait on the other side.

His fingers brushed the polished metal handle.

The cooler door whipped open, smashing him in the face and knocking him onto his back. The Python was knocked from his grip.

Karbuly Ghemenizov stood wreathed in the cool mists wafting out of the cooler, his smile completely feral.

CHAPTER TWENTY-ONE

Ashgabat, Turkmenistan

The men of Phoenix Force pulled the quick-release tabs on their high-altitude, low-opening chutes and let the harnesses fall. There was no need to bury the chutes, no need to pretend to be operating covertly. It was time to take direct action against a pitiless dictator and mass murderer. They had dropped directly into the grounds of the fortified, militarized, hardened presidential palace in the Turkmen capital of Ashgabat.

"Can't believe they didn't have more air defenses," James said casually. He was using a handheld thermal-imaging monocular to scan the grounds ahead of them. "But I think I see what they did spend their money on."

"What have you got?" McCarter asked.

"Looks like the grounds are covered in overlapping high-tech sensors," James reported. "I don't see any active countermeasures. No turrets or mines or anything like that. But they're going to know we're here the second we get any closer. They may already know."

"Then let's not keep them waiting, lads," McCarter said. He hefted the M-16 he carried. There had not been time to outfit the men of Phoenix Force with more specialized weaponry, so they had borrowed arms available at the Afghani military base from which they'd caught the jet that air-dropped them over Ashgabat. The logistics had been arranged by Stony Man Farm. Each member of the team carried an M-16 A-4 with Picatinny rail-mounted red-dot optics, an M-9 pistol and various other munitions on his Army-issue combat gear. Manning's rifle had an M-203 40 mm grenade launcher, too.

The team had also opted to continue to carry the Jordanian combat knives provided to them by Ghaem Ahmadi. In McCarter's case, at least, it was partly a tribute to the capable intelligence operative who had done so much to ensure the success of the Tehran mission.

The briefing from Stony Man Farm included extensive details of the presidential palace in Ashgabat before the changes instituted by Ovan, and satellite imagery had been used to provide updates and tentative schematics. As much information as could be supplied by U.S. intelligence had been uplinked and downloaded to their secure satellite phones.

They made their way through the field, moving quickly and quietly, but making no real attempt to conceal themselves. As James had indicated, there was little hope of penetrating the surveillance net in the palace undetected. They simply did not try. They were already on the grounds of the fortified palace. No doubt Ovan thought a small force represented no threat to him.

That might be true of any force but Phoenix Force.

An access road, newly plowed and still smelling of fresh dirt, waited for them ahead. On it stood a small convoy of canvas-covered troop trucks. Hawkins saw them first and signaled to the others. The Phoenix Force commandos fanned out and approached in gliding crouches, ready at any moment to unleash the full firepower at their disposal.

"Wait for it," McCarter said.

The flaps on the trucks were pulled back and RPK light machine guns on bipods were pushed through the openings. McCarter signaled for Phoenix Force to scatter as sustained automatic fire ripped into the field all around them, showering them with clumps of dirt.

"Gary!" McCarter called. "Now!"

Manning aimed his M-203 and fired a grenade into the engine of the lead truck. It exploded, burning with an orange-red blossom of liquid flame as it was pushed up and away from its position. The men in the rear of the truck were toppled from the bed, the RPK in that vehicle firing wide. As Phoenix Force moved in along scattered vectors of approach, Manning fired a grenade into the last vehicle. When its cab turned to flaming fragments, spraying the soldiers in the truck ahead of it with burning shrapnel, the rest of the convey was effectively trapped between the two fireballs.

Phoenix Force, operating as a mobile fire team, flanked and surrounded the troop trucks, moving from vehicle to vehicle, spraying down the ranks of men within. The M-16 A-4 rifles fired in semiautomatic or 3-round-burst modes. The Phoenix Force commandos used their understanding of trigger control to milk from the weapons precisely the fire they wished to lay down. Ovan's enforcer troops, by comparison, were poorly trained. The veterans of Phoenix Force scythed through them as if they were wheat.

Gary Manning leaped up onto the running board of one of the few trucks that had yet to be significantly damaged by gunfire or the explosions of the other trucks. His M-16's bursts sprayed the driver of the truck all over the inside of the cab, at which point he ripped the door open and yanked the dead driver out. Then he climbed in and broke out the glass separating the cab from the rear troop compartment of the truck.

The men crouching in the truck bed turned as one to see the snout of Manning's rifle pointed at them. He sprayed down the rear of the truck, dropping them, scattering them, then allowed his rifle to fall to the end of its sling as he hauled himself out of the truck cab and into the bloody bed.

The big Canadian picked up one of the RPK rifles and used what ammo it had left to make short work of the men nearest the truck. Then he leaped from the rear of the truck onto the hood of the one behind it. Hurling the RPK to the ground, he brought up his M-16/M-203 combination and burned down the men in the truck before similarly burning away the troops in the truck bed.

McCarter watched all this chaos while contributing to it himself. When they had fully destroyed the convoy of enforcement troops, he called to the other members of Phoenix Force. The team wore conventional operational radios and earsets provided for them at the Afghani military base, suitable at least for this operation if not for more covert uses.

They moved, running in erratic patterns, verifying their positions to each other by radio as they spread out wide to prevent being targeted in one mass. As they moved, always closer to the presidential palace, they did so under fire. Machine-gun nests and sniper positions close to the palace were popping away without any real idea of where the Stony Man force was, for their defenses were designed to prevent a breach by a large invading or revolutionary force—not an insertion by five highly trained and highly mobile veteran special operators.

They reached the palace proper. Manning used up the last of his 40 mm grenades blowing apart machine-gun nests and fortifications. The very last round, he used to put a hole in the palace itself. Mortar and bits of stone rained down as the smoking crater ripped a wound in the building.

"Through the breach, men," McCarter called.

Phoenix Force moved into the presidential palace. Their target was twofold. The fortified palace housed the private offices of President for Life Nikolo Ovan, whose terrorist activities against the people of Iran and of the United States were now widely known. The palace was also, however, the headquarters of Ovan's state television station, nestled right in the grounds of the palace to make it convenient for Ovan to address his oppressed people. If Phoenix Force could secure that television station and broadcast the evidence of Ovan's machinations to the Turkmen people, it would help unseat the dictator by robbing him of any pretense of legitimacy. Without that pretense, the grip of fear with which he held his people would be loosened, and rebellion would be encouraged.

In other words, it might yet be possible to liberate Turkmenistan from Ovan's regime.

They began to encounter heavy resistance as they moved through the opulently furnished palace. Everywhere portraits of Ovan in various historical costumes glared down at them. The scene would have been funny if not for the fact that Ovan's enforcers were firing on them.

The presidential palace was a long, rectangular structure with huge open halls in the center of each level. Smaller rooms, each of them with exterior windows, were clustered on the wall space to either side. The halls themselves were free-fire zones, with troops in the rooms on the sides firing from multiple levels through the open great hall space in the center. Had they tried to run through that unprotected, Phoenix Force would have been cut down before they ran twenty paces. It was necessary to employ more intelligent tactics.

Starting at the ground level, they leapfrogged from room to room. McCarter, Encizo and James took one side of the hallway, while Manning and Hawkins took the other. They moved from one small room to the next. First, a man would charge forward, using his M-16 to spray out the room ahead, clearing it of resistance. He would do so under the cover fire of the team member or members behind him. Once he reached his cleared room, he would provide cover fire so the man or men behind him could come up and do the same. The pause at each leapfrog stop enabled the men of Phoenix Force to reload as needed, always bringing maximum fire-power to the engagement.

It was slow going. The palace was large, and the number of armed men guarding it was immense. Phoenix Force had exhausted the supply of ammunition they had brought with their weapons by the time they reached the third level of the palace, continuing their leapfrog sweep-and-clear tactics with consistency and efficiency. They simply picked up Kalashnikovs and magazines as they went, trading their M-16s for the local equivalent, taking the ammo they needed off the troops they killed.

It was bloody difficult work, McCarter would freely acknowledge, and involved some of the heaviest fighting Phoenix Force had seen in a while. When they reached the top level, where Ovan's offices were supposed to be, they hit a wall in the form of an armored barrier.

The commandos assembled, with Manning and Hawkins watching their backs in case any stragglers or reinforcements showed themselves.

"Well," James said, "now what?"

The armored barrier was emblazoned with what McCarter assumed to be Nikolo Ovan's personal crest. More giant posters, these prints of photos of Ovan glaring at the camera, were plastered over the barrier. There was also a picture of a television camera in silhouette on one smaller door inset in the barrier.

"Well," McCarter said, surveying the larger double doors, "we can try to blow it. We have grenades."

"I'm not sure that's going to get through that armor plate," Encizo said dubiously.

"Well," McCarter said, "we could always—"

The double doors swung quietly open.

"Wait for the doors to open?" Hawkins finished hopefully.

Without warning, a group of men screaming in Farsi and wearing the paramilitary uniform of Iranian Internal Security came streaming through the doorway.

CHAPTER TWENTY-TWO

The Iranians wielded pistols and truncheons. Their first volley came dangerously close, but the men of Phoenix Force managed to fend off the onslaught, taking cover behind the metal desks, chairs and other furniture that was stacked in the hallway outside the armored barrier to Ovan's inner sanctum.

"Who is this now?" James said indignantly, firing his field-acquired Kalashnikov into the crowd of Iranians.

"Looks like Magham wasn't too happy to see us go," McCarter called back. "Wanted to make sure we knew he missed us."

"Say it with Iranian assassins," James intoned.

McCarter would have laughed at that, if one of the assassins in question wasn't trying to bash his brains out with an expandable baton.

The gun battle waged first, but the large force of Iranian killers hurling themselves at Phoenix Force quickly pinned down the commandos. They couldn't rearm themselves, so when their Kalashnikovs ran empty, they were forced to use their pistols. These, too, quickly started to run low on ammunition. The sustained fire from behind the armored barrier was whittling away at their cover in the hallway.

"This is rapidly proving unsustainable," Manning said.

"I agree," McCarter said. "We've got to go for broke,

lads," he announced. "Fight our way beyond the barrier while we still have some ammo left."

"On three?" James asked.

"On me!" McCarter said. He charged.

He emptied his pistol into the opening through which the Iranians had come. He threw the empty weapon down and grabbed at a pistol clutched in the hand of a fallen assassin. He emptied that, too, and managed to acquire an expanding baton. The men of Phoenix Force behind him were likewise picking up whatever weapons they could, fighting desperately hand-to-hand through the armored portal.

McCarter drew the Jordanian knife that Ahmadi had given him, grateful now more than ever to have it. He wielded stick and knife with great skill, slashing, thrusting and hitting as he moved in and out among the crowd. Phoenix Force became a living organism, a single combat body made up of five individual cells, all of them capable of dealing death and destruction at close range. They slashed with their knives. They stabbed into vital organs. They smashed their expanding batons into joints, into heads, into faces. They kicked. They used hand-to-hand techniques, gouging eyes, smashing throats, crushing vulnerable joints. They moved, always onward, fighting through the crowd of Iranians that was even now steadily dwindling.

McCarter remembered the first training he had ever received in dealing with multiple attackers. In the SAS, it was long before the advent of mixed martial arts made groundfighting popular. The Briton was dimly aware that a plethora of movies built around the popularity of mixed martial arts and various groundfighting styles of martial arts had risen up in popular culture, to which he was not terribly well connected. As he understood it, the folks who enjoyed mixed martial arts bouts on television were running around proclaiming that style of sporting, one-on-one groundfighting, grappling and wrestling to be a self-defense method.

Whenever he heard that, McCarter couldn't help but flash back to his days in the SAS, from the earliest parts of his training through the lessons fought and won through hard experience. His instructors had drilled into him time and time again that to go to the ground in a combat situation, be it on the battlefield or even in civilian self-defense, was to invite your death. If you fell, if you tripped, if you were taken to the ground, you had to do absolutely everything in your power to get back up. The reasons, as they told him over and over again, were threefold: to survive in combat, you had to stay mobile, you had to avoid getting stomped and you had to avoid getting stabbed.

In combat, McCarter knew, playing the lessons over in the back of his brain as he fought for his life, you never knew truly how many enemies you faced. You never knew what weapons would come into play. If you hit the ground, multiple enemies could swarm you and stomp you to death. He'd seen that happen before, both in street crimes and during mass riots in some of the world's less civilized environments. A man on the ground could take a beating from a single man standing over him. A man alone who was surrounded by multiple assailants would be stomped to death, the way skinheads used to perform curbings as part of their night's wilding activities.

That same man could take a knife in the ribs as easily as not, and once on the ground, his vulnerability to such weaponry increased. The only way to deal with all the possible threats—and this was the key to multiple-attacker defense—was mobility.

McCarter, staying on his feet, his weapons lively in his hands, moved among his opponents. There were those who advocated attempting to, as Sun Tzu said, "attack the corners," piling enemies on top of each other so they would get in each other's way. That worked sometimes, but it was most often a function of luck. It was very hard to make it happen purposefully. No, to circulate among one's enemies as McCarter now did required, not complicated geometry, but simple forward drive and aggression. McCarter charged his foes, and as he did so, he did his best to hurl, push, kick and stomp them into each other. His mobility, his aggression, combined with his willingness to stab them, stomp them and beat them, proved decisive, as it was proving for the other men of Phoenix Force.

But that, of course, was no surprise. That was why they were elite fighting men. That was why they were chosen for missions such as this. That was why the thought of facing overwhelming odds didn't faze them. No man wanted to face such odds…but the Stony Men did so because it was required, and they won.

Once firmly on the other side of the barrier, in the midst of their enemies, they were forced to move back-to-back. The enemy was all around them, ducking and dodging in with a kick here, a knife blade there, the metal of a truncheon over there. McCarter had never heard so many joints snap in one battle in his life; this was hand-to-hand fighting on a truly bloody scale. The knives Ahmadi had given Phoenix Force truly got a workout as they carved their way from man to hapless man, engaged in the most primitive of combat with one of man's most ancient tools.

All five Phoenix Force commandos were splattered with blood, most of it not their own, by the time they reached the inner entrance to the state television studio. McCarter realized, as two more foes dropped under the blades he and Calvin James held, that no more Iranians had taken their place. Similarly, none of Ovan's enforcers were anywhere to be seen. Calvin James, experienced knife fighter that he was, looked relaxed and ready, although the fatigue of the battle clearly showed in his eyes.

The commandos looked around. Manning finished off the last of his opponents, bouncing his man off the armored barrier and cracking the man's skull open. The big Canadian turned to his teammates and then pointed to the door of the television station.

"Shall we?" he asked.

"Great idea, mate," McCarter said.

There were a few technicians in the television station, but they were not armed. They offered no resistance as the bloody Phoenix Force commandos, looking like fugitives from a horror movie, tracked blood and gore through their midst, moving slowly, carefully assessing the aches and pains they had sustained during the vicious, protracted hand-to-hand fighting that had gotten them to this point.

"Anybody know how to run a television station?" James asked. A couple of the technicians tentatively raised their hands. "You speak English?" he asked.

"Yes," the man responded. "Yes, sir."

"Oh, I like him." James grinned. "He's polite."

"Computer feed," McCarter said. "I want to display pictures and audio, and I want to transmit them. Can you do it?"

The technician nodded. "Do you wish me to put you on camera, sir?"

"No," McCarter said. "Cameras off. Just the video and audio files I'm giving you are to go out."

"Yes, sir," the technician responded. He remained poised despite the presence of the gory, battle-weary veterans in his midst. It occurred to McCarter that the man was probably no fan of Ovan, who had nationalized the country's television stations to exert an iron grip on all forms of public media. According to their briefing from Stony Man, the country's newspapers were all being censored by state officials who had been sent to approve every scrap of what the papers' reporters tried to print. Well, that bit of trivia wouldn't do them much good, unless they decided to excoriate Ovan in a strongly worded editorial…but it was a thought, nonetheless.

"I'm going to check the presidential residence," McCarter said. "Calvin, take this," he said, handing James the memory stick. "Make sure we start transmitting things that will embarrass Ovan."

"You got it," James said. "Good luck, David."

"Thanks, mate," McCarter said.

On his way out of the television station, he did his best to clean his knife on the shirt of a fallen Iranian assassin. He sheathed the blade and found a Makarov pistol on one of the dead men, with two spare magazines. He checked the pistol, pocketed the magazines and moved out. His destination was the suite of offices beyond the television station. Beyond those offices were Ovan's private residence chambers. If the Turkmen dictator was anywhere close by, he would be there, possibly either hiding or perhaps holed up with a weapon.

A couple of well-placed kicks got the Phoenix Force leader past the door to Ovan's private offices. He found no one inside the anteroom. When he hit the next set of doors, he started taking fire. The Kalashnikov clatter was unmistakable. He crouched behind an antique desk, listening to the Kalashnikov shred the upper portion of the helpless piece of furniture, and when he heard the weapon click empty, he popped up.

The second man almost took his head off. They'd gotten smart, it seemed, and when the first fellow had run out of ammo, his partner was waiting to shoot whoever was bloody fool enough to stick his head up. Well, McCarter thought. That would teach him to look after himself a little better.

The two AK gunners traded off like that for a while. McCarter simply hunkered down and let them do it. They stopped, eventually, and then tried to wait him out, but like all relative amateurs, they lacked the patience for it. Finally, one of them, perhaps thinking they had killed their opponent by simple luck, stepped out from cover to take a look beyond the desk.

McCarter raised the Makarov and drilled the man through the face. His partner immediately started shooting again, but this time most of the AK rounds went through the already dead body of the man who'd come looking for McCarter. Using the corpse as a shield of sorts, McCarter eased himself up just far enough to bring the sights of his pistol in line with the gunman's face. Another quick pull of the Makarov's heavy, gritty trigger, and he had dropped the second man where he stood.

He finally reached the ornate doors that were, he was quite certain, labeled with grand titles for Ovan's name, though he could not be sure because he couldn't read them. The doors were locked. He kicked them in and then threw them open, expecting at any moment to have to dodge a bullet once more. None came.

McCarter made a thorough search of the residence. He found the place looking as if it had been ransacked. It had to have been an inside job, however, because the bolt holding the doors that he had broken had been thrown from the inside.

He found, at last, Nikolo Ovan's inner office, just off the man's bedroom. Here, he pictured, in the large chair behind the desk that dominated the room, Ovan had done his planning and scheming. He looked over the desk, wondering if perhaps a clue to Ovan's whereabouts would be offered. He found only a pair of very old photographs. The pictures were blurry, but they depicted two teenage boys who were clearly Karbuly and Ebrahim Ghemenizov. The boys had not been photographed together, but the two black-and-white photos had been combined in one hinged, dual frame.

Well. Even heartless dictators had their soft spots.

McCarter was about to leave the room when he spotted the hatch.

He would not be able to say, later, what about it caught his attention. From across the room it appeared to be little more than a loose seam in the floor paneling. Perhaps he had a hard time believing that a dictator like Ovan would allow something like an unsightly floor tile to remain unseated in his presence. Whatever the reason, notice it he did, and when he crept closer to investigate, mindful of booby traps, he found nothing more high-tech than a concealed passageway in the floor.

He moved the hatch aside. It was on hinges that appeared to be counterweighted so that it moved easily. The hinges were smooth, well-maintained and oiled. They made no sound. He took a small angle-head flashlight from his web gear, switched it on and flashed it down the opening of the hatch.

A ladder led into the darkness. He lost count of the rungs when the darkness shrouded them, beyond the range of his little light. He could pursue, but there would be little point. Unless he was trapped in a cave-in somewhere in his escape tunnel, Nikolo Ovan was gone. He had escaped, fleeing the presidential palace before he could be caught and brought to justice for his crimes. Evidently, Ovan knew a coup was in the offing when he saw one.

Certainly, had they taken him into custody, McCarter would have brought him in expecting to see the man "disappeared" into a black bag prison if not put on public international trial to answer for his terrorist crimes. Either way, it was an outcome that a proud, dictatorial man like Ovan would not favor. Had he not had the tunnel in place, it was just possible that McCarter would have entered to find Ovan's corpse slumped over the desk. More than one dictator of his type had chosen to eat a bullet rather than be caught. Most if not all of them couldn't stomach the thought of being on the receiving end of the power they enjoyed wielding so much.

McCarter slowly made his way back out through the private offices and chambers. He had a few rounds left in the Makarov and the two spare magazines, but he felt underarmed. The Kalashnikovs wielded by the dead guards he'd killed had too little ammunition left to be of much use.

He was almost back at the television station when a vase exploded next to him.

He returned fire instinctively, then dropped the Makarov's magazine and reloaded. He burned through that one, and then his remaining magazine, laying down enough fire to make a hole through which to run. The shots were coming from a gunman concealed on the other side of the armored portal. Lyons heard the man's gun run dry, heard a curse in English and then heard rapid footsteps as his unseen foe ran away.

That had been odd, but McCarter wasn't going to worry about it. You simply could not take out every opponent in a situation like this, and a foe that had chosen to run was not one you needed to pursue in this context. He and his Phoenix Force teammates would have to pick their battles getting back out of Turkmenistan. They had arranged for an airlift through hostile territory, which would be possible with Turkmenistan's government in disarray following Ovan's hasty retreat from power, but they would still have to get to the rendezvous point. Wasting what little resources and energy he had on chasing down someone who'd dared to take a shot at him—even one who, strangely, swore in English and was therefore perhaps something other than a Turkmen or an Iranian—just wasn't on the program.

He found Phoenix Force at the ready inside the television station. James was bent over a console and conferring with the technician. The two seemed to be getting along famously. Someone else in the room—two someones, actually—was talking, and McCarter realized he was hearing a recording of Ovan and Magham colluding.

"Everything going all right?" McCarter asked.

"Splendidly," James said. "This here is my friend Vazily." James indicated the technician. "Vaz, this is my friend Jack. Jack, Vaz here was just telling me that these conversations are being watched on televisions all across Turkmenistan and even over the border."

"Are they, now?" McCarter said. "Well. Isn't that just a bonus?"

"I'm pulling the memory card from their board," James reported. "I think we've given them enough to accomplish what we needed to accomplish. Just wait until this gets syndicated. It'll be bigger than that show with the pretty people who sit around doing nothing. What's it called?"

"I wouldn't know, mate," McCarter said. "I think I watch about as much television as you do."

"Well, I have to say I like the programming on this station." James grinned. "Let's go, then."

"Yes," McCarter said. "Let's. Give Vaz there my regards."

"He's right there, man."

"Yes, well, I haven't known him as long as you have."

"Right."

The door behind them creaked open.

Garret Aimler stood there.

CHAPTER TWENTY-THREE

"I have to admit," Aimler said, "that I didn't think any part of this plan was going to work."

McCarter was the first to recover from the surprise. "Aren't you dead?" he asked.

"I was," Aimler said. "For a little while. But then I realized that there was really only one thing I wanted. And that was to make sure you and the rest of you bastards didn't get away with taking my life from me. You can't get away free. I won't let you."

"Don't think you have much choice, mate," McCarter said. He was keenly aware of his lack of a firearm. Aimler, however, did not appear to have a weapon, either, unless he had a hideout gun somewhere.

"Destroyed my life," Aimler said again. "Walked into the country I spent my blood, my energy, years of my waking hours, trying to arrange for the benefit of a country that didn't deserve it. You're thugs, all of you. I won't let you do it."

McCarter decided he had had enough of this nonsense. He drew the Jordanian combat knife. It was still smeared with the blood of the foes he had dispatched not long before.

"Oh, well," Aimler said, drawing a black boot dagger from a sheath clipped behind his hip. "I guess we can play that game if you want."

"You're not walking away from this, Aimler," Mc-

Carter told him. "You're a traitor to your country and a threat as long as you're allowed to continue walking around. You'll be sent to prison, 'disappeared' so bloody hard you'll forget your own name. If you surrender, I can at least put in a good word for you. Let us take you into custody."

"And who are you, really?" Aimler said. He held the dagger loosely at his side. "NSA? Not CIA, surely. Some other agency? Something I've never heard of? Don't think I don't know. There have been rumors at CIA for a long time about people like you."

McCarter had time to wonder if perhaps this man had some inkling of the existence of Stony Man Farm. Could he have a clue about the covert counterterrorist function of the Farm? Did his intelligence contacts go deep enough that he might know just what function McCarter and his team truly fulfilled? A leak at this level would have to be plugged. Aimler had already written a crackpot tell-all book, some of it probably just true enough to be dangerous when combined with the vast quantity of lies, distortions and conspiracy theories that it seemed made up of at first blush. He could not be allowed to go on telling the world about the Farm. He would have to be terminated to prevent the possible exposure he represented.

"You need to mind what you're saying, mate," Mc-Carter said.

"You're one of them, aren't you?" Aimler demanded.

"One of whom?"

"The reptilian aliens!" Aimler demanded. "The creatures who secretly run our government, control our money supply. I used to think it was just torture. Well, mostly torture. I used to think the wrongs our country was committing had to do primarily with how it treated those it declared its enemies. Taking prisoners without giving them access to jury trials. Forcing high-value terrorist suspects to undergo interrogation just because they might have information that would save a few paltry American lives. What are a few lives, the lives of soldiers, warmongers, baby-killers, compared to human rights? Where is the respect and the regard for humanity? Where?"

Wait a minute, McCarter thought. Reptilian aliens? He risked a glance at James, then Encizo, who were both within the field of his vision. James shook his head and mouthed the words "No idea."

The man had gone completely around the bend, it seemed.

There was no reason to continue listening to the man rave, however. McCarter was ready to step in, take the knife away from him and end this. He moved as if to do so.

"Stop right there," Aimler said. He held up his left hand, the hand that did not hold the knife.

In his hand was a single metal sphere about the size of a baseball.

"Stop right there," Aimler repeated. "This is an Iranian smart bomb pod. It's been rigged to go off on impact. If I drop it, we all die, and so do they." He jerked his chin at the technicians standing in the background. "Don't want any innocent deaths on your conscience, do you?"

"What do you want, Aimler?" McCarter asked.

"Maybe I want justice," Aimler said. "Maybe I want payback. You took everything from me. Do you have any idea what that feels like? To have aliens rip you away from your humanity? To know that they travel to the center of the world every night, laughing through their

Rolex radios, dictating what will happen to stock prices in the morning? If I don't tell the world, who will?"

McCarter couldn't help himself. "You're bloody crackers, you are."

"Am I?" Aimler asked. "I'm the one holding the bomb. Now, you and your people are going to walk out of this place with me. I'm going to give you to the people of this fine country and let them know what you really are. Then we'll see how they choose to judge you."

"You're going to walk us out of the presidential palace and tell the Turkmen public that we're reptilian space aliens," McCarter said deadpan.

"That's right," Aimler said. "Let them judge you. They'll be so grateful that I'll be given safe passage—"

The blade of Aimler's knife whistled past his face. McCarter almost didn't see it coming. He brought the Jordanian blade up to protect himself, dancing and wheeling back, staying out of range of Aimler's thrusts.

"Stay back!" Aimler warned. "Tell them to stay back, or I'll drop the sphere and we all die! Face me like a man and maybe, just maybe, there's a chance that some of your hired killers can live."

McCarter ignored his braying, focusing on the sphere. He would need to stay well clear of the blade of Aimler's knife while trying to figure out how to stop the sphere from connecting with something hard enough to set it off. As Aimler lurched around, McCarter allowed himself to think that it wasn't going to be too hard not to get knifed. The man wasn't very good. He was clumsier than he had any right to be, in fact, and McCarter was going to have to—

The edge of Aimler's knife caught him across the arm.

Bloody stupid! He chided himself. Of course. Aimler, cracked nut though he might be, was an experienced intelligence operative. Of course he'd deliberately concealed his skill level, hoping to lull McCarter into a false sense of confidence, getting the Stony Man operative to commit himself in a way that brought him within range of Aimler's knife. Well, two could play *that* game, as well.

It was a difficult situation. Aimler blocked the door, so there was no way to send the technicians or any of the rest of his team to safety. The sphere in Aimler's hand meant that the crazed intelligence agent controlled the rules of the engagement. Any attempt by the Stony Man teammates to interfere, and the sphere would drop. Kill Garret Aimler, and the sphere would drop. Admit to being a space alien, and the sphere would... Wait. Could that work?"

"You're right," McCarter said finally. "I've been an alien all along. You can, er, join the new world order, mate, if you'll just gently set that explosive aside and talk to me..."

"You bleed red!" Aimler shouted. "You're not an alien! You're a ghoul!"

Bloody wonderful, McCarter thought. He dropped the games and went back to the dirty business of trying not to get cut or stabbed, as his team looked on anxiously.

Aimler's dagger cut in and out, describing figure-eight patterns in the air. McCarter, who was no slouch with a blade himself, tried to determine if he could learn anything from Aimler's movements. Was he obviously educated in some form of blade mechanics? Was it simply common sense and street smarts combined with good reflexes? Was it some sort of Filipino or Indonesian martial art?

The two men danced around each other, circling and weaving. Several times Aimler cut patterns that McCarter thought he recognized, but just as quickly, he abandoned them. Each time McCarter tried to make use of an opening, Aimler would change tactics. As he did so, the expression on his face transformed from one of concentration to a feral snarl. The Central Intelligence agent wanted nothing more than to plunge his knife into McCarter, killing the man who embodied so much that the sadly deranged man had come to hate.

If he had ever been a good operative, no part of the man in front of him was recognizable as such, except for the technical skill Aimler exhibited. And he was indeed skilled. McCarter realized finally what the expression on Calvin James's face meant: McCarter was dealing with a truly experienced knife fighter. Aimler had been toying with him, trying to misdirect him. Misdirection was the fundamental theme to Aimler's career. It was his defining characteristic. Should McCarter be surprised that the man employed it here?

He watched the bomb sphere balanced precariously in Aimler's left palm. If he took Aimler, if he disabled him or killed him, he would have only one chance to catch the bomb before it exploded. He could try a disabling cut to the non-knife arm, but if he did that, he would have to focus on catching the sphere. That would leave him vulnerable to Aimler's knife hand. He could well end up spitted on the end of Aimler's knife, or have his throat cut wide open, even as he caught the bomb.

If he did so, would he be able to stop the bomb from striking the floor? Would one of his people be fast enough to catch it before he, in turn, dropped it? He looked from face to face among his team as he moved cautiously around Aimler. Yes, he decided. They were all watching intently, poised on the balls of their feet, ready for action. If he took the knife while catching the bomb, one of them would step in and try to take the bomb from him.

It was worth the sacrifice. To save his team, he would gladly give his own being.

He went for it then, but Aimler knew what he was trying. The agent scored another minor cut against McCarter's knife arm, not deep enough to disable the Stony Man warrior. It was going to have to be the disarm, then. McCarter was going to have to take Aimler out to stop him from countering McCarter's attempt to neutralize him. It was no longer a question of noble sacrifice; he had to take away Aimler's ability to use his knife to take away the agent's ability to oppose him.

Well, he thought, here goes nothing.

He waited, timing Aimler's thrusts and slashes. The agent finally made a committed thrust straight in. It wasn't a move he had made often, not so directly or so exaggerated. McCarter recognized the trap for what it was. Aimler was hoping McCarter would go for the disarm and expose his own arm in the process.

McCarter had a different idea in mind. He subtly shifted his body, delivering a painfully hard, vicious slap to the outside of Aimler's knife hand, moving quickly enough that Aimler would not have time to draw the blade back and cut him with it. As he slapped the arm, he inverted his own blade, drawing the blade down over the inside and top of Aimler's forearm. He pushed deep, carving Aimler like a Christmas goose, forcing the man's knife arm into the blade with the brutal simultaneous slap.

Aimler howled. His dagger fell from suddenly nerveless fingers and blood began to ooze from the deep wound. It fell in spatters to make large pools on the floor. It was, if not treated, a mortal blow, but Aimler, far gone as he was, barely seemed to notice save to lament the loss of his ability to grip his blade.

He tried to scoop up the knife with his injured hand but failed miserably. The attempt put him off balance, and McCarter, seeing the opening, drove the point of the Jordanian knife into the hollow of Aimler's exposed throat notch. The knife went in deep and stuck there. Aimler's eyes bugged. He tried to speak, choked and sprayed blood from his mouth as his face went deathly pale. He collapsed dead on the floor—but not before feebly tossing the explosive sphere into the air, using the last of his strength.

"Bloody hell," McCarter said. He lunged.

He dived for the sphere, trying to catch it in his hand. The metal casing fell, and he watched it in agonizing slow motion, reaching for it, hoping to catch it, knowing that his hand would be just a fraction of a second too slow. He had time to wonder if he would see old friends who had passed on before him, the brave men and women who had died before their time in the service of their country and of the ideal of freedom. He hoped that he, David McCarter, would be remembered well, and that his stewardship of Phoenix Force would be regarded positively by those who took up the mantle after his team....

The metal sphere hit the floor, bounced and rolled into the metal wheels of a rolling television camera. It split open along the seam in its center. The two halves rolled loudly to a stop, shaking in ever-smaller rotations until they had spent their momentum.

The sphere was hollow.

McCarter's eyes went wide. The man was truly bonkers, threatening them with a bomb casing that had no bomb in it. It must have been something he'd had on hand back in his office, something he'd taken with him, or perhaps something he'd found here in the presidential palace.

CHAPTER TWENTY-FOUR

"Hello, little man." Karbuly grinned. "Do you know how much I am going to enjoy this?"

"Not nearly as much as I am," the Able Team leader said.

Lyons launched himself at the giant, plowing into Ghemenizov with every foot-pound of force he could channel into his body. The two men went down, crashing into the walk-in cooler and upsetting metal trays bearing supplies and plastic-wrapped desserts. Lyons knew that he had only one chance, and that was to finish the giant quickly, before Ghemenizov could make use of his greater size and strength. Lyons was by no means a small or weak man and usually he was the more powerful one. In Ghemenizov, he faced an opponent whose advantage over Lyons was at least as great as the ones Lyons usually enjoyed himself.

Oh, how he'd wished for this moment. He could see the contempt in Ghemenizov's face. The giant had never faced an opponent he hadn't beaten; that much was obvious. He was used to fighting, used to using brute force. Lyons had seen the type many times before. Such brutal men always thought they could never be beaten, always thought they were the toughest people in any room. Ghemenizov was as close to a subhuman monster as any enemy he had faced. The need to rend, to crush, to tear, radiated from him almost like heat. When Lyons looked into Ghemenizov's eyes he saw two black pits of hate and pain. To be close to Karbuly Ghemenizov would make most decent people sick.

It was those decent people that Lyons thought of now. If he wasn't stopped here, if he wasn't stopped now, Ghemenizov would go on hurting people. He would go on murdering. He would go on preying on any and all people who were weaker than he was...and Ghemenizov, strong as he was, had a pretty wide field of victims from which to choose.

No. The line in the sand was here. The end of the line for this murdering monstrous terrorist was in this place, breathing cold air and surrounded by the last mundane objects he would ever take notice of in life.

Lyons punched Ghemenizov in the gut. It felt like punching stone, but he did it again and again and again, picturing tearing his knuckles bloody on a cliff face. He was rewarded with a grunt of pain from the giant, and then another, and then another. His hands were stinging. His body was reeling. But he kept fighting. He realized suddenly that he was surrounded by potential missiles, objects he could use to deal pain to Karbuly Ghemenizov...and he saw no reason to spare the giant one moment of distress and discomfort if he could dish it out.

"Tell me again how you're going to break me, you big bastard!" Lyons yelled. He was psyching himself up, programming himself, forcing himself to keep stepping forward into perhaps the hardest hand-to-hand fight he'd had in years. He smashed two fists into Ghemenizov's stomach, then slammed a boot into the big man's crotch. Ghemenizov let out a whoof as the air was driven from his lungs. The big ex-cop smashed hammer fist after hammer fist down on the back of the terror-master's head. He pictured himself driving nails, beating the big man down, rooting him to the spot so that he could never again rise to terrorize the decent.

It was not enough, but Lyons was not nearly finished.

He began grabbing plates from the nearby racks and smashing them against the giant's face. He threw plate after plate, hitting Ghemenizov as viciously as he was able, shattering each plate across the giant's craggy visage. Ghemenizov lashed out with a kick that smashed Lyons against the wall of the cooler, so Lyons grabbed a full jar of pickles and used it like a battering ram to smash Ghemenizov in the face. Blood spurted from the big man's nose.

The two fighters started trading punches again, with Lyons slipping and dodging as many of the massive strikes as he could. More than once a ham-fisted punch landed, jarring his teeth in their sockets and sending pain exploding through his blood-streaked body. Lyons ignored it, fighting through the pain, fighting through the effort with sheer force of will. Karbuly Ghemenizov stood in front of him, and Karbuly Ghemenizov was not going to leave under his own power. Lyons owed a great many people some payback from the terror-master, and that payback was coming out in blood.

Lyons smashed a full container of heavy frozen hamburger patties across the giant's head, feeling the muscles in his back and shoulders screaming in protest as he wrenched them. He ignored these, too. He fired kick after vicious stomping kick, going for the giant's knees, trying to crush the joints. He stomped on the giant's toes. He grabbed, threw, slashed, thrust and smashed every single object he could get his hands on, the pure ferocity of his attack staggering Ghemenizov in a way the brutal giant had probably seldom experienced.

The glass bottles on the shelf had potential. Lyons began grabbing them and smashing them down on the giant again and again. The bottles didn't break but they were very heavy, full of liquid weight that crashed against the giant's malformed skull and caused him to sway under the barrage.

Under Lyons's vicious attacks, the bigger man finally retreated, backing out of the cooler and stumbling into the kitchen area.

"Oh, no, you don't," Lyons said, breathing heavily. He pursued, and narrowly missed the large steak knife that Ghemenizov threw at him. He grabbed a cutting board from the countertop and held it up like a shield, battering away the poorly thrown knives and even a meat cleaver that Ghemenizov hurled. Then Lyons shifted the heavy cutting board in his fists and smashed it across the giant's face, corner first, drawing blood and knocking out one of the giant's teeth.

Karbuly Ghemenizov howled in anger. Lyons wouldn't relent. He wrenched one of the benches free from its place mounted to a cafeteria table, smashing it into Ghemenizov's chest. The giant roared again, and this time, he managed to connect with a brutally powerful mule kick that cracked one of Lyons's ribs.

The big ex-cop went down, the pain in his side excruciating. Ghemenizov came down on top of him, intent on crushing him with his weight. Blood streamed from the giant's mouth. When he talked, he spit blood.

"I am going to break you," he said. "I am going to crush your skull until your eyes come out. I am going to show you what it means to face Karbuly Ghemenizov."

He managed to get his arms around Lyons then, squeezing like a python, and this time, Carl Lyons knew there would be no escaping from that iron grip alive.

"You," he gasped as Ghemenizov squeezed, "are one…ugly…bastard!"

"Americans." Ghemenizov laughed. The sound was like the roll of thunder from deep within the big man's throat. "You are all soft. Weak. I would kill you all if I could…but that will take a long time. I think I will start…with…you." The big man punctuated his words with quick, brutal squeezes. Lyons could feel himself losing consciousness.

"You forgot," Lyons said.

"Forgot?" Ghemenizov asked, laughing his rumbling laugh. "I forget nothing. I have a long memory, American. I enjoyed fighting you the first time. But I will enjoy fighting you the last time a great deal more."

"Forgot," Lyons said, "that I can…reach my pockets."

The giant's eyes shot wide and looked down.

The little Raven .25-caliber pistol was in Lyons's fist. He pulled the trigger again and again, then three more times, emptying the weapon's magazine into his adversary's chest directly over his heart.

Ghemenizov let out a choked sound that was neither a scream nor a gasp. The tension in his arms immediately slackened, and he dropped Lyons to the floor. The Able Team leader fell to his knees, the empty pistol still in his hand. Ghemenizov hit the floor like a tree being felled. His pumpkin-size head rebounded off the polished fake marble.

"How…" he was saying weakly. Lyons thought he could hear the death rattle in the big man's words. "How…"

With difficulty, Lyons pushed himself to his feet. He limped over to stand above Karbuly Ghemenizov, holding his chest, favoring his cracked rib. He held up the little chromed pistol so Ghemenizov could see it.

"A .25," Lyons said. "It fires a tiny, underpowered bullet. It's small and weak, Ghemenizov. Maybe like the American people you hate so much. Maybe not. But each one of these little bullets, while it may be weak by itself, is strong when accompanied by others. The more there are, the stronger they are."

"I…" Ghemenizov breathed. "I…"

"You lose," Lyons said. "Because a bunch of small, weak opponents worked together to put you down like the dog that you are."

The light faded from Ghemenizov's eyes. The look on his face was one of disbelief leavened with horror.

They always looked like that, Lyons reflected, in their last moments. None of the predators ever wanted to believe that death could come for them as it had for so many of their victims.

Justice was like that.

EPILOGUE

Virginia

The diner in rural Virginia was as ageless as any Mc-Carter had ever stepped into. Warn linoleum covered the floor, and the chipped Formica counter and shiny leather stools testified to the many decades that the diner had been serving fresh coffee and home-cooked meals.

McCarter opened the door and walked in, looking for Carl Lyons.

The big blond ex-cop was seated at the far end of the counter, a cup of coffee and a half-eaten meal in front of him.

McCarter joined his friend and fellow Stony Man commando, sliding onto an adjacent stool. Lyons didn't turn to look at him.

"How're the ribs?" McCarter asked.

"Healing," Lyons said. "At least I'm still pretty."

McCarter laughed.

He looked up at the television mounted on the wall above the counter. A football game was playing.

"If this was a movie," Lyons said quietly, "there'd be a news report up there about Iran's presidential election."

"Funny thing about televisions." McCarter nodded. "They rarely serve as convenient tools of exposition in real life."

"How'd you find me?" Lyons asked. His tone was low, almost flat, but McCarter recognized the edge to it. Lyons was in a bad mood, and it was wise not to antagonize such a man when he got that way. McCarter had his own moods; he would respect his friend's, as one warrior to another.

"Your phone," McCarter asked. "You left before the debriefing. Barb was concerned."

"I wasn't in the mood," Lyons said. "I filed all the reports before I left. I didn't feel like sitting around jawing about it."

"Nobody's accusing you of shirking your duty, mate." McCarter shook his head. "I just thought you might be curious about what's going on out there in the world. Apart from this entertaining game of American football. How I wish this was a World Cup year."

"I got enough of those dumb plastic horns the last time around," Lyons said.

"Didn't we all, mate," McCarter replied.

The two men laughed about that. They sat in silence for a while before McCarter said, "It looks like the UN will be passing a resolution. The new regime in Turkmenistan will be recognized. Ovan's gone into hiding, probably gone to polish Imelda Marcos's shoe collection or something. Seems a coalition of more moderate influences have taken over in Turkmenistan. Some analysts are saying the power vacuum's going to make it a mess, but...well, there's some hope for them."

"There's that."

"Magham's trying to suspend the election results in Iran, for his part," McCarter continued. "He's lost but he won't admit it. CNN, Fox News, the other networks... they're all running clips from the tapes Ghaem Ahmadi recovered for us. Bear and his people are running through the copy we gave them to see if they can isolate any juicier bits. The CIA and NSA are busy arguing over it, too, but the cat's out of the bag, so it's too late for them to do any redacting. The Company's got some egg on its face in all this, but the big story is the news leaking out in Iran itself. Seems Ghaem's friends have taken to the internet to help spread the word, like the dissidents did during the previous election. Slowly, freedom's taking hold."

"Slowly." Lyons nodded. "Hal or Barb hear anything about Ghaem?"

"Seems he's up for a commendation." McCarter smiled. "I might have had something to do with that. He's been put in charge of rebuilding the Agency's network out there. I guess they needed somebody they knew they could trust."

Lyons nodded slowly but said nothing for quite a while.

"What's bothering you, Carl?" McCarter finally asked.

"I'll tell you what's bothering me," Lyons said. "It bothers me that no matter how hard we work, no matter how hard we fight, no matter how many predators we remove from this Earth, there are always more. Good people die, David. Innocent people. People who don't deserve to be murdered. People whose only crime is being in the wrong place at the wrong time. People who should have had full lives ahead of them, in a lot of cases. The Ovans and the Ghemenizovs and the Maghams of the world just grind them underfoot for their own gain. It wears on me, David. I don't like to see good people killed."

"Oh, about that," McCarter said. "Hal had a message

for you. Asked me if I'd bring it to you. He said you made some friends in Vermont. A married couple?"

"Yeah?" Lyons looked at McCarter suspiciously.

"Seems the Man got wind of it somehow," McCarter winked. "Seems that couple's going to meet with the Man himself to receive some new Presidential Citizen of Liberty medal. Something like that."

"The President's actually going out on a limb to praise them?" Lyons asked, incredulous. "Isn't he worried about condoning vigilante violence or something like that?"

"Normally, you'd think so." McCarter shook his head. "But I get the impression Hal pulled some strings, called in some favors. He seemed to think it was the right thing to do."

"Yeah," Lyons said. He reached for his coffee cup.

"What we're doing is the right thing," McCarter said.

"I know that," Lyons agreed. "I never thought otherwise. I just hate to see good people die." Lyons knew McCarter was right. They were doing what was right, as they'd always done. It had never been easy. It never would be. It would never come without cost…and as long as there were predators within society, innocent people, good people, would be in danger.

As long as that danger existed, the warriors of Able Team and Phoenix Force would be there to stand between evil and the innocents it threatened. They were the last line. They were the guardians of hope in a troubled time.

They were the men and women of Stony Man Farm.

Don Pendleton's Mack Bolan®

Stealth Sweep

A madman's war games are poised to plunge the world into chaos....

A rogue major mastermind from Chinese Intelligence has the patience and resources to execute an attack to expand Chinese territory into world domination. Remote-controlled stealth-attack drones carrying nuclear bombs are being smuggled to strategic strike points, and Mack Bolan must infiltrate and terminate the conspiracy before the bombs are released.

Available July
wherever books are sold.

TAKE 'EM FREE

2 action-packed novels plus a mystery bonus

NO RISK
NO OBLIGATION TO BUY

AleX Archer
TEAR OF THE GODS

The early chapters of history contain dangerous secrets…secrets that Annja Creed is about to unlock.…

A dream leads archaeologist Annja Creed to an astonishing find in England—the Tear of the Gods. But someone knows exactly what this unusual torc means, and he will do anything to get his hands on it…even leave Annja for dead. Now she is fleeing for her life, not knowing the terrifying truth about the relic she risks everything to protect.

Available July wherever books are sold.

GOLD EAGLE®

JAMES AXLER

DEATH LANDS®

Perception Fault

From the rubble of the future comes potential…and peril!

In Denver, Ryan Cawdor and his companions are offered a glimmer of
hope: a power plant, electricity, food and freedom. But the city is caught
in a civil war between two would-be leaders and their civilian armies…
and Ryan is caught in the middle, challenged by both sides to do their
bidding. Tomorrow is never just a brand-new day in the Deathlands.

Available July wherever books are sold.